PAULA RAWSTHORNE

For my Mum, Veronica, the heart of the Rawsthorne clan.

Scholastic Children's Books
An imprint of Scholastic Ltd
Euston House, 24 Eversholt Street, London, NW1 1DB, UK
Registered office: Westfield Road, Southam, Warwickshire, CV47 0RA
SCHOLASTIC and associated logos are trademarks and/or
registered trademarks of Scholastic Inc.

First published in the UK by Scholastic Ltd, 2018

Text copyright © Paula Rawsthorne, 2018

The right of Paula Rawsthorne to be identified as the
author of this work has been asserted by her.

ISBN 978 1407 18025 0

Printed by CPI Group (UK) Ltd, Croydon, CR0 4YY
Papers used by Scholastic Children's Books are made
from wood grown in sustainable forests.

1 3 5 7 9 10 8 6 4 2

www.scholastic.co.uk

CHAPTER 1

GOODBYE

I watch as Mak rummages through her bag. It's so good to see her. She must have gotten a real early flight from Houston to El Paso to make it all the way out to the clinic for this time. Mak just used to be my best friend but, since I got sick again, she's turned herself into my health guru, entertainer and make-up artist. She's armed with trashy magazines, "spirit-lifting" music, "inspirational" books, and every comedy ever made because "you can't underestimate the healing power of laughter."

Yeah right, Makayla, I'm just going to laugh away every last freakin' tumor! I want to say it, but I don't; she's trying so hard.

"Found it." She waves an ornate bottle of perfume in front of me. "I got it from this new boutique in the Galleria. I'll take you there when you get home."

She tips droplets on to my pillow. She's careful. She knows not to put it on my paper-thin skin. The scent of my favorite flowers sails up my nose, masking the smell of hospital disinfectant and sickness.

"It's freesia. As soon as I smelled it I knew it was for you. Do you like it?" she says, expectantly.

"I love it," I whisper, forcing a smile for her.

Her face lights up. It always does when she thinks she's made me happy.

My body aches as she plumps the pillows and props me up. She holds the beaker while I suck the water through a straw.

"I can do this myself, you know," I tell her.

"I know." She smiles, straightening the beanie hat that slides off my bald head. She produces a pot of chocolate mousse from her bag. "My mama made it specially for you. She sends a big fat kiss, by the way."

How can I refuse as she spoons it into my mouth like I'm a baby? The thick goo clings to my dry throat.

I watch for her reaction as I blurt out, "They want to put in a feeding tube."

I see her face freeze before she reminds herself to stay upbeat. "Yeah, I heard. It'll just be for a while, Lucy; you know, to build you up ... get some nourishment in you," she answers cheerfully, taking my hand. I look down at our entwined limbs and, for a split second, I don't recognize my own. It keeps happening; I can't remember when they started looking like they belong to an old lady.

"Your hands are icy." Mak shudders on my behalf and

2

delves into her bag of tricks, pulling out one of her lotions. "This is one hundred per cent natural. Nothing in here to irritate you." She gently massages the rich cream into my hands and up my stick-thin arms. It feels so nice; so soothing.

"Hey," Mak says. "I saw your grandma a couple of days ago. She told me that her pastor has the whole congregation praying for you."

The thought of Grandma makes me smile. "I know. I think she has half of Texas praying for me. She writes me every day; sends me all these scripture quotes. I wish I could see her. She's desperate to visit but Mom won't let her; she says it'll be too much for her."

"Have you had many visitors?" Mak asks.

"Dad has fit in a few visits around work, but mainly it's just Mom," I sigh heavily. "She's here night and day. I'd really love to see Arthur but there's no pets allowed. They worry about infection. Anyway, Arthur gets so travel sick that the journey from H-Town would be terrible for him."

"Well, how about, when I get home, I go over to your place and shoot a video of him? I'll get him waving his paw at you and cute crap like that."

"Thanks, Mak, I'd love that." Tears swell in my eyes at the thought of seeing Arthur. I feel my top lip quivering. I shouldn't cry.

"Hey, that better not be your Elvis snarl I see on those lips." Mak narrows her eyes. "No crying allowed in here."

"Oh, shut up, Mak," I say, playfully. "Come on and tell me the gossip from Bailey Heights?" I'm a fraud; I'm not really

3

interested, but I need to keep Mak talking. I'm too tired to make conversation and she's not good with silences; she's worried I'm going to fill them with words she doesn't want to hear. Anyway, I like to hear Mak talk; I like to listen to the melodic rhythm of her voice, especially now that mine is so small and lifeless.

I wish I could stay awake, be more alert. I seem to have spent the last two weeks drifting in and out of sleep. Each time I open my eyes I'm gripped by the same panic as I wait for my spidery vision to clear, but so far, I'm still here, in this clinic in the desert, surrounded by these whitewashed walls, lying in this bed, the IV needle still embedded in my collapsing veins.

"Okay, how about this; I was in Memorial Park yesterday and guess who I saw with his tongue down the throat of a girl who *isn't* his girlfriend?" Mak says, her eyes wide.

I smile inwardly – this is the Mak I know and love, in full flow, regaling me with her stories.

"Don't know." I shrug.

"It's someone from school. Someone you know."

I try to picture my classmates as Mak feeds me more mousse. I haven't seen them since I had to give up school again. It's not like any of them would think of visiting me. They probably haven't even noticed that I'm gone. Anyway, even if I *was* Miss Popular, I doubt they'd want to hang out with someone who's a depressing reminder that being young doesn't make you immortal.

"I can't think," I say.

"Come on. He's a major-league douchebag. We hate him."

4

"Josh Dartmere?"

"Correct!"

My face screws up.

Josh Dartmere! I cringe at the thought of him. I can't believe I wasted my precious time in remission dating him. I was pathetic. I genuinely believed that a member of the football team was interested in me. It didn't take long to realize that he was just doing it so everyone would think he was a great guy for dating "the girl with cancer." When Mak made me summon up the self-respect to dump him, he told me that he'd only done it because he felt sorry for me. What an asshole!

I tune back in to Mak as she finishes her rant about Dartmere.

"He's such a two-timing scumbag," Mak declares.

"I feel sick even thinking about him." I shudder. "Let's talk about you and Mr Kendrick instead. Has he proposed yet?" I smirk, thinking about Mak's unrequited love for our English teacher.

"You can mock all you want, but one day me and Mr Bret Kendrick will be together. We'll live in one of those big, rambling houses in Montrose, surrounded by artists and writers, and I'll work on my latest poetry collection while Bret changes the diapers on our three . . . maybe four, super-adorable babies."

Laughing hurts my chest but I can't stop it rattling out as I get a sugar rush from the chocolate mousse. "You do realize that he lives with his girlfriend."

"So? I happen to know that she's an accountant!" she says

5

with disgust. "What Bret needs is someone who shares his love of words, of literature. Anyway, think about it – what man in his right mind wouldn't want a Jennifer Hudson lookalike? I am *all* woman!" she proclaims with a shimmy.

"Well, stop stalking him," I chuckle. "If they lock you up, you won't be able to visit me."

She makes a face, but I can see that she's delighted to have made me laugh. "Enough lecturing me, Lucy Burgess. What you need is one of my makeovers."

"No," I groan, pulling the bed sheets up for protection. "I can't deal with this, not today."

"And that's exactly why you need one. Let's put some color in those cheeks, although the vampire look will never go out of fashion." She winks.

Her face is an expression of manic cheerfulness as she gets to work. I wish she'd be brave and drop the act. We still tell each other everything; we've always trusted each other with all the embarrassing stuff that would be certain social suicide if we ever fell out. But now she avoids talking about the one thing that really matters. She sticks to the same script as Mom and Dad: the clichés about "when you're better," "it's just a bad patch," "we're going to have the best summer ever together."

"Looking good!" she announces, penciling in my eyebrows. "Selfie time. Hat on or off?"

I hold my beanie hat down. "On."

I'm not having Makayla posting a photo of me looking like a moon-eyed alien. I don't want people to remember me like that. I've even picked out the photo I want on my funeral program. I emailed it to Mom weeks ago. I keep asking her whether she got it but she just changes the subject. There's no way I'm having her choose the photo. She loves the ones where I look a complete dork. I've picked one from last year in Barbados. Dad actually took some time off work and rented the most incredible beach house. I got to go horseback riding along the sand every day. I felt so good, so healthy. I couldn't even imagine it coming back. But now, looking down at this skeleton of a body, I can't ever imagine being well again, and I hate it that Mom and Dad are keeping up the pretense that I'm going to get better. Do they really think they can protect me from what's going to happen? They're forcing treatment on me when we all know that pumping my body full of more poison isn't making any difference. It's just making whatever time I have left feel like hell on earth. I'm ready for it all to stop now, even if they aren't.

Mak places an arm delicately around me, afraid that I'll break; her warm body dominates mine. She pulls out her cell. "On three I want a sexy mega pout. One, two, three!"

"You look gorgeous!" she coos, showing me the screen.

I stare at myself. The brown foundation on my face suddenly gives way to translucent skin on my scrawny neck, making it look like the two don't belong together. She's tried to hide the dark rings with concealer but it makes my eyes look even more sunken. The blusher only highlights my hollow cheeks, the lipstick is plaster filling in my cracked lips, and the eyebrows ... they're so arched, I look like I've been shocked.

My eyes shift to her image and I'm suddenly overwhelmed with jealousy. I crave her thick glossy curls, her flawless skin, her full, smooth lips.

Mirror, mirror on the wall... I want to offer her the ruby-red apple and take all her glowing health for my own... I've turned into the evil witch. Inside I cringe with shame.

"I look like a drag queen." I give a hollow laugh.

"No!" She tuts. "You look glamorous."

"You should do my make-up for the funeral. Give people something to laugh at as they file past the coffin."

Her face clouds. "Don't say stuff like that. It isn't funny."

"Do you think anyone from Bailey Heights will turn up for it?"

"Shut up, Lucy."

"I suppose if the funeral is during school time some might volunteer just to get out of class," I muse. "Don't get me wrong, I know that people don't hate me. To hate someone you'd have to notice them first, but it's not like I've 'touched people's lives', is it? I'm not expecting them to rename the library after me or anything."

"Would you stop it with all this self-pity crap?" Mak snaps.

She's rummaging in her bag again, ignoring me like I'm a naughty, attention-seeking toddler. "Look, I got that new thriller everyone's saying is awesome." She reaches for the laptop, but my bony hand grabs hers.

8

I'm determined she's going to listen. I can't handle everyone avoiding the subject any more.

"We need to talk about it. It's going to happen soon. I don't want to die, Mak, but there's not going to be any miracle. You know that, don't you?"

She looks at the floor, doesn't answer.

"It's not like last time. This is different. I can actually feel my body shutting down."

She shakes her head violently. I feel cruel, but now that I've started, I can't stop as the words start spilling out of me.

"I've been peeing myself. I'm losing control of everything. They've put a catheter in." I lift the sheet to reveal the bag of warm yellow liquid attached to the frame of the bed. "And this thing is my new best friend." I shake the syringe driver at her. "One press and the pain is put in a cage ... for a while. You should try it – it's seriously trippy." I wanted to sound calm but it comes out vicious. "You've got to listen, Mak. Mom and Dad won't stop treatment but they've got to. It's pointless. I can't take any more chemo. I'm all worn out."

"Stop talking like this!" Makayla orders, her cheery face gone. "You're not a quitter. You've got to keep your attitude positive. You're just having a bad day. Tomorrow will be better. You have to keep fighting this thing."

A wave of anger heats up my insides.

"That's such bullshit," I rumble. "I've been 'fighting' this thing for three years but it's a disease, not a freakin' opponent; some people get better, some live with it for years; others, like me, it will kill. It won't mean that I didn't *fight* hard enough, so don't make me feel like a failure." My body's fired up. The worn-out veins in my arms pulsate blue.

Tears stream down Mak's face. I've made my best friend cry, but I've got to get through to her.

"I'm sorry," she splutters. "I never meant to make you feel like that. You're the bravest person I know."

I can't suppress a bitter laugh – ME, BRAVE? I feel such an urge to let her glimpse the terror that lurks inside me and raises its monstrous head when I'm least expecting it; when I've fooled myself that I've got it tamed; when I've transported myself to a safe place, away from its clutches, a calm place where I see death as my friend. To share the terror with Makayla would haunt her forever; it would taint every happy event in her life. I can't do it to her, so I hold my tongue.

"I feel so useless, Lucy. Tell me what I can do to help you."

She's desperate; now's my chance.

"Do you really want to help me?"

"Course I do!"

"Then speak to my mom and dad. Please. Tell them it's cruel to keep up the treatment. They're not prolonging my life. All they're doing is making my dying longer."

Mak chews her bottom lip, mumbling, "They know what's best for you."

Is *that* her response? I glare at her with contempt. My energy levels come crashing down. I'm clammy, hot. Beads of sweat sting my eyes. A wave of nausea hits me. I gag, once, twice. She grabs the cardboard tray from under the bed but it's too late. Stinking chocolate-stained bile heaves up from my belly, burning my throat before spewing out over the sheet. Mak recoils; her hand covers her nose and mouth. She offers me water. It stings as I suck it down.

"I'll get the nurse." She heads towards the door but it swings open and Mom sweeps in.

"No need for the nurse. I can sort this little mess out," she says breezily.

Mom, my permanent shadow. Has she been listening outside the door? I wouldn't be surprised. This illness has been a double whammy; the cancer eats me from the inside while Mom suffocates me from the outside.

I feel like a rag doll as Mom fusses over me. She bundles up the puke-soiled bed sheet. Rolling her grey-blue eyes in mock frustration, she dabs away the slime that clings to my chin as though I'm a baby. Why do people treat me like I'm an infant? I may be riddled with cancer but my brain still works.

I try to focus on her through watery eyes. She still dresses like she's going to work – expensive tailored suit, high heels that leave imprints on the floor, but there's a smudge of lipstick on her teeth and, as she bends to get a clean sheet, I notice grey roots are showing at the top of her sleek chestnut bob. Three years ago Mom wouldn't have left the house with a hair out of place. But that's before she went from kick-ass corporate lawyer to a full-time carer – her choice, not mine. She went back to work for a few months when I was in remission and that made all of us feel a whole lot healthier. When she's only got me to think of, she gets obsessive.

11

I know that it's my fault; my illness has made her like this, but it hasn't helped that Dad has buried himself in his job. He seems to have become obsessed with earning even more money, despite the millions he's already made. He and Mom must think they make a dream team. She researches the latest experimental treatments and Dad makes sure I get them. In fact, he's like the Santa Claus of cancer treatments: "Go ahead, choose anything you want." But the problem is you can't buy a cure that hasn't been developed yet. We all know that nothing's worked, but they won't admit it. I've tried to talk to him, tell him that I'd rather we spent what time I have left as a family, enjoying myself, making memories for them for when I'm gone. He just looks at me blankly. "We've got years to make memories, sweetheart. To get you well, I need to make money."

All this money from Dad's hedge fund firm has bought me to Doctor "Call Me Leo" Radnor and his clinic in the middle of nowhere. Before him I'd seen so many physicians that I'd lost count. Sure, this one is charming and handsome in a silver fox kind of way, and he looks like he works out, but I don't understand why Mom treats him like he's some kind of god when basically he's just another person who won't let me talk about dying.

"Let's focus on the positives, Lucy," he says. "Yes, the tumors have spread, but it's still worthwhile pursuing aggressive treatment; it will give us more time."

More time for what? For me to be terrified that they won't be able to control the pain? For Dad to work 24/7? For Mom to keep hoping for the impossible? Dr Leo is supposed to be the professional. Why isn't he telling us all the truth? Is he just trying to make as much money as possible out of rich, desperate parents?

Mom tucks in the clean sheet while Mak stands awkwardly in the background.

"Sorry, Mrs Burgess, I gave her some chocolate mousse," Mak says guiltily.

"Not to worry. No harm done." Mom's smile is forced.

"Mak?" I signal to her to talk to Mom, pleading with my eyes.

She shuffles, looking embarrassed. She's not going to help me; she's itching to get out of here.

"I need to get going. My flight's in a few hours and it takes forever to get to the airport. I've got to go back for a field trip tomorrow. It's mandatory otherwise I wouldn't go." She looks at me apologetically, but that's not what she needs to be sorry for. "I'll be back in five days."

"Five days!" I echo in alarm.

"Yeah."

"But I might not have five days."

Mak looks horrified. "Don't be silly. Now give me a kiss and say *arrivederci*."

That word! It's part of her survival strategy. She's convinced herself that if we say "till we meet again" instead of goodbye it's going to keep me alive, but I can't afford to play along with her game this time.

"Don't say *arrivederci* to me, Mak, say *goodbye*."

She's scared. "You know we don't use that word. *Arrivederci*, Lucy . . . now you say it back!"

I don't answer.

13

"Say it!" she pleads.

Mom goes over and hugs her, lifting up her head so they're eye to eye. "Makayla, honey," she says gently, "Lucy isn't being mean. She's right, you need to say *goodbye*."

I'm stunned.

"Mrs Burgess, no," Mak protests.

"Yes." Mom's voice is steely.

Tears flood Makayla's eyes. She shakes out of Mom's embrace and leans down to kiss me. "*Arrivederci*, Lucy. I *will* see you in five days." She glares at Mom as she gathers her things and rushes out.

"Mom?"

She doesn't answer, but we both know that this is the first time she's acknowledged that I'm dying. I've been desperate for her to admit it but now that she has, it hits me that all hope is gone. The realization sends my body into panic; a searing pain is unleashed in my crumbling spine. I cry out, reaching blindly for the syringe driver. Mom takes it and presses.

She holds my hand in silence. We have so much to talk about, there's so much I need to say to her, but I can't. I'm distracted. Something has entered the room. It has no form but I feel its presence becoming stronger and stronger. It's indescribably beautiful. I'm overwhelmed by a feeling of joy. I hear my sobs of happiness as a great weight suddenly lifts from me and I'm moving into the very heart of it. I look back and see my lifeless body lying in the bed. All pain and fear is gone. There is no sickness, no suffering, only euphoria. I am released.

CHAPTER 2

OPEN YOUR EYES

"Open your eyes, Lucy."

I recognize that voice.

"Lucy, can you hear me? Open your eyes, please."

It's Dr Leo.

"Lucy!" His voice is commanding. "Please do as I ask and open your eyes."

I open them, only it's still black. Why can't I see anything?

"Reduce the sedation."

Who's he talking to?

"Lucy, open your eyes."

I'm trying, but I can't. I think that I keep opening them, but they must be closed still. I visualize myself stretching them as wide as an owl's, but my eyelids won't obey.

Suddenly I feel more alert, like I'm being shaken out of a hundred-year sleep. I can hear the shuffling of feet, the beeping and hissing of machines. I feel something hard around my mouth and nose.

"The sedation is wearing off. There's eye movement. Pass me the flashlight." It's another voice: a woman's voice.

A painful brightness momentarily penetrates the darkness, leaving white spots dancing behind my eyelids.

"Lucy, open your eyes!"

Please, please open! I need to see what's happening to me. Come on, do it, do it, do it! ... My eyelids begin to flutter frantically, like an injured butterfly trying to take off. They open. The air around me crackles with excitement.

"They're open!" The woman sounds ecstatic.

But all I can see are blue, blurred images against a stark white light. I sense people all around me.

I want to get up but something is gripping my head.

"Lucy, this is Doctor Leo. You must not try to move." His voice is behind me. "You've got an oxygen mask on. It's covering your mouth and nose but you should still be able to talk. Lucy, if you understand what I'm saying then say 'Yes'."

I can't form the word. My mouth is numb. I bite down into my bottom lip but feel nothing and yet my whole face is uncomfortably tight and stretched. Each time I try to summon a sound it feels like broken glass is cutting the inside of my throat.

"She's trying to speak," the woman reports.

"Take your time, Lucy. Just say 'Yes'."

Despite the pain in my throat I keep trying again and

again; eventually a grunt rises out of me. I hear a communal gasp fill the room.

"Okay, well done, Lucy. Don't worry. The fact that you've made a sound at all is good."

Dr Leo sounds more than pleased. But why? Last time I was awake I could talk, I could see! What's happened to me? I felt myself dying. Did they resuscitate me? Why would they do that? Did Mom make them?

"How's her BP and heart rate?"

"Both stable."

"Time check," Leo asks.

"Operating time so far, thirty-six hours and twenty-four minutes."

What? That can't be right. What are they doing to me?

"Okay, we need to move quickly now; test her critical function. Map out the area of eloquence. Have you got the tags?"

"Yes, Doctor."

"Then let's begin. Lucy, blink if you can see anything."

With each passing minute my sight has been slowly coming into focus. The blurred shapes are more solid. I can't make out any small detail but I can see that the room is busy with people in blue scrubs and masks. My head is elevated and fixed sideways but I cast my eyes downwards, past the oxygen mask, and I can make out that my sheet-covered body is lying on an operating table.

I blink. One of the medics in front of me whoops with delight.

"Please restrain your celebrations," Dr Leo says. "We've got a long way to go."

The figures and voices fade away and Mak is standing over me, holding my hand, grinning.

I'm flooded with relief to see her. What are they doing to me, Mak? You've got to help me get out of here.

She doesn't speak; she just starts laughing hysterically. Her head thrown back, gasping for breath like I've said the funniest thing that she's ever heard.

Stop it, Mak! Stop it! Why won't you help me? ... She fades away as a blackness descends.

"Lucy ... Lucy?" It's the woman again. Where has Mak gone? "Her eyes are open, Doctor. She's back."

"Well, let's keep it that way. We can't have her drifting. Keep sedation levels to a minimum."

Where are Mom and Dad? I want to see them. I'm scared.

"Lucy, you must focus on staying awake, okay?" Dr Radnor's voice is so gentle. "It won't be too much longer."

What won't be too much longer? What happens when it's over?

"Okay, let's continue, team. I'm beginning with establishing motor skills."

I feel something probing my head. I'm relieved that there's no pain but it makes my fingers twitch.

"Movement in fingers," one of them reports.

"Yes, I can see it on the monitor. We've got the right area but we need more than an involuntary reaction. Now, Lucy."

18

His voice addresses me. "I want you to lift your right hand. Can you do that for me?"

I look down at my hand. It's bloated and red where the IV tube is inserted. I try to lift it off the table but it's like it's not even attached to me. I can't make it move.

I feel a tug and pressure on my head.

"Try again."

My eyes bore into my hand, willing it to obey me. It starts to tingle into life. As it rises it's like I'm observing a levitation trick. My fingers touch a clear plastic sheet that seems to be suspended around me. I try to reach farther but I feel the grip on my head restraining me.

"That's wonderful, Lucy, but try to keep your head still. Now, can you feel anything in your feet?"

As he talks I feel something pricking the soles of my feet, one after the other. I try to say yes but it comes out like a growl.

"Good, the nurse just pricked you with a needle to test for sensation. Now, you'll feel another probe in your neck area and I want you to move your toes, okay."

My toes twitch and seconds later I feel them wiggling. Delighted laughter fills the operating theater.

"Tag this section. Good girl, you're doing so well. Now let's see if we have movement in your right leg."

It was one thing wiggling toes, but moving my leg is asking for a miracle.

I try and try but nothing happens. My hot breath steams up the oxygen mask as I pant. Maybe they took too long to resuscitate me and I've been left brain-damaged ... crippled. Are they just patching me up so I spend my last few days on earth locked inside a broken body? Why are Mom and Dad letting him do this to me?

The air in the operating theater is heavy with people's tension. Their eyes flit from a monitor to the sheet covering my leg. But Dr Leo isn't giving up. After each of my attempts he tugs and probes at the back of my neck, asking me to try again and again. I'm exhausted, I just want to sleep, but he's insistent.

"Try again," he orders for what seems like the hundredth time. My leg obeys, making the sheet jerk.

The room bursts into applause. People are high-fiving each other. Why are they so excited? Has he cured me? Has he gotten rid of the cancer?

"As long as she holds stable we ought to test just a couple more functions," he says.

I'm beginning to feel like a performing monkey. I don't want to do anything else. I want them to leave me alone. I need to sleep. People shift in front of me, checking monitors and adjusting my drip. I catch flashes of another operating table alongside mine. There's something on it, but it's covered with a sheet. I strain my eyes trying to make it out. The top of the sheet is blood-soaked; a congealed pool of deep red has formed on the floor below it.

What's going on? Why won't someone tell me why they're operating on me? Where are Mom and Dad? I need to get out of here!

I force my head forward but it's useless. My legs only twitch when I command them to run. I want these people to stop. I shout at them, but the noises coming out of me are like desperate grunts; like a pig being led into the slaughterhouse.

"Her heart rate is soaring. Her BP is dropping. She's going into distress!"

My heart is going to explode out of my chest. Everything starts spinning. I'm Alice tumbling down the rabbit hole.

I hear barked instructions. There's panic in the room.

"It's too dangerous to do any more assessments; we'll lose her. Put her under immediately and let's close her up."

I feel fluid pumping into my veins. I can't let them put me to sleep. What else are they going to do to me? I fight to keep my eyes open but the lids are metal shutters rolling down. I must stay awake, I . . . must . . . stay. . .

CHAPTER 3

REST IN PEACE

The tent billows above the crowd seated in rows in front of the gaping grave. Ladies clutch their black hats as the sudden breeze tries to lift them off their heads. The congregation holds their breath as the wind wobbles the enormous photograph of the girl perched on the stand next to the closed casket.

Strains of hymns rise from the solemn gathering. At the front, an elderly lady is supported by a glamorous middle-aged woman. The elderly lady's voice soars above everyone else's as she declares "Amen" at the end of the pastor's prayers. Standing apart from the congregation, Mak keeps her lips buttoned shut. She doesn't feel much like singing in praise of someone who has let her friend die.

The pastor speaks words of redemption as the pallbearers lift the casket off the pedestal and rest it on the bars across the open grave. He inhales deeply before delivering his lines.

"Earth to earth, ashes to ashes, dust to dust, in sure and certain hope of the resurrection to eternal life through our Lord Jesus Christ who will transform our frail bodies that they may be conformed to his glorious body."

Makayla shudders as the bars are removed and Lucy's coffin is slowly lowered into the ground.

She watches as Lucy's grandmother clutches her daughter, the sound of weeping carried to her on the breeze. She sees Lucy's mom reach out to touch her husband's arm, only for him to pull away, stony-faced.

Another hymn springs up as the congregation processes to the grave to offer a silent prayer and throw earth on to the coffin. But when Makayla reaches the soil-filled basket, she hesitates.

"Go on, honey," her mama encourages her.

Mak looks down at the coffin; a layer of soil already covers the lid. Her belly twists.

"I can't," she says, rushing out of the tent.

CHAPTER 4

AWAKE

There's an excruciating pain in my head. Is Dr Leo still operating on me? Has the anesthetic worn off? Oh, God, I have to get him to stop!

My eyes shoot open. Everything is blurred but I try to keep calm, giving them time to focus. Slowly a softly lit room appears. I can see one window down at the far end, but there's no light shining through it. Is it dark outside? Is it night-time? How long have I been asleep? Hours? Days? Weeks?

I'm lying in a bed but the image of the table I saw in the operating theater flashes into my mind; I see the stained sheet draped over the shape and the pool of blood on the floor. I screw my eyes up to chase it away. I feel so strange, but I shouldn't panic. I just need to talk to Dr Leo. He'll be able to explain what happened. I've got to focus on my surroundings. My head isn't restrained any more, it's free to look around, but every slight movement feels like a hammer-blow to my skull.

I must still be in the clinic. The room looks familiar, only now I'm hooked up to a whole load of monitors next to the bed. My eyes inspect my hands lying by my sides. They still don't look right, but the swelling and redness has gone down despite the drips inserted in them. I'm breathing without an oxygen mask but when I suck in the warm air my lungs ache.

I notice Mom's scarf draped over a chair next to the bed and feel a jolt of relief. It's okay. She's been here, watching over me, keeping me safe. I see my hand reaching to press the call button on the wall, but when I look again it hasn't moved . . . I'm imagining things. I've got to get a grip on this. I concentrate on my hand and make my fingers twitch. I focus harder and it starts to rise off the bed. I reach it out to press the call button but the movement makes me woozy. I'm going to be sick! I need to sit up. I try to push myself upright but every muscle in my body protests. I feel like I've been run over by a freight train; I can't do it. I lie very still, looking up at the ceiling, just trying not to throw up.

The red blinking light of a camera high up in the corner of the room catches my eye. I try to call out, producing a barrage of grunts as I'm overwhelmed by panic. What has happened to me? Is it brain damage? A stroke? Is that why I can hardly move – why I can't speak?

The door opens. Dr Leo hurries in with his staff; behind

25

them I can see Mom and Dad. Hot tears stream down my face at the sight of them.

Dr Leo gives me the most joyous smile. "It's so wonderful to see you awake."

He ushers his staff forward to look at me. "Note her tears, her emotional response. The limbic system is functioning correctly and there's no sign of facial nerve damage."

Mom rushes over and sits on the bed. She looks terrible, like she hasn't slept for days. Her quivering fingers float above my cheeks, but she doesn't touch me. Her stare is so intense it's frightening me.

"Do you know who I am?" Her voice shakes.

Why's she asking that? Of course I know who she is.

"Mom," I grunt.

"Yes, yes, Mom." Her eyes fill with tears. "And who's that?" She points to Dad, who stands in the background, his eyes cast to the ground.

"Dad." I'm saying the right word, even if it doesn't sound like it.

"Yes, Dad. Oh, Lucy, my Lucy!" She kisses me so gently.

She must see the fear on my face. I need to know what happened. Tell me what happened!

Dr Leo looms over me, smiling calmly. "I understand that you're confused and more than a little frightened right now, but believe me, everything is going to be all right. You've been in an induced coma for a while, to help with the healing. You see, you've had major surgery ... pioneering surgery, and we are all very optimistic about the outcome."

How can he say that? Can't he see me? Surely I'm in a worse way than I was before?

"Don't worry," he says gently. "I'm confident that your voice will come back, and the signs are that you'll regain full mobility. The surgery wasn't just about extending your life for weeks, even months. This operation has given you a whole new life and, with rehab, you'll get stronger and stronger."

"How? Cancer!" I grunt at him angrily. He's lying. I know that my cancer is terminal. He's put me through this pointless operation to keep Mom and Dad hoping.

He shakes his head, his brown eyes sparkling with excitement through his frameless glasses. "While you've been sleeping . . . healing, you've had scans, tests, and I can guarantee you are cancer-free. Everything looks great."

I gasp. It can't be true. I look to Mom and Dad for confirmation. Mom looks elated but Dad's face is so solemn, it's almost as though I've been given bad news.

"It's true, honey. The cancer is gone. Dr Radnor has done something miraculous," Mom says, her expression ecstatic.

I stare at Dr Radnor in awe, tears running down my face. I can't get the words to come out, but even if I *could* speak, nothing I could say could express how grateful I am. The overwhelming relief of being free from this disease that has taken so much of my life, caused me such pain, such terror. How do I thank a man who has saved me from death?

"It's okay, you don't have to say anything." He touches my hand. "I know that you'll be in pain right now." He presses a

27

button on one of the machines. The medication it releases makes me sink deep into the bed.

Mom leans down and kisses me. "We'll be here when you wake up again."

"Tell Mak! Tell Grandma!" I smile to help Mom decipher my words, but she must not understand; she suddenly looks so sad.

CHAPTER 5

THE GIRL IN THE WINDOW

Someone is rubbing my hand, stroking my cheek.

"Lucy. Lucy." Mom's soothing voice is in my ear. It's her soft hands I can feel.

Am I late for school? I'd better get up!

As my eyes open I look around, confused. This isn't my bedroom . . . I'm still here, in the clinic, but my heart swells with relief at the memory of Dr Leo's words – he said the cancer is gone. He's made me well again.

Dr Leo is at my side, studying the beeping monitors with his staff.

Mom sits in the chair next to me, smiling. "Well, that was another long nap you had, young lady."

I've lost all sense of time but I think Mom is in different clothes and the darkness from the window means that it's night-time again.

"You're definitely looking better today, don't you think so, Lewis?" She beckons Dad forward but he stays put. He looks well-dressed – he always looks well-dressed – but his eyes are bloodshot and he's all on edge, like he'd rather be anywhere else than here.

I stare at him, wishing he'd come over. I want his reassurance. I don't understand why he seems so upset.

I glance down at the sheets. My shape seems bigger in the bed. Whatever drugs have been pumped into me have made my shrunken body bloat. I've seen it happen before; the cocktail of drugs turn my body into a balloon, inflating and deflating as they mess with it.

"Well, hello again," Dr Leo says cheerfully. "Let's just sit you up a little." He instructs his staff to ease me up. Everything aches, especially my head: it feels like a constant stabbing in my skull.

"Kate, our physical therapist, has been working on you while you've been asleep. She reports that you've been responding well."

I wince. I don't like the idea of someone "working on" me when I'm unconscious; not knowing what they're doing to me, not being able to say no.

"Are you in pain?" Dr Leo asks.

"Hurt," I grunt. My hands seem to rise without much effort as I place them on my head. I gasp as my fingers explore my bald scalp. My fingertips bump over staples around the top of my skull, continuing a short way down my spine. I shudder inside. Dr Leo must have had to open my skull. I don't dare to imagine what it looks like.

"Why?" The sound of my voice is more human.

Mom hesitates. She looks to Dr Leo for help. He steps forward as she shrinks back.

"It was a vital part of the surgery," he says, pouring a cup of water and placing it by my bedside. "I can hear an improvement in your voice already, but your throat needs lubricating. Lean across and take the cup."

I need to get my voice back, make myself understood, so I do as he asks even though my body protests. He seems to be assessing me as I reach for the cup. At first I miss it and on the second attempt I knock it over, the water spilling on to the floor.

"Don't worry," he says, refilling it. "It'll be easier using your right hand."

But I'm left-handed; it's only going to be harder using the wrong one. I concentrate and pick up the cup using my right hand. It's definitely easier. How did he know?

He nods with satisfaction. He opens a medicine cabinet in the corner of the room and takes out two small pills.

"Swallow them one by one with the water. They're a heavy-dosage painkiller. They'll control your headache. Brain surgery can leave the patient with an initial intense discomfort, but we can manage it with these drugs until things get back to normal."

I hesitantly put the first pill in my mouth and take a sip of water. It feels like a pebble is stuck in my throat. I gulp down more water in a panic. I cough and splutter as the pill goes down.

"Good," Dr Leo says. "Now, the second one. It'll be easier, you'll see."

He's right. The other pill isn't so hard to swallow.

Mom is beaming at me. "You're doing so well, honey."

"I think that we need to get you moving," Dr Leo announces. "Kate has done a great job with your physical therapy, but the longer you lie in bed, the more chance you have of developing blood clots."

He can't expect me to get up. I'm not ready! I look to Mom in a panic, but she's smiling and nodding.

"Come on, there's nothing to be afraid of. I wouldn't ask you if I didn't think that you could do it." Dr Leo bends down to me.

He carefully removes the IVs from my hands and unhooks me from the monitors. He pulls the sheet clear, revealing my gown-clad body. He slowly swings my legs out of the bed so that my feet dangle just above the floor.

"Okay, up you get! I'm here to hold you, but only if you need it," he says encouragingly.

The whole room holds its breath as I plant my feet on the floor. I push my hands into the mattress and make it halfway up before collapsing back down again. I feel sweat escaping every pore, like someone turned a tap on.

Dr Leo tuts playfully when he sees how frustrated I am. "Don't give up before you've even started." He takes both my hands and pulls me back on to my feet. He waits a minute before releasing my hands, but I feel like I'm falling forward.

"Straighten up!" he says encouragingly.

He's right. I'm hunched over like a crooked old lady. I breathe through the ache as I pull my shoulders back and look straight ahead. Wow! That's better. It's like my spine has clicked into place.

"Good. Now take a step towards me," he says.

I can do this! I lurch forward but my feet don't come with me. He reaches out to steady me.

"Tell your feet to move," he says.

I look at him, puzzled.

"In your head you must instruct your feet to step forward."

He lets go of me and I straighten up again, taking my time. Beads of salty sweat are running into my eyes. I feel damp patches bloom under my armpits.

I ... can ... do ... this. I visualize each foot moving as I command my body. *Right foot – step forward.* I watch in excitement as it moves. *Left foot – step forward.* It obeys. *Now, feet – you're going to walk!*

I start to move. I'm wobbling and lurching like I'm on the deck of a tiny boat in a violent storm. My arms instinctively stretch out in front of me in case I fall, but my legs remain stiff as iron rods.

Dr Leo is holding out his hands inches away from me, like a father encouraging his baby's first steps. "Soften your knees. Let them bend. Tell them what to do. Take control."

Take control! Take control! I tell my legs to relax, my knees to soften. My feet stop shuffling and start lifting off the floor,

33

but I'm still wobbling. I bump into Mom and she maneuvers me back on track, like I'm a go-kart. With every step my tight, aching muscles are easing; even my headache feels less intense. I'm growing more confident, getting giddy with excitement as I circle the room. If I can make improvements this quickly, imagine how I'll be after more physical therapy, more exercise.

The thought of it makes laughter bubble up in my tight chest. A noise explodes from my throat, sounding like a goose honking. Mom responds with peals of laughter and tears start to roll down her face.

"Lewis! Lewis! Look at her. It's incredible, isn't it?" Mom says to Dad, but he looks so serious, so tense that I can't stand it.

He needs a hug. He needs to know that I'm okay. He won't have to stress about me any more. I was upset that he's been working all the time, but he did it for me. He did it so we could afford to have this . . . this miracle surgery.

I stumble towards him and fall into his arms.

"Thank you, Dad," I croak, wrapping my arms around him.

I feel his body stiffen. He isn't returning my hug.

"It's okay," I tell him.

I look up and see his whole face crumple. God, what's wrong? He looks like he's going to cry.

"No, Lewis!" Mom shouts as he eases my arms from around him and steps away. I'm unbalanced. I grab the windowsill for support and suddenly I see a girl, standing outside in the darkness, looking through the glass. She startles me. She's a ghostly figure, barely there. She's wearing a white gown. Her head is shaved. Her eyes are sky blue, like mine, but she has hooded lids and thick lashes. She's taller than me, with long limbs and a heart-shaped face. Her mouth is petite with full lips and the poor girl looks like she's had a beating. Her face is discolored and bruised. She looks puzzled, confused. I wonder what she's doing here.

I wave at her and she waves back ... no, not back, she waved at the same time ... didn't she? I wave again. She did ... it was ... it was exactly the same time. How's she doing that? I touch the glass and she does it simultaneously. I run my hands down my face, and watch through my fingers. She's mirroring my every move. This isn't funny, it's freaking me out.

"Stop it!" I shout, and see her mouth shape the words at the same time. God, she's creepy. How is she doing this?

I know how to stop her copying me. I pick up the medical file that's lying on the windowsill. I close my eyes and hold it in front of me. She can't copy something that she hasn't got. I open my eyes, ready to declare myself the winner, but she's there, holding up the same medical file, the one with my name written on the cover, only now it's backwards.

Our hands fly to cover our mouths as we gasp. I turn to Mom and Dad, trembling.

"Do you see her?"

They don't answer. Dad is looking at me pityingly. Mom's face is ashen, her mouth pinched shut.

I say a silent prayer to ward off the girl. I turn back, but she's still there. She looks terrified.

But then I realize what's going on and the girl and I laugh, our shoulders shaking in relief. She's nothing but a hallucination. I must be as high as a kite with all the drugs the doctor has given me. This is tame. I could be seeing a pink elephant flying around the room.

We stick out our tongues at each other. We flick a finger at each other. I can't stop laughing although it hurts.

Dr Leo places his hands on my shoulders. He leads me away from the window and sits me on the bed.

"No more drugs. Messing with my head," I splutter. He doesn't smile. He crouches down in front of me and holds my hands.

"I'm going to explain something to you and it's extremely important that you stay as calm as possible. Do you understand?"

The tone of his voice puts a stop to my manic laughter. Dread starts to creep over me.

"Yes."

He produces a mirror from his pocket and holds it to my face. The girl who's stolen my eyes is back again, but this time her image is sharp and in technicolor. The stapled ridge around her bald skull looks hot and angry. Her lips are pulsating red, her eyes shine and her heart-shaped face is covered in fading bruises. She has an old scar just above one eye that leaves a track through her thick, dark eyebrows.

"Not real," I tell him. "In my head."

"No. You're not hallucinating. She is real. She is *you*."

The girl in the mirror looks furious. Her lips twist, her eyes narrow.

"Liar!"

Mom is at my side. "Lucy, listen to me. I know this is unbelievably hard for you, but be brave. Everything is okay. You mustn't be afraid. Dr Radnor isn't lying. The girl you can see is you."

I stare into the mirror. The girl's eyes are frozen with shock, her mouth a perfect circle of horror. Her face contorts as a strangled scream fills the room.

CHAPTER 6

TRAPPED

Hands grip me as I lash out hysterically, unable to catch my breath. Mom and Dad retreat into the corner of the room as Dr Leo inserts a needle into my arm, saying quietly, "We don't want you injuring yourself. This will just calm you down. Don't worry."

The hands continue to hold me as my rigid body begins to relax and stops resisting. Somewhere in the back of my mind I know that I should still be panicking, terrified, but now I can't summon up any of these emotions. A calmness has been forced on me and I can't fight it.

"Good girl," Dr Leo says gently. "Sit up now." He signals for me to be released and motions for his staff to back away.

He makes me have more sips of water and I do it obediently.

He takes a deep breath, saying, "I'm going to tell you everything and, of course, you'll have a lot of questions, but please try to just listen and take it in. You need to know that this has all been done with your parents' consent and it's all been done to save you. But, before I explain, you must understand the most important thing, and that is that despite everything, *you* are still *you*."

What? Why is he talking in riddles? What have my parents let him do to me?

He sits down on the edge of my bed, looking me in the eye. "You know that your cancer was incurable and you were very close to death. You're only sixteen years old – too young to die. Your parents came to me because they found out about my specialist area of research. They understood that no one could cure you, but for decades I've been working on a procedure that can offer people a chance of another life. And now, after years of experimentation, I've finally succeeded with you." He tries to suppress his elation.

"What have you done?" I whisper.

"I performed an operation that put your brain, which was unaffected by the cancer, into a donor body."

I stare at him blankly. I feel numb. I heard what he said but I can't understand it.

"This has saved you," he says. "All indications show that the operation has been a triumph. I was even able to retain your own eyes: the windows to your soul."

Those sky-blue eyes I saw in the mirror? Is he saying that they're all that's left of me?

"A small number of scientists around the world have tried

39

and failed to perform this operation. Most of the scientific community believe it's impossible. One of the major barriers was the ability to successfully connect the donor's spinal cord to the recipient's brain. Without this connection, the procedure is useless, leaving the recipient without any movement or sensory function. But I have succeeded where all the others have failed." He looks at me expectantly, as if he wants me to congratulate him.

"I used your own stem cells to build bridges between you and the donor body," he continues, unable to hide his excitement any longer. "You clearly have a fully functioning central nervous system. And with rehabilitation, your mobility and function will only get stronger."

My brain in someone else's body? I pull at the hospital gown and it comes away, exposing a naked body.

"Lucy, not now. Cover yourself up," Mom gasps, hands fluttering to find a blanket.

I ignore her and gaze down at it. The skin is plump and creamy, not sagging and grey. There are no rivers of blue veins flowing under a paper-thin surface. The breasts are full and pert, not shrivelled like popped balloons. The belly is taut with no trace of a hollow. The pubes are jet black and neat. The legs are toned and slender with muscular thighs and calves; there are no jutting-out hip bones and toadstool kneecaps on withered limbs. I flex the arms and small, hard biceps rise up. This body is strong, not weak. This body is full of life, not on the verge of death.

"Whose body is this?" I murmur, in a daze.

"It doesn't matter whose body it was. It's yours now," Dr Leo says firmly.

"No! Tell me." I gaze at the elegant hands and long fingers, knowing that they don't belong to me.

"A donor. A girl your age," Dr Radnor replies.

"She died suddenly of a brain aneurysm," Mom interrupts. Dr Radnor seems to scowl at her, but she continues. "Her parents were devastated, of course, but they wanted to donate her body to help others. It has brought them great comfort to know that some good has come out of their tragedy. You can understand why, can't you, Lucy?"

A girl my age? Donated by her parents? The words float around my mind.

"What's her name?" I insist.

"No." Dr Radnor shakes his head. "I'm sorry but I'm afraid all that information is confidential. We'd never let a patient know those details. It's a breach of trust."

My breath catches in my throat; I suddenly think of the blood-soaked sheet covering the shape in the operating theater. Was that me? It *must* have been me! "Where's *my* body? What's happened to it?"

"It was of no use to you any more," Dr Leo says gently.

"It's gone, Lucy. It's been buried," Mom whispers. "We had a funeral. All the people who love you were there. They all came to say goodbye."

A funeral? I ought to be hysterical, but my breathing remains steady as the medication does its job. "But I'm not dead. Why would you tell everyone I am?"

41

"No, but ... but ... you see, Lucy..." Mom can't finish. She looks at Dad pleadingly. "Please, Lewis, help me."

Dad walks over, his whole body rigid with stress. "Everyone thinks you're dead. People knew how sick you were; they've all been expecting it. We had to hold a funeral to make sure that no questions will be asked." His voice cracks.

Dr Leo looks at me gravely. "This operation is revolutionary ... ahead of its time. You must understand that even before the first organ transplants there were moral objections fuelled by ignorance and suspicion. Sometimes we scientists have to wait for society to catch up with us. Once people realize that I have made whole-body transplants a reality, they will come to appreciate that this is the future – that this incredible operation will save countless numbers of people who would have died prematurely, but we couldn't wait for years of medical-committee approvals and endless legislation, so in the eyes of the law, what I've done to save you is illegal."

"Do you have to burden her with this now?" Mom protests to him. "Don't you think that she has enough to take in?"

"It's best that she knows where we stand right from the start," Dr Leo says, silencing Mom. "You want to understand, don't you, Lucy? You wouldn't want me to keep the facts from you? If people found out about the transplant, your parents and I could be imprisoned and you would be left alone. There are people out there who would use you, exploit you, but we're here to protect you. We'll keep you safe but, for your own sake as well as your parents', you can't tell anyone who you are."

I want to cry but the tears won't come. "But if I can't be me, then who am I?"

Mom tries to sound confident as she covers me up and fastens the gown. "We've put things in place. You'll always be our Lucy, of course, but Dr Radnor has sorted out a new identity for you, a new history. But there's no need to think about all that now."

I feel sick. "But Grandma . . . Mak? Won't they know who I am?"

"You'll see them but you can't tell them. I'm so sorry, but this is for your own sake. No one must know the truth," Mom says, not meeting my eye.

"Why have you done this to me?" I want to scream it, but there's no volume.

"Because we love you, Lucy, and we couldn't let you die." Mom wraps her arms around this stranger's body.

"But this isn't me," I say, bewildered.

"You must not think like that," Dr Leo says firmly. "It is you. The donor body is merely a vessel, but it's your brain, and what it contains, that makes you who you are. I'll assess everything during your rehab but the signs are good – all your thoughts, memories, attitudes, experiences should be intact, and *they* are what still make you Lucy Burgess. Your brain is the boss. It will map itself to this new body. It will take control of it, so the two work as a whole, in harmony. Soon your brain and this body will work so naturally together

43

that you'll forget that this isn't your original form. You must believe me. You are still who you were before the operation."

I feel a room full of eyes burning into me, scrutinizing me, waiting to see what I'll say and do next. I know what I am; I'm a freak, a fascinating freak that they're in awe of.

"Get out. All of you get out." My voice croaks and cracks when I want it to roar.

Dr Leo gestures to his staff to leave. "Of course. You need time to digest all this."

"I'll stay." Mom pulls up a chair.

"Go!" I glare at her.

She looks wounded and I'm glad. "I'll wait outside until you're ready; it doesn't matter how long you need." She leans over to kiss me but I turn away.

The door closes behind them and I'm left alone, wishing that this drug-induced calm will never wear off. I don't want to feel the reality of being trapped inside another girl's body.

CHAPTER 7

REHAB

I stare out of the rehab room window, watching as the wind outside gathers strength. Pretty soon it'll whip into a sandstorm that will turn the hot air yellow and pelt the glass so hard that I always think it's going to crack. The gusts are sending sand skittering around the clinic's garden. Not that it's much of a garden: a few desert plants fighting for survival in the cracked earth, a couple of benches against the high surrounding walls, a fancy fountain with water cascading down a marble statue of some naked goddess. My thoughts turn to Mak and Grandma. I miss them so much. I can't stop worrying about them. How must they be feeling when they think that they've lost me forever?

"Renee, should we continue?" Tess asks.

I snap back to attention, bristling at the sound of my false name. At first I protested every single time they used it, but after four months I know that they're not going to stop. They can say it all they want, but I know my *real* name.

"Sure," I reply. I'm actually glad to be having the speech therapy sessions with Tess. I look forward to them ... and the physical therapy with Kate. Dr Leo is astounded by my progress and is having them push me more and more each day.

The only side effects from the surgery seems to be the slight hand tremors that I've developed, but they don't happen very often and I try to play them down. I don't want Dr Leo keeping me here for months of more rehab and tests. I hate it in here. This ghost town of a clinic is so claustrophobic. He doesn't let me go anywhere. He won't even let me have my cell or use the internet. He insists that it's for my own good and Mom just agrees with him.

I'd be better off in a prison; at least there I'd have other inmates to talk to. In here, it's just Dr Leo, his staff and Mom, of course – how could I forget her? She's taken up residence down another corridor and, just like before the operation, she never lets me out of her sight. Dad, on the other hand, is still avoiding me. He's always full of apologies, says that work's keeping him away, but he's lying. When he *does* visit, I've noticed that he hardly looks at me. People used to say, "You're the absolute image of your daddy." I always knew that Mom was the good-looking one and that Dad and I weren't going to win any beauty pageants, but our similarity created a special bond between us. I'd always been a daddy's girl, but since the surgery he can't see *me* any more.

"Come on, Renee, concentrate," Tess says, in mock frustration. "Try some deep abdominal breathing and let's do ten 'oh' sounds as you exhale."

I like Tess. She's nice ... middle-aged, maternal. She's friendly without actually being my friend.

I take a deep breath and start repeating a deep, reverberating "oh". I sound like an ape. "Am I ever going to sound like I used to?" I ask despondently.

"Listen, you've made such great improvements. Every word is clear. Your voice has a husky quality now, but that's not a bad thing ... it's an attractive tone." She smiles.

"But Dr Leo keeps telling me that my brain is in control of everything. That I can get this body ... **her** body to do as I want, but I can't, can I?"

"You have the donor's vocal chords so, after sixteen years of being shaped by her accent, they're not going to adapt enough to sound like your original voice. But you can talk clearly and that's the important thing."

I know that I should be grateful to be able to talk at all after what Dr Leo has done to me, but it's painful to realize that I've lost *my* voice forever.

Weeks slip by, but it's hard to tell what season it is in the desert. Each month just seems to bring varying degrees of scorching heat outside. I long for the lush gardens back home. I picture myself chasing Arthur around the paddocks and going to see Moonshine at the stables.

I help Kate put the mats out in the physical therapy room. I always feel better in here. Kate is my favorite person in this place. She makes the exercises fun. We race around the room on the Swiss balls. She hangs a net up and we play volleyball, but more important than that, Kate seems to understand how hard I'm finding all this. She doesn't tell me that I'm lucky; that I should be grateful. She doesn't just expect me to accept being trapped in someone else's body.

"Do you think that you can manage to look at how you're standing? It will help with your posture," Kate says gently, pointing to the wall of mirrors.

"No, sorry." I turn away. I can't do it. I don't want to see **her**. I've got to try and keep hold of Lucy Burgess and that means not looking at **her**; not being reminded of what they've done to me. I told Dr Leo to get rid of all the mirrors in this place, but he insists that it's good for me, that it will help with my "psychological adjustment". But how am I supposed to "adjust" to being a freak?

"How long have I been here now? It feels like years," I groan to Kate.

"It'll be six months come Friday," she says sympathetically. "Listen, I know that it feels like an eternity, but the rehab has paid off. Look at you! Your mobility is beyond anyone's expectations. Soon you'll be able to take advantage of how supple you are."

"But it's not me who's supple, is it? It's **her**. I don't even walk like I used to."

It was obvious from the beginning that **her** feet angle slightly outwards. When I position them straight it aches and within seconds they're pointing out again. When Mom first noticed, she declared with delight that I walked like a ballerina.

"It can't be changed, but it's fine," Kate says. "Just let the feet position where they want to. The tendons and muscles are set this way."

"I don't want to walk like **her**. I want to walk like *me!*" I protest.

How can **her** body ever be mine when she has power over it, like dictating the way I speak and walk? But I also know that in the months before the transplant I couldn't walk at all without getting breathless, without feeling a hundred years old. Didn't every minute that I was in pain feel like a lifetime? Didn't I spend my days too exhausted to do anything, to be anyone?

I catch a glimpse of **her** reflection in the mirror. I should be thankful to this girl, but I can't face **her**.

As I turn from the mirror I see Dr Leo heading into the room with two men I don't recognize.

"Good afternoon, Renee. You're looking well." Dr Leo gives me one of his charming smiles. "These two gentlemen are colleagues of mine. They're interested in learning more about what we've achieved and it would help them greatly to meet you."

"I'm not sure, Dr Leo." I suddenly feel vulnerable. I sense the men's eyes inspecting me as I stand in my sweatpants and tank top.

"Don't you want to let others learn from what we've achieved?" Dr Leo looks disappointed in me. I don't know what to say. Am I being selfish? I've had months of being examined ... tested. I should be used to it by now, but this feels different.

"Are you okay, Renee?" Kate squeezes my arm supportively.

"I'm not sure." My voice is quivering.

Kate's expression hardens as she looks at the men, then to Dr Leo.

Dr Leo holds her stare. "Kate, please reassure Renee that everything is fine."

"It's okay, Renee," she says hesitantly.

I nod reluctantly.

"Good, just relax, Renee. Could you bend your head forward for us?" Dr Radnor asks.

I feel **her** cheeks blazing as he invites the men to feel the scars on **her** skull and explains the details of the surgery.

I can't even bear to look at **her** body and now these strangers are pawing it. I close my eyes but Dr Leo asks me to open up so the men can shine a spotlight into them.

"I was able to keep her original eyes," he tells them with pride, as they nod in admiration.

He encourages the men to move me this way and that, asking me to bend and stretch as they run their fingers down **her** spine. I feel like a piece of meat in a butcher's shop.

The two men talk to each other in hushed tones, making notes enthusiastically.

Dr Leo promises to talk them through the video of the operation.

I feel sick at the thought of it.

"I think Renee needs to rest," Kate intervenes, putting her arm around me.

"Yes, you're right. I don't want to tire her." Dr Leo looks pleased. "Thank you, Renee. This has been invaluable."

I'm slouching in the chair, staring at Mom across the cafeteria table. I'm so sick of her company, week after week, month after month.

"Let's try it again. Repeat after me – my name is Renee Wodehouse. I was born June 1, 2002, in San Diego, California," Mom says impatiently.

"My name is Lucy Burgess. I was born August 4, 2002, in Houston, Texas," I fire back.

Mom gives a heavy sigh. "Come on now; you can't keep this up forever. You've got to start helping us to help you. It won't be safe to let you out of the clinic until Dr Radnor is satisfied that you're ready. Don't you want to get home and see Arthur?"

I stare at her with such contempt. She knows that I ache to see Arthur. It's cruel to use him as a bribe.

"Don't look at me like that, Renee."

"My name's not Renee. You're supposed to be my mother, you should know that." I scowl.

"Dr Radnor says that it's best if I only ever call you by your adopted name. It'll help you adapt to your new identity."

"I don't want a new identity," I snap.

"How many times are you going to make me go through this? You know that you have no choice," she says, exasperatedly.

"Yeah, and whose fault is that? You did this to me without

asking. You've made me into a freak and now you expect me to be grateful." I feel **her** fingers suddenly tapping on the table. **Her** hands are shaking again.

Mom masks her unease with a bright smile and upbeat voice. "Don't worry. It'll pass. Now come on, let's keep practicing. When where you born, Renee?"

I try to control the tremor as I gulp down the glass of Coke in front of me.

"You've developed a real taste for that," Mom says.

"I haven't developed a taste for it; it's **her**, *she* loves it. **Her** taste buds override my memories of what I like; why else do I crave ketchup and burgers and coffee? I've never liked any of that stuff," I protest.

"I've been telling you since day one; you've got to stop saying 'she' and 'her'," Mom warns.

"Well, I'd call her by her name if I knew it," I snap.

"It's not good to think of this body as someone else's. It's yours now. It belongs to you."

"No, it doesn't; it never will. You should have just let me die!" I shout.

"Just think about what you're saying. Is that how you *really* feel? That you'd rather be dead than alive?" Mom flares up.

I hesitate, confused. She's right; I don't want to be dead, but how can I live like this?

"I hate you for doing this to me," I hiss.

"I refuse to feel guilty," she says defiantly. "You're my child and I did what I had to do to save your life. And now it's up to you whether you waste this incredible second chance

52

or you make the decision to embrace it and start living again."

I grab the Coke glass and hurl it across the room. It smashes into pieces as it hits the wall. I look at **her** hands; they're steady again. I can't help but get a kick out of the strength of this body. I storm past Mom and stride through the silent corridors, passing the restricted area that leads to the operating theater and Dr Leo's labs. I shudder as I hurry past them.

As I walk faster I'm aware of an odor coming off **her** body; it's not unpleasant, it's slightly sickly sweet, but it's not a smell I recognize as myself. Before they did this to me, when I was practically bedridden with the cancer, I'd be aware of the sharp, chemical smell of my sweat as I lay there festering. The chemo drugs would seep out of my pores, turning my belly. I try to remember what I used to smell like, not just before this body, but before I got sick . . . but I can't.

I reach my room and slam the door behind me, pulling down the blind to block out the sunlight. Everywhere is shrouded in darkness. I feel my way to the windowless bathroom. I turn on the walk-in shower and strip off in the darkness, eyes closed, listening to the jet of water hitting the tiled floor. As I step under, the warm water cascades over **her** body, pummeling the muscles, making me relax. I squeeze the lavender-scented shower gel on to the hands and massage it into the scalp. I can feel the soft, short bristles that have erupted on the surface. **Her** hair is trying to reclaim **her** head. I run fingertips along the raised surgery scar; she won't be able to take this back; no hair will ever grow there again. My eyes remain closed as I tip the head back; the top of the spine crackles but doesn't hurt. The water beats down on **her** face. I let go of the constant voice in my mind that tells me this isn't my body and, instead, I allow sensation to take over. I smother every inch of the firm body in foaming gel. Palms glide over smooth arms, boobs, belly, thighs, butt. My body was never like this. I'd barely hit puberty when I got sick. From the age of thirteen it was shaped by cancer and the drugs trying to stop it. I only ever got to see my real body when I was in remission; tantalizing glimpses of health before it was snatched away again.

I feel **her** armpits, spiky with new hair growth, lower legs stubbly, finger and toenails getting longer. I'm appalled and in awe of how **her** body continues to grow with me in it. I open my eyes, hands in the air, suddenly not wanting to touch **her**.

I turn the shower off and cover up with a dressing gown. I feel my way to the bed and crawl under the covers, pulling **her** knees up to the chest, closing my eyes and trying to conjure up memories to remind me who I am. It's easy; they come flooding into my mind.

I can smell the towering Christmas tree in our living room, sparkling with baubles and lights. I'm ten years old, wearing my fleecy PJs. It's dark outside. I'm surrounded by presents. Dad walks towards me carrying a big box with a red bow tied around it. He places it carefully down in front of me and I tear at the wrapping, opening the flaps. A black nose pokes out and then the box tilts over as a bundle of golden fluff with floppy ears crawls out. The puppy jumps up at me, licking my face and yapping. He's the cutest thing that I've ever seen – Arthur.

It's my first day at Bailey Heights. I'm such a dorky little kid with train tracks on my teeth. Mom drops me off but I don't want to get out of the car. There are hundreds of students swarming through the entrance. They all look older, bigger, cooler than me. How come the girls are all so pretty? They flick their hair and laugh with the boys and I feel like I'm from another planet. Mom kisses me, tells me not to be silly. I open the car door and get my bag strap wrapped around my ankles. I topple out of the car, scrambling to get off the ground. I hear slaps of laughter as people pass by and I want to die. But then I feel hands around me, helping me up.

"You okay?" the cute, plump girl asks.

"Yeah, just feeling stupid," I mumble.

"Don't worry about it, everyone just saw my mama crying and shouting, 'Good luck, baby.' Now that's embarrassing!"

We laugh and walk through the gates together and that's that; me and Mak, joined at the hip.

Escaping into my memories is making me happy … relaxed, but I'm aware of my breathing getting heavier: sleep is overpowering me. I'm drifting into it.

*I'm looking at **her**. **Her** hair has grown into a flowing ebony mane; the heart-shaped face is blemish-free. There's a serenity about **her**; **her** eyes … my eyes, seem calm and languid.*

Now is the time to ask. "Please give them back to me."

"Of course, Lucy." Her voice is like honey.

*I watch, paralyzed with horror, as she gouges out the eyes from **her** face with **her** fingernails. She holds the Jell-O–like orbs towards me, blood dripping from the empty sockets in her face.*

I gasp awake, flinging off the covers. Sobs build up in my throat. Then, like a dam wall breaking, my wailing fills the darkness.

The light stutters on as Dr Leo rushes into the room.

"I was asleep . . . I keep having nightmares about me and **her**," I sob at him.

He sits down on the bed, close to me. "It's okay. I understand that you get distressed. But you're not helping yourself, Renee. You must stop referring to your body as if it doesn't belong to you. You're only making things more difficult for yourself."

"Don't you understand how hard this is?" I thump the bed in frustration.

His warm brown eyes look full of sympathy. "You can't change it now. You've got to stop fighting and accept what happened; then you can start to actually enjoy what I have done for you."

"But you never even asked whether I wanted this. You just went ahead and made me into a freak," I mumble.

He shakes his head. "Your parents made the decision for your own good and, as for being a freak . . . well, you're looking at this all wrong. You're not a freak; you're an extraordinary human being, unique on this planet. You are living proof that I can go on to save the lives of countless young people. You're at the very center of something magnificent, world-changing; how many people can say that about themselves?"

I feel tears well up in my eyes again. "But I'm not me any more," I splutter.

He wipes my tears away with his soft hand, his voice full of passion. "Yes, you are. These are your thoughts that you're expressing, your emotions; they belong to Lucy Burgess and no one else. All I've done is give you a fit and healthy body to replace a disease-ridden shell. Doesn't it feel wonderful to be free of all that pain?"

The memory of the terrible pain triggers a shiver through **her** body.

"Did you try this operation on anyone before me?" I ask apprehensively.

"Yes," he replies solemnly. "I've been attempting the procedure over a number of years. Three of my patients died on the operating table and a fourth was left paralyzed from the neck down."

"What happened to him?"

"He only survived a few weeks," he says sadly. "These patients were like you; they had nothing to lose by attempting the transplant."

"So why has the operation worked so well on me?" I ask in confusion.

"Because of the advances I've made, because of techniques that weren't available to me even five years ago, because of the boundaries that I've pushed to make this happen." He looks deep in thought.

"What boundaries?"

"Well, boundaries that held less committed scientists back, but I was determined that with you I'd be successful, and the results have proved beyond my expectations." His face lights up. "I know that you won't waste my gift, and as soon as I think that you're ready, you'll be able to go home. That's what you want, isn't it?"

"Of course it is." I'd do anything to get home. He knows how crazy I'm going in here.

"So you just need to show me that you've accepted your body and that you can live convincingly as Renee."

"But how can I be around people like my grandma and Mak and pretend to be someone else?" I protest.

"You *have to* live as Renee. You know the discovery of this operation would risk putting me and your parents in prison – that would leave you with no one. I know that you don't want that to happen. Your parents and I have an agreement; I won't discharge you from the clinic until you are fully adjusted."

"What if I can't?" I ask in trepidation. "You can't just keep me here."

He smiles confidently. "It won't come to that, Renee."

CHAPTER 8

PLAYING THE GAME

"Don't let me interrupt." Dr Leo strolls into the physical therapy room.

"We're just practicing fine motor skills with a writing exercise," Kate tells him.

I look up from the desk as he approaches.

"How are you feeling, Renee?" he asks.

"Great, thanks!" I plaster on a smile.

I'm getting better at this. I've spent the last month trying so hard to be the model patient. No mention of **her**, no more telling them about the nightmares and thoughts that plague me. I don't want to give him any excuse to keep me in this place.

"And have you experienced any hand tremors today?" he asks

"No, they don't happen often. It's no big deal." I try to sound laid-back.

"Kate, Renee's MRI scans consistently show that everything is functioning well. However, there's some irregular activity in areas of her motor cortex, which explains the tremors. But I'm confident they'll settle down."

"I'm keeping an eye on them," Kate replies.

I can explain the tremors, but I'm not going to tell Dr Leo; he'll say I'm being ridiculous and that I'm not ready to go home, but I've realized that they're **her** way of fighting back: Rebelling against the orders sent by my brain; letting me know that I'm not in charge of her body.

"Renee, please carry on with your exercise," he requests.

He leans over me as I write.

I was placed in foster care at the age of eleven. My mom was a drug addict and neglected me. I never knew my dad. I have no siblings and no contact with my mom. When I turned sixteen I opted to live semi-independently but found it difficult. I was lucky enough to meet Mr and Mrs Burgess at a charity fundraiser for children and family services. I felt a real connection with these warm, generous people. They told me about their daughter, Lucy, who had died, and my heart went out to them.

Her lips start to quiver. I won't cry, not in front of him.
"You okay, Renee?" he asks.
"Sure." I nod.

"I know it's hard, but writing your new history is cathartic. It's all part of your journey to acceptance. You write so well with your right hand," he says.

"I used to be left-handed." I try to hide the bitterness in my voice.

"By all means keep trying. There's no reason why you can't master writing using the left hand; the donor's muscles and digits will learn to adjust."

I change hands but it feels awkward, and the letters forming on the page are spidery as I continue to write:

We kept in touch over the last few months via email. When I was having trouble finding a place to stay they invited me to come and visit with them in Houston. Of course, I was reluctant to do this, especially as their daughter had died so recently, but after a few weeks they asked me to stay for as long as I wanted. They said it brings them comfort having me around.

I rub **her** aching hand.

"That's not bad. The more you practice, the easier it will get," he says. "I'm glad you listened to me, Renee. I'm delighted with your more positive attitude. I told you, didn't I, that once you mentally accepted your body, everything would be so much easier." He sounds pleased with himself.

I remind myself to smile and nod. My mind is still my own and I won't let him know my true thoughts.

"Would you do some floor exercises for me?" he asks.

"What? You mean stretches and stuff?"

"No, I want you to try something more challenging, something more gymnastic," he says enthusiastically.

I laugh incredulously. "You're asking the wrong person. I've never even been able to do a somersault."

Mom would have loved me to be a dancer, gymnast, on the cheer squad, but I've always been terrible at all that. She'd been the flyer for her high school senior cheer team. She doesn't boast about it, but she keeps an old framed photo on her dressing table. She looks amazing doing a one-leg stunt at the top of the team pyramid. I can't imagine what a disappointment I was to her when she realized how badly coordinated I was.

"Just trust me. Do a few warm-up stretches and then try a somersault," Dr Leo insists.

This is ridiculous but I need to keep him happy.

Kate walks with me to the floor mats. I look away from the wall of mirrors opposite. She coaches me as I stretch the legs and circle the arms. She makes me crouch down and positions the hands, tucking in the head.

"Give it a try," Dr Leo says encouragingly.

I begin to rock on the balls of **her** feet, hoping that they'll propel me forward, but I can't make myself go over. Instead I'm a rocking horse, moving but going nowhere. I'm getting dizzy. I stand up, huffing. "I told you I couldn't do it!"

"That's because you're overthinking it. Just empty your mind and let your body do what comes naturally," he says calmly.

"What? You can't have it both ways," I say, irritated with him. "You keep telling me that my brain controls this body; now you're telling me to let the body control the brain. Make your mind up!"

"Just do it!" he bawls.

His anger shocks me. I don't even register my movements as I feel myself rolling over before springing up, arms in the air.

Kate claps her hands in delight.

Dr Leo is beaming at me. "I'm sorry that I had to shout, Renee, but I needed to distract you so that you did it instinctively."

"But how? I didn't do that. I can't do that," I say in shock.

"Of course it was you. This body is a lot more flexible than your original body. I chose the donor well," he replies.

I screw my face up.

"Come on," he says hurriedly. "Don't you want to practice more? See what else you can do."

Despite myself, I'm excited to see what **she** is capable of. I do another somersault, then another and another. Each time it's more elegant, more rounded; I spring higher as I come out of it.

"Try a cartwheel," he says, clapping.

Kate moves to the center to support me, but I don't need her. I take a run up and spin across the length of the mat, legs and arms straight and strong, heart pumping. I'm flushed, exhilarated. I want to do more.

I attempt a handstand. At first I wobble like Jell-O but

then I find my balance. As I smile, upside down, I see Mom's feet walking into the studio.

"Oh my God!" Mom trills. "Lucy, look at you!"

I topple over at the sound of my real name.

Dr Leo shoots Mom a disapproving look.

"Sorry. It was the shock, the excitement. Renee, honey, it's amazing to see you do that." She bends down to hug me, but I bristle.

"I think Renee has done enough for today," Dr Leo intervenes. "I don't want her to get too tired. Let's just do one more thing to reinforce her tremendous progress." He hauls me up and leads me over to the wall of mirrors.

I keep my eyes to the ground but he lifts **her** chin with his fingers.

"Look at yourself, Renee."

I glance.

"No, really look. I want you to really see yourself."

He's not going to leave me alone until I do. He stands behind, watching as I stare in the mirror.

"What do you see?" he asks.

*I see a pretty girl in a grey sweatsuit. **Her** hair is short but dense; it covers most of **her** head like a mound of jet-black grass. An old scar cuts across **her** thick right eyebrow, breaking the symmetry of **her** heart face. **Her** full lips sit red against **her** creamy, blush-tinged skin. Hooded lids and dark, long lashes frame blue eyes that have spent so long dulled by illness, but now shine with the rush of adrenaline.*

I don't know what to think, but I know what I've got to say.

"I see me," I answer.

"And who are you?"

"I'm Renee Wodehouse from San Diego, California. I've recently come to live with Mr and Mrs Burgess."

"Good girl." He nods with satisfaction. "I really think you might be ready to go home."

CHAPTER 9

HOMECOMING

Dad has hardly said a word the whole journey but Mom hasn't stopped talking. She keeps gushing about how wonderful it's going to be to have me home; talking about all the great things we'll do as a family, telling me about all the tutors she has lined up to teach me. I wish she'd shut up. When we left the clinic, I was tearful with relief, but it's overwhelming to be outside, in the real world: on the plane from El Paso I could feel the knot in my belly tightening and now we're in the car, getting closer to Houston, I think that I might puke with nerves.

Dr Leo gave me a hug as I left the clinic. He squeezed me so tight, as if he didn't want to let me go. I surprised myself at how emotional I got. I kissed him on the cheek; I kept thanking him! I think that I even meant it. Despite what he's done to me, despite all my messed-up feelings, the facts are that he saved me.

"I'll miss you Renee," he said, "but we'll see each other soon."

"But I thought that I was discharged?"

"No. These are still early days. I'll be checking up on you. Getting you back for regular tests. For a start, we have to figure out your tremors," he said, taking my hands.

"And if they can't be figured out?" I replied nervously.

"You should know by now that 'can't' isn't in my vocabulary," he laughed.

I sit in the back of the car tugging at my wig. The scalp is itching and hot under the long strawberry-blonde hair that's been glued to **her** head. Mom and Dr Leo insisted that I need to wear it to cover up the scarring; they don't want people asking awkward questions.

"Mom, no one else is around; I need to take this thing off," I say, clawing at it.

"No, honey, you'll rip your scalp if you try to pull it off. You'll get used to it. It looks fantastic, so natural." She looks delighted.

"There's nothing natural about me," I reply bitterly.

"Come on now, you've been making such great progress. Let's keep up the positivity, Lucy!"

"Renee – we've got to call her Renee," Dad warns.

"It'll be okay, Lewis. I'll be careful. We can call her Lucy when it's just us. It'll be better that way, won't it?" she says to me, conspiratorially.

"Yes. I'd really like that." I smile. I'm not Renee. I'll *never* be Renee.

"This is your new beginning, Lucy, and we're not going to look back. From now on it's all about our future," Mom trills, excitedly.

"Are you looking forward to our future, Dad?" I ask anxiously.

Dad hesitates, keeping his eyes firmly on the road as he drives.

"Of course he is," Mom answers for him.

"I asked Dad."

"Sure, I'm looking forward to our future together," he replies softly. Mom squeezes his arm in approval.

Dusk is falling and the street lamps start lighting up on the Loop as we head towards downtown.

"It'll be dark by the time we reach the house. At least it'll be easier to sneak me in," I say.

Mom tuts. "We don't need to sneak you in. We've got nothing to hide. You're Renee, a girl we're helping out. We've told everyone about you."

"I had no idea you were such a good liar, Mom."

She pretends to ignore me.

"But what do I say to Maria when I get to the house?"

Mom doesn't answer.

"Mom?"

"I've let Maria go," she says quietly.

"Why? She's been our housekeeper forever."

"Exactly; that's why I thought it best that she wasn't around. It will mean that you can relax in the house. You won't always have to be thinking about saying the right thing.

68

Maria knows you too well. If I need help I'll get agency staff," Mom says, regaining her confidence.

I feel terrible. Is this my fault? Has Maria lost her job because of me?

"And what about Jim? You haven't fired him as well, have you?" I ask anxiously.

"No, he's still looking after the stables. He's not so much of a problem; he doesn't come up to the house much."

"Then what about Arthur? He knows me too well. Have you gotten rid of him, too?" I say sarcastically.

Mom rolls her eyes. "Stop being silly. Arthur is fine. The Dawsons have been looking after him for a couple of days. They'll bring him by in the morning."

"I can't wait that long. Can't I see him as soon as I get home?" I plead.

"Well, I didn't want to tell you at the clinic, because I knew it would be upsetting, but poor Arthur has been pining for you all this time. He's been inconsolable; scratching at your bedroom door, looking for you all over the house. In the end Dad gave him your old Bailey Heights sweatshirt and he's been carrying it around like a security blanket. He sleeps with it in his basket. The other week, on one of my trips back home, I tried to get it off him to wash and he wouldn't let me near it," Mom laughs.

I feel tears pricking my eyes at the thought of Arthur missing me so much. "Can he sleep in my room?" I ask, knowing that Mom never lets him do that. She says he leaves hair everywhere.

"Sure he can, as long as it's not on your bed."

I smile to myself as we glide towards our neighborhood but, as the car turns into our tree-lined boulevard, **her** mouth goes dry. It's been over eight months since I've been home, and it feels like a lifetime ago. I was so sick when they took me to the clinic that I honestly believed that I'd never see home again. Now here I am, back, but I'm painfully aware that I'm not the same girl who left this place.

The electric gates swing open and we cruise up the long, winding driveway. As we take the last bend, the house comes into view, glowing invitingly. The gardens are all lit up; the sprinklers on the lawn hiss as they try to keep the grass lush after a day in the baking sun.

"Did you get rid of all the mirrors like I asked?" I say in a panic. I can't stand to see **her**. The more that I can just live in my head, the bigger chance I have of holding on to Lucy.

"Yes, all the mirrors in the house have been taken down. I didn't dare tell Dr Radnor; he wouldn't approve," Mom says.

"Who cares? We're out of that place. He'll never know," I say triumphantly.

Dad stops the engine and turns around to look at me, his face so serious. "You can't ignore anything that the doctor said. He knows what's best for you. You have to be Renee now, for all our sakes, okay?"

"Okay," I reply bitterly.

Mom opens the front door and ushers me in with a flourish. "Welcome home, honey."

The cavernous hallway gleams. The chandelier sends

sparkling light dancing across the marble floor. The ornate staircase sweeps up to the galleried landing and the vaulted ceilings. Everything is so big and grand after the confines of the clinic. Mom has been busy. The air is perfumed by the bouquets of flowers that are dotted around every surface.

"It's lovely, Mom."

"Well, I wanted to make everything nice for you," she trills. "But I haven't changed anything in your bedroom or your den. It's just as you left it, before ... before, well you know." She flushes.

"Sure, thanks." I smile at her reassuringly.

She leads me into the kitchen.

"Lewis, open the champagne; it's in the fridge. We need to celebrate."

Mom claps excitedly as the cork whizzes into the air and the bubbles spill into two of the three glasses.

"Don't I get any?" I ask.

"No, young lady. You stick to soft drinks," she replies, pouring me out a glass of Coke. "I'd like to make a toast." Mom beams. "To our amazing daughter and the many happy years we have ahead of us."

"To our daughter," Dad echoes flatly, raising his glass.

"To me, whoever I am," I whisper under my breath before gulping down the Coke.

"We'll get the bags in from the car. You look around, get used to things again," Mom says, leading Dad out of the kitchen.

The excitement of being back home is making me feel

light-headed. I walk into the utility room to find Arthur's basket. I kneel down to the hair-encrusted blanket and inhale its musty scent. A volley of sneezes fires out of me. My eyes suddenly itch. I hurriedly leave the room and the sneezing subsides.

I head to the end of the corridor to the basement door. I swing it open and turn on the lights. I grin as I look down on my illuminated den. The pool table is all set up. The screen is pulled down ready to show a movie. The Xbox has all my games neatly stacked next to it. I rush down the steps and check the record player; Mom wasn't lying, they haven't touched a thing; even Springsteen's "Born in the U.S.A." is still on the turntable, just where I left it. It was Dad who converted me to the wonders of The Boss. After that first concert he took me to, I was hooked. He used to play me all his albums on this turntable; real old school. I loved spending time with him in the den, especially because there's no signal down here, so we'd never be interrupted by his calls about work. It was bliss.

I pick up the mic connected to the karaoke machine. Mak and I used to sing diva anthems at the top of our out-of-tune voices, imagining we were playing Carnegie Hall. For a moment, I visualize Mak here, right now, singing and dancing with me. The sight of it makes my heart swell.

I bypass the leather sofa and sink into my favorite armchair. Mom got it years ago from a flea market. It's all plump and floral and old-fashioned, just like something Grandma would have in her place. Maybe that's why I like it so much. I could sit here all night, but I want to see how the rest of the house is looking. I want to soak in every last detail. A few months ago, in the clinic, Mom asked me whether I'd find it easier to relocate; move away from Houston and make a fresh start. I told her that I wasn't running away; that I could deal with seeing people; with pretending. Houston is my home; the place I grew up. All my memories are here; Grandma and Mak are here. If I've got any chance of holding on to who I really am, then this is where I need to be.

I head up into the living room; it's just as I remember, except for the large painting of a wild meadow that's hung over the fireplace. It's replaced the gold-framed mirror that used to be there.

"Thanks, Mom," I whisper.

My eye is caught by something else that's new: in the corner of the room is a glass display cabinet. The spotlights shine down on a collection of my things. There's my first pair of shoes, a crayon drawing of the family I did in day care and an embarrassing poem about my feelings that the hospital therapist made me write when I first got sick. They're surrounded by framed photographs. Each one shows me at different ages: as a chubby, toothless baby with red cheeks; my first day at school; sitting on Elmer, my first pony; graduating from elementary school in a ridiculous mortar board; blowing out candles on my thirteenth birthday cake; standing in between Mom and Dad on a sun-drenched beach in Barbados. Looking hot, sweaty and ecstatic at a Springsteen concert with Dad ... then a more recent photo, a close-up of me and Grandma sitting on the swing chair by the pool. She has her arm around my bony shoulders, a rigid smile on her face. A scarf covers the tufts of my remaining hair. I look like a ghost sitting beside her. It was taken just before I was admitted to the clinic. That was the last time I saw her.

The display makes me shiver. Mom has built a shrine; is it just for show for any visitors, or is she in mourning for me too?

I need to get away from it. I rush up the stairs and into my bedroom. Everything is just how I left it; I feel safe here, I feel like me. I open the door to the balcony and look out on to the softly lit gardens, inhaling the fresh night air.

I wander around my room, touching everything. Mom has draped a pretty shawl across the dressing table mirror and on the table stands one of Mak's "inspirational" cards. It shows two old women, one white, one black, doing the can-can, flashing their bright red bloomers. Inside she's written, *Looking forward to being outrageous old cougars together! All my love, Mak*

My belly twists. When am I going to see her? What do I say to my best friend?

Among the clutter of make-up, bangles and earrings sits my hairbrush. I pick it up and caress the fine strands of mousy-colored hair entwined in the bristles. Grief washes over me – is this all that's left of the real me? I place my precious artefact in a drawer and lock it for safekeeping.

Half-empty bottles of body lotion and perfumes litter the

surface of the table. I spray "Dawn Dew" on to my wrists, rubbing them together. The familiarity of the scent makes me smile. I find myself skipping over to the walk-in closet. The rows of clothes are a mixture of things I've chosen and expensive dorky outfits that Mom bought for me. I felt ridiculous in them, but Mom loved to dress me up and I couldn't refuse her.

Flicking through the rails, I find my favorite pair of jeans and purple sequined top. Stripping off, I try to pull on the jeans, but they won't even go past the calves. I lie down on the carpet and strain to get them up, but it's like trying to fit into dolls' clothes. I drag them off before picking up the top and squeezing it over **her** boobs; it's so tight that I can hardly breathe. As I fight to get it off, my wig gets tangled in the sequins, pulling painfully at the scalp. I tussle with it, screwing up the top in frustration. I forgot that my clothes size shrank as the cancer ate away at me. **Her** body is too healthy, too curvy for my old clothes. I don't know whether to laugh or cry.

I need my music. I search around the bedroom in my underwear, opening drawers and cupboards until I unearth my iPod. I plug the earphones in, fumbling as I find the right track and put the volume up.

The sound of the harmonica and piano penetrates my mind, then the gravelly voice of The Boss kicks in and I'm away; eyes closed, swaying arms in the air, singing along so loud that the lungs might burst. "Hey, it's okay, Thunder Road!" I feel drunk on happiness. As I sway faster I lose my balance and topple on to the thick carpet, rolling around with laughter. I manage to scramble halfway up, ready for my solo. I'm matching Clarence on the sax, note for note with my air saxophone. The music soars and takes me with it. I spring towards the bed, doing a somersault across to the other side. I'm dancing on air, twirling and leaping. I haven't felt this alive for years.

"Honey, are you okay in there?" It's Mom shouting through the door.

I pull the earphones out, turn off the music. "Yeah, I'm fine," I pant.

"Well, can we come in? We have someone who wants to see you."

"What? No! I'm not ready to see anyone!" I grab my dressing gown from the closet and cover up.

"It's okay, it's not a person." There's laughter in Mom's voice. The bedroom door opens and Arthur bounds in, his tail wagging madly.

I squeal in delight but Arthur skirts past me and searches around the room, into the closet, the bathroom, under the bed. He's sniffing the air, trailing his nose on the ground.

"Arthur! Arthur, come here, boy!" I crouch down with open arms to welcome him, but he's keeping his distance. His huge liquid-brown eyes take me in; his head cocks to one side.

"Come on, Arthur. It's me, Lucy!"

He lets out a sharp bark at the sound of my name.

"Please, baby, it's me. Come here and get your belly tickled." As I lean towards him he backs away.

"Arthur, go to Lucy!" Mom orders.

Arthur looks at Mom with uncertainty. Mom takes him by his collar and drags him towards me.

I hold out a hand and he sniffs it cautiously. He must be able to smell my perfume but he picks up **her** scent too, I'm sure of it. He looks confused, scared. I gently stroke his soft golden head but he flinches.

I try to hold his face but I'm distressing him. His shaggy body is shivering. He whimpers, shaking out of the grip and fleeing from the room.

"Don't worry. Just give him time," Mom says with forced cheerfulness.

My euphoria comes crashing down. A choking lump forms in my throat.

Dad shakes his head sadly at Mom and walks out of the room.

My eyes are itchy. I press the heels of **her** hands into them but suddenly I'm sneezing uncontrollably. I can feel my eyes swelling up, face getting hot.

"Go wash your hands," Mom says.

"What's happening to me? I was sneezing downstairs when I was by Arthur's basket."

Mom bites her lip. "It looks like you might be allergic to him."

"*I'm* not allergic to Arthur, this body is!" I shout. "She's made my own dog afraid of me and now I can't even touch him! It's not fair! It's not fair!"

CHAPTER 10

GRANDMA

*Arthur is trapped in a windowless whitewashed room with me. He claws at the door, desperate to get away. "Here, boy, come to Lucy," I call, but he only scratches more furiously, barking for someone to rescue him. I have to show him that it's me. I know what I've got to do; I dig the nails deep into **her** skin and start to tear at the impostor's body. I let out a roar like a wild animal as I rip at **her** arms, legs and face, turning the white room into a bloodbath. Arthur stops barking; he approaches, no longer scared but curious. He starts to see that it is me underneath. I kiss his head as he jumps up, wagging his tail, barking in delight to know that I've returned.*

"Arthur!" I open my eyes to my bedroom. My T-shirt sticks to me with sweat. I've been scratching my arms during the nightmare, causing stinging, hot red tracks along **her** creamy skin.

It's an effort to get out of bed. I feel shaken, but I've got to throw it off; it's my first day back at home. I have to enjoy it. I shower, get dressed and head to the kitchen.

"Hi, Lucy, you're looking tired this morning," Mom says as she flips a pancake on the griddle. "Didn't you sleep well in your own bed?"

"Yeah, I'm fine," I brush her off.

She lifts a sizzling pancake on to a plate and hands it to me. "Is it nice being back home, honey?"

"Sure, besides my dog being scared of me and your weird shrine thing in the living room," I reply.

"You mean the display cabinet? That wasn't me, it was your dad. I told him not to, but he insisted," Mom sighs.

What? I can't believe Dad made it. What's going on with him? He hardly came to visit in the clinic and yet he's making shrines to me at home.

"Where is Dad?" I ask.

"He had to go to work. It was something he couldn't delegate," she says apologetically.

I wince with disappointment. "Our happy family thing didn't last long, did it?"

"He's going to make an effort to be around more. He's promised."

"Don't think I haven't noticed that Dad can barely look at me. He doesn't want to be around me."

"Shush now, Lucy. You're talking nonsense. Dad has a lot of work, there's nothing more to it," she says brightly, pouring me juice.

I shake my head at her. There's no point talking to her

about it; she's not going to tell me the truth.

"You've shut Arthur in the utility room," I say sadly.

"Yes, I thought it best to keep him out of the way until we can deal with your allergy."

"Sure, but that won't cure the fact that he's terrified of me." I stare at Arthur through the glass utility door, lying in his basket, head flopped on the floor. I tap on the glass and wave at him.

"Arthur, how you doing, boy?"

He looks up and his whimper cuts right through me. Even the sight of me is upsetting my beautiful dog. I can't stand it.

"Let's go for a walk. I need some air," I say.

Mom looks pleased. "Okay, I'll get my boots on."

It feels so good to be striding through the gardens and across the paddocks with Mom. I breathe in the sweet air, swish through the long grass, soaking up the morning sun. It's like my senses have been turned up to eleven; as if I'm seeing everything for the first time.

Mom picks a cluster of bright wild flowers and slides them into my wig, making a perfumed crown. Her face glows with happiness as she takes my hand. As we get nearer the stable block I can see the horses' heads poking over the stall doors. Moonshine shakes her chestnut mane in excitement as she spots us. I was too weak to ride her before I went into Dr Leo's clinic. Now, the thought of being able to gallop around the fields again fills me with happiness. But, as I get closer, the atmosphere changes. The horses get jittery. Their heads start bobbing up and down, their hooves clattering on the ground. I stretch out my hand to Moonshine but she snorts, her eyes widening in fright.

"Moonshine, it's me, Lucy," I say desperately, but it's no good. She pulls away, trying to move as far from me as possible. She wedges herself against the back wall and kicks at the side of the stall as if trying to create an escape route.

I move along the stalls, calling each horse by name, pleading with them to be still . . . calm, but they feed off each other's distress as squeals and snorts fill the air and they bare their teeth to form terrified smiles.

Tears fill my eyes. I can't believe this is happening. Do animals know that I'm a freak? Can they sense what I am?

Mom puts her arm around me and pulls me away. She tries to comfort me, but I feel her anxiety too.

"They've just got to get used to you, that's all." She kisses my forehead. "Arthur and Moonshine will figure out that you're their girl. You'll win them over."

I wish I could believe her.

"Look, forget about the animals for now. I've got a plan for today," she says enthusiastically. "I want us to go shopping at the Galleria. None of your old clothes fit you any more and you'd only let me buy you sweatsuits in the clinic, but you're home now. You need nice clothes. You can choose whatever you want. I won't interfere, honest." She holds her hands up as if she's surrendering.

"But I might bump into someone I know! People will stare. I'm not ready to go out," I say anxiously.

"You'll be fine. If you see someone you know the only reason they'd stare is because you're so very pretty." The pride in Mom's voice stabs me. She never said that about me before I had the transplant.

I look down at her hands as she gets her phone out of her purse. "Hey, what about my cell?" I ask. "Now that I'm home you've got no reason not to give me it back," I say firmly.

"Why do you want your phone?"

I look at her like that's the dumbest question ever. "Because it's mine! It's got my SIM card with all my contacts on it."

"You don't need your SIM card. You can't contact those people. They don't know who you are any more."

Her words take my breath away. For a moment, I'd forgotten what they'd done to me. I'd forgotten the reality of my life now. "They don't know who I am," I echo.

Mom looks at me anxiously. "You can't tell anyone, Lucy. Promise me you won't tell. I'll buy you a new phone so you can contact me and Dad. For now, that's all you need it for. *We're* all you need."

The mall is so busy, bright and loud. After months of only ever seeing a handful of people in the clinic I'm finding our shopping expedition overwhelming. We've had to buy boxes of new shoes and sneakers, as **her** feet are two sizes bigger than mine. Mom is insisting that I get "measured up" in the ladies' department of Saks and now she's bought me tons of lacy underwear; the kind she used to say I was far too young for. Mom is loving all this; as she picks out yet another top from the rails it's like I'm a grown-up doll that she can dress up.

"You'll look so cute in this. Go try them all on," she says, maneuvering me to the changing room.

"I thought you were going to let me choose my own clothes," I huff.

"I am, but you've hardly picked up anything. I'm just helping. I'll wait outside. Come out and show me." She shoos me into the cubicle.

Mom hasn't chosen her usual dorky designer dresses that are more suited to a little girl; these clothes are for her new, cool hippie chick of a daughter. I try each outfit on, avoiding the reflection in the cubicle's full-length mirrors.

Mom coos as I reluctantly model every outfit. "That style is so great for you. Do you like it, honey?"

I shrug.

"Come to the checkout with me. You might as well keep that on."

"Can we go home now?" I beg. I'm tired of being on display.

"Sure, but let's pay and I'll take you for a coffee before we head home. It's good for you to be out ... to be around people."

A sea of shoppers washes by as we sit in a café in the middle of the mall, our shopping bags surrounding us like flood defenses. As I stare blankly into the distance, a figure approaches and blocks my view.

"Hi, Mrs Burgess?" The boy is speaking to Mom, but he turns his gaze to me. Oh my God, it's Josh Dartmere! I feel the heat radiating from me. Why's he looking at me like that? Does he recognize me? No . . . no, don't be stupid, how could he when I don't even recognize me?

"Yes, that's right. It's Josh, isn't it?" Mom says.

"Yes, ma'am, Josh Dartmere. I dated Lucy for a while. I'm so sorry I wasn't able to make the funeral. I really wanted to be there. Lucy meant a lot to me."

Mom starts fiddling with her coffee cup. Silence hangs awkwardly in the air. She's struggling. "Well, that's nice to hear," she says at last.

"Anyway, I'm glad to see you out, Mrs Burgess. Is this your niece?" he asks.

"No, this is Renee. She's a friend of the family. She's staying with us," Mom replies more confidently.

He extends his hand to me, giving me his most winning smile. "Well, it's a pleasure to meet you, Renee. How long are you in town for?"

"As long as Mo . . . Mrs Burgess wants me to stay." Come on, Lucy, get your act together.

"You're not from around here, are you?" He's picked up on my strange voice.

"No." I don't offer any more information.

"Well, I'd be happy to show you the sights." His eyes linger on me. "I know all the best places in Houston."

I'm not imagining it; he's actually coming on to me. He's such a creep.

A pretty girl with short brown hair and olive skin comes towards us, calling out, "Josh, where did you get to? I've been waiting for you outside Macy's." She takes his hand when she sees me.

"Sorry. I was just on my way," he says. "Lovely to see you, Mrs Burgess . . . Renee. Hope to see you again sometime." He smiles, staring only at me.

I shudder with relief as he walks away. "God, he is such an asshole," I hiss.

To my surprise, Mom laughs. "You're right. He was a jerk when he dated you. But I'm so proud of you – you did it!"

"Did what?"

"That was our first test; you just met someone who knows you and you held it together. Good job!" she beams, clinking her coffee cup with mine.

Mom's upbeat mood is infectious. All the way home, she's telling me tales from her high school days. My eyes widen at her stories about dating unsuitable boys, skipping school to go to music festivals, being sent home by the principal for having her tongue pierced. Grandma was convinced that her perfect daughter was turning into a juvenile delinquent and actually forced Mom to see a shrink! All this is a revelation. She's never told me stuff like this before. It's like sitting in the car with a gossipy big sister rather than my uptight mom. I'm still laughing as we pull up the drive and I suddenly realize that I haven't thought about **her** the whole journey.

We're so laden down with shopping bags that we practically fall through the front door. Arthur appears, avoiding me and jumping up at Mom, barking excitedly. He grips her sleeve between his teeth and tries to pull her towards the living room.

"What is it, boy?" Mom asks.

"Gemma, it's just me! I let myself in. I love all the flowers in the house, but where have all your mirrors gone?" A familiar voice rings out from the living room. Grandma! I let my bags fall to the floor and run towards her. She's elegantly dressed as always and her hair and make-up are perfect, but she's lost weight; she looks older, frailer. Instinctively I throw my arms around her.

I feel her whole body go rigid. My arms shoot away, remembering that she doesn't know me.

"Gemma, who is this?" Grandma asks in alarm.

"Sorry, Mama, I think Renee has gotten a bit overexcited!" Mom glares at me.

I step back, apologizing. "I'm so sorry, Mrs Kendal. That was ridiculous of me. I know that we've never met but Mrs Burgess has told me so much about you that I feel like I know you already." *God, that sounds pathetic.*

"So, you're the young lady Gemma has told me about." Grandma is talking slowly, like I'm simple or something.

"Yeah, I'm Renee Wodehouse." I'm grinning like an idiot, but I can't stop.

"Gemma told me you're from San Diego, but that's not a California accent, is it?" She's scrutinizing me.

"I moved around a lot with my mom. I suppose I've just picked up a bit of everything," I reply with my rehearsed answer.

"So you're visiting for a while?" Grandma asks.

"Yeah, Mr and Mrs Burgess have been so kind to me."

"Yes, I can see that!" Grandma looks disapprovingly at the pile of shopping bags.

"Renee arrived with one outfit to her name. I just bought her a few things to keep her going." Mom sounds nervous.

"Well, that's very generous of you, Gemma," Grandma replies, unsmilingly.

"Renee, why don't you go put those clothes away. Just move the things out of the closet to make space," Mom says, trying to get me out of the way.

"Move what things out of the closet?" Grandma asks. "You don't mean Lucy's clothes, do you? Surely you haven't put Renee in *Lucy's* bedroom?"

Mom is too flustered to speak.

"Mrs Burgess just thought it would be good to use it," I say, cringing.

"*Really*, when there are six other bedrooms in this house that she could have chosen from?" Grandma says curtly.

"Mama, I don't want Lucy's room to be some kind of mausoleum." Her voice is steely.

Grandma huffs. "Fine, you must do what you think is best, Gemma, but it's only been a matter of months since the poor child passed. I still haven't touched your daddy's study after eight years."

"Well, maybe you should start moving on before life passes you by," Mom replies harshly.

87

Grandma's face crinkles in anger. "I don't think we should be having this conversation in front of a stranger." Her words feel like a slap. She means me. I'm a stranger to my own grandma.

"Sorry, Mama. I'm feeling a bit tired and snappy," Mom says contritely. "Come on through and have some coffee."

"No, thank you. I think I ought to go. I just came by to let you know that I've instructed my lawyers to set up the memorial trust in Lucy's memory. I've decided to call it The Lucy Burgess Foundation Trust. I had wanted to discuss a fundraising auction with you, but I think it best to leave it until another time, when you aren't quite so *preoccupied*." Grandma flashes her eyes at me.

"Setting up the foundation is wonderful, Mrs Kendal. I know that Lucy would have been so happy about it," I gush, unstoppably.

Grandma can't disguise a scowl. "But you didn't know Lucy, did you? You never even met her."

"No," I mumble. I'm flushing with embarrassment. She thinks I'm insincere.

"You're doing a great thing, Mama, thank you," Mom intervenes.

"Well, some good has got to come out of this." Grandma's voice cracks as she turns to go.

"I promise to phone you to discuss the foundation, Mama," Mom says, kissing her on the cheek.

"Bye, Mrs Kendal, I hope to see you again soon," I call out to her.

"Goodbye, Renee. Enjoy your visit," she replies coldly as she shuts the door behind her.

I slump on the stairs, clasping **her** hands together as the tremors start up. "Grandma doesn't like me."

"She does. It's just that she's so upset about ... about..."

"About me dying. Say it, Mom, say it out loud and realize just how screwed up this is!" Anger fills my voice. "I can't spend the rest of Grandma's life lying to her."

"We can't tell her," Mom pleads. "She won't understand."

"But you do realize that when she sees that 'Renee' isn't going away, she'll resent me even more."

"No, she won't. She'll get to know you; she'll grow to love you," Mom says, passionately.

I stare at her in disbelief. She's living in a fantasy world.

CHAPTER 11

HOMESCHOOLING

We're sitting at the table in the library. That's what Mom calls it, anyway. It's an impressive room with Persian rugs on the floor and oak bookshelves lining the walls. It's the kind of room just perfect to study in, but I'm not going to. Six weeks I've been stuck at home with tutors and I can't stand it.

Mrs Bentley has her arms crossed. I can tell that she's losing patience.

"How did you do with that question on Texas agriculture?" she asks.

"Sorry, I didn't get around to doing it." I shrug.

"Oh, well, that's a shame, Renee. I was hoping we could move on to another topic today."

"I'm not really in the mood to study," I mumble.

"Well, if you don't mind me saying, you quite often don't feel 'in the mood'. Mrs Burgess is paying me a good salary to teach you and I feel like you're not making the most of it."

"Then maybe she shouldn't waste her money," I sigh.

I know Mrs Bentley thinks I'm an ungrateful brat, but I can't help it. I hope that she and the other tutors have been feeding back to Mom; telling her how uncooperative I'm being and that homeschooling isn't working out. I'm not spending any more time being cooped up, not seeing anyone.

There have *been* visitors to the house but they're not the people I want to meet. Over the last few weeks, a trickle of neighbors and friends of Mom and Dad have been coming over; they're curious about the girl Mom has taken in; they come to take a look at me. Most of them I've known all my life. It's so stressful having to lie, but each time I'm getting better at "my story". I don't hesitate so much. It doesn't sound so rehearsed and people seem to accept it. But I can tell they think that it's odd Mom has installed me in their home so soon after their daughter died.

When I complained to Mom that I need to be with people my own age she said that she'd take me to her tennis club to meet some of the girls there. But I don't want to; they're not my kind of girls. The only friend I want is Mak. I miss her so much that a dull pain weighs down on me every time I think of her. When I ask Mom to invite her over to meet "Renee", she evades the question. The only thing she said was that she'd heard that Mak was upset that they had a new girl living with them. A "new" girl . . . me.

I get up from the table. "Sorry, Mrs Bentley, do you mind if we leave it there?" I walk out of the library, not waiting for her answer.

I just want to go and lie on my bed again but I know Mom will come up and hassle me; tell me to make the most of the day, but what else does she want me to do? The thought of getting home was the only thing that got me through all those months in the clinic, but now that I'm here I'm having to spend my days with tutors and go everywhere with Mom because she's too nervous to let me go out on my own. It's like I've just swapped one prison for another.

I wander into the acres of lawn . . . it's beautiful. I know it ought to lift my mood but I can't get rid of the greyness that's dragging me down.

I spot Arthur in the distance, chasing a bird as it flutters from bush to bush. I skirt around the pool and into the tennis court, where I pick up a ball before approaching Arthur, cautiously.

"Here, boy." I use **her** strength to throw the ball across the lawn. "Go get it, Arthur! Go get it!"

He doesn't move. He just stands there eyeing me anxiously. I clap and jump around, trying to get him excited. "Arthur, it's Lucy. Your Lucy." He looks poised to run and as soon as I make a move towards him, he bolts.

I close my eyes in despair. The blackness envelops me. **Her** hands begin to shake, **her** lip starts to quiver. I find myself walking towards the pool and when I get to the edge I don't stop. I hit the water and sink to the bottom but as I start to rise I force myself to stay down, holding my breath, **her** lungs beginning to burn.

I hear muffled shouts. There's a splash and I'm grabbed,

pulled up and dragged to the side of the pool. The chlorine stings my eyes as I see Dad holding on to me. He's in his suit, soaking wet. He didn't even stop to take his jacket off.

"What were you trying to do?" he splutters in horror.

I struggle to find any words. I look around in a daze. "I don't know," I gasp, shocked with myself.

CHAPTER 12

CHECK-UP

After the pool incident, Mom and Dad insisted that I needed a check-up, but what they really meant was that they want Dr Leo to fix my head. I'm embarrassed about the pool "thing" and I've tried to reassure them that I wasn't thinking straight, but it has rattled them. Mom keeps hovering over me like I'm on suicide watch.

I fidget as I sit in Dr Leo's office. Being back in the clinic feels like I never escaped.

"Personally, I think Renee would benefit from antidepressants. Just until her spirits lift," Mom says to him.

"I don't need pills to stop me feeling like this. I just need you to let me live a normal life. Well, as normal as *I* can. Give me some freedom . . . let me do things other teenagers get to do."

"That's unfair. We've been going out and doing nice things together," Mom says, smarting.

"Exactly – together. Hanging out with your mom all the time isn't normal."

Dr Leo is silent. He takes his glasses off and cleans them. Then he nods, pointing at me. "I agree with Renee. Antidepressants aren't the answer and anyway, I don't want her on any other medication when I'm still investigating the tremors. You should give her more freedom, within limits. Let her spend time with other teenagers. Let her join clubs and then she'll find the homeschooling more tolerable. Renee's mental health could affect her physical well-being and we want her to stay healthy, don't we?"

"But with all due respect, you're the one who has made us so nervous about all this," Mom protests. "You encouraged us to keep her away from her friends in case she couldn't cope with the emotional turmoil."

"Just be sensible. Renee knows what's at stake. She'll be careful," he says, his warm brown eyes smiling at me.

Yes! I could kiss him.

"In the meantime, I need you to stay overnight. There are a few tests I have to complete to try to identify the source of the tremors, and I'd like you to write down a thorough history of when you've experienced them and what was happening immediately before each incident. There could be a trigger," he says.

"Okay," I reply, compliantly, but I already know that he's wasting his time trying to find a trigger because the "trigger" is **her**.

*

It's ten-thirty and I've spent too long sitting in the empty cafeteria trying to recall all the tremor incidents. Mom thinks that she's helping by suggesting times and dates, but she just confuses me. I beg her to go and get me a Big Mac and fries from town. Driving there and back should keep her occupied for at least an hour.

I wave her off and watch her tail lights disappear into the dark. The desert air is chilly; goosebumps have erupted on **her** arms. I rub them as I walk back inside. The clinic is unnervingly quiet. I don't like hearing my own footsteps echoing down the corridors.

"Hey, is anyone still here?" I shout, but no one replies to break the silence.

I pace through the whitewashed corridors, looking into darkened rooms, until I come to the double doors that lead to Dr Leo's lab and the operating theater. I know that it's strictly off limits and I've never wanted to go in, not when it holds such nightmarish memories, but the lights are on. If he's in there, I could do with some company. I'm regretting sending Mom off; this place is creeping me out. I give the doors a shove but they don't open. I knock but no one appears.

I retreat down the corridor and head to his office, maybe he'll be there.

I groan. His light is off and the door shut. I try the handle and the door swings open. Curiosity pulls me in. I switch on his desk lamp and sit in his swivelling desk chair wondering what it must be like to be him. Cheating death through his surgery must make him feel like a god, invincible.

His office is pristine, just like him. Nothing is out of place. He even keeps his potted plants watered! His screen saver flashes in front of me – it's a painting of a handsome young man staring at his reflection in a pond. I've studied this painting in art class. He's Narcissus, the boy who fell in love with his own reflection. I snort. Is that what Dr Leo wants me to do? Fall in love with the image I see in the mirror – **her** image? But someone as smart as Dr Leo must know that Narcissus's obsession with his reflection killed him in the end.

I get up to leave but my eye is caught by the three drawers down the side of the desk. The bottom one is open, just a fraction. I know that I shouldn't but I'm itching to look inside, already imagining that I'll find his fatal flaw: maybe a bottle of Jack Daniels, maybe a baggie of cocaine. How else does he perform operations that last days and nights?

I look at the office door, listening out for footsteps, but everywhere is silent. I nudge the drawer with my foot, as if I'm doing it accidentally. The drawer glides open.

The sight of a handgun gleaming in the dark jolts me. My heart starts racing; I can't resist picking the black-handled weapon out of the drawer. I've never held a gun before. It's heavier than I'd expected and feels cool to the touch. I hold it up to the light, making its silver barrel glint. Is it loaded? Is the safety even on? I give myself a mental shake – I shouldn't be touching this. As I go to put it back in the drawer a photo attached to a file captures my attention. I gingerly lower the gun on to the desktop and pick out the file. Beneath it is a whole bundle of them, all with photos attached. There are four boys and six girls. All prom king and queen types, beautiful and gleaming with health.

I feel a twinge of guilt – this is confidential. I know I should put them back. But I can't – are these kids like me? Is Dr Radnor planning to help them? I start to flick through the files. There are no names but each file is full of medical information. What did I expect? I can't understand most of it, but there's page after page of test results, X-rays and scans. It looks like these patients have had every test under the sun. What's wrong with them?

"What are you doing?" Dr Leo's voice cuts through the silence.

I gasp at the sight of him in the doorway. "Oh God, Dr Leo, I'm so sorry," I garble, backing away from the desk.

"This is *my* office! Those files are confidential!" His face is twisted with anger. "How dare you come in here uninvited. Why have you touched my gun? It's not a toy. You could have shot yourself!"

I'm so ashamed I can't look at him. "I . . . I was all alone. I've been looking for you. Your office was unlocked and I got curious . . . carried away. The drawer was open and I just . . . I didn't see anything about your patients, honestly. I don't even know their names." I shrug helplessly, wishing I was anywhere but here.

He picks up the files and gun and places them back in the drawer before locking it. He's breathing deeply but his face is calmer. His silver hair is ruffled and there's a line around his forehead. He must have just taken off a scrub cap. *Was* he in the operating theater?

"I should have kept the drawer locked to secure the gun. I just didn't expect an intruder tonight," he says, his tone mellowing.

"Why do you have a gun?" I ask nervously.

He looks at me like I'm stupid. "I'm in a clinic in the middle of the desert, full of medical equipment worth millions of dollars. I'd be crazy *not* to have a gun out here."

I nod slowly. Of course he needs a gun. He must think I'm so naive.

I spot a fresh bloodstain spreading on the cuff of his shirtsleeve.

"Did you cut yourself?" I ask, concerned. He looks down at the spot where I'm staring.

"No," he says abruptly. "I've been in the lab examining your blood samples. I'm still trying to figure out the cause of the tremors."

I feel even worse. He's been working late to help me and in return I break his trust.

"Those files that you were looking through. . ." he says.

"You don't need to tell me. It's none of my business," I say guiltily.

"No, it'll be good for you to know. They're all young people who need my operation. They're all terminal, just like you were, and time is running out for them." He massages his temples, looking stressed.

Their images flash in my mind. They all looked so

healthy ... so full of life. The photos must be from before they got sick.

A lump forms in my throat. "I'm so sorry. Do you think that you can help them?"

"I'll do my best." He smiles wearily.

I suddenly think about him doing other transplants. It's weird but I actually find the idea of him making another person like me comforting. Maybe I wouldn't feel like such a freak if I wasn't the only one.

"Listen, Renee, I won't tell your mom about you breaking into my office. I don't want to get you into trouble, not when I've just persuaded her to give you more freedom. So, let's both keep all that happened in here to ourselves, okay?"

"Yeah, thanks." I flush, embarrassed. I don't deserve his kindness.

"Have you finished documenting the tremor incidents for me?"

"Nearly." I feel **her** cheeks burning with embarrassment. "I'll go finish it right now."

CHAPTER 13

CONDOLENCES

The pills Dr Leo gave me don't seem to be working yet, but I'm getting better at realizing when the tremors are building up, so I can get out of the way of Mom and Dad before they become visible. I don't want them hauling me back to the clinic again.

I'm going through my closet taking the last of *my* clothes out so that Mom can take them to the thrift store. Mom seems so eager to deal with them; sometimes it feels like she wants to get rid of any evidence of me before the transplant. At the end of the rail I see Mak's denim jacket. I borrowed it last year when I got cold on one of her "life-affirming trips". It was a visit to the planetarium. I think Mak was hoping we'd have some profound experience about our place in the universe or something, but we both got bored and headed to the multiplex to catch a movie instead. I'd forgotten to give the jacket back and she'd never asked for it.

I slip Mak's jacket on and inhale deeply; there's still a scent of the tutti-frutti body lotion that she was into last year. A dull ache builds in my chest. I've got to see her! I need to know how she is.

There's a knock on the door and Mom appears. "Hi, Lucy. It's time for studying," she says, holding the laptop aloft. Mom has been using a new strategy since Mrs Bentley and her successor quit due to my "lack of engagement". She's letting me use my laptop for "independent learning", even though she insists on staying in the room when I'm on it and hiding it away as soon as I've finished.

"I don't feel like it." I shrug.

"Oh, come on. You can choose the topic. We could even sit by the pool. Study al fresco!" she says with a flourish.

"How about you let me study without hovering over me? Just leave the laptop on my bed," I say, irritated.

"That's not a good idea."

"Mom, I know that you're paranoid that I'm going go on social media and announce who I really am."

"No, you wouldn't do that." It sounds like a question.

"Of course I wouldn't. Do you think that I'd want to expose myself as a freak to the world?"

"Please don't call yourself that." Mom winces.

"You need me to study, don't you? All I want is some space while I do it. Will you give me that?" I implore, trying to make her feel guilty.

Mom is twitchy. She's weighing things up, but she knows that nothing has worked so far. "If I leave you the laptop, do you promise just to use it to study? No going on social media?" She uses her "I mean it" voice.

"Promise," I say, wide-eyed.

"Okay, then." She puts the laptop on the bed and walks hesitantly out of the room.

I listen to her footsteps going downstairs and open the laptop excitedly, then log in to my Facebook account. I know that I promised, but surely it doesn't count if you're forced to agree to something completely unfair. Anyway, I only want to look. I bring up Mak's page. There's only one post since "my death". There's a photo of me and her on the rollercoaster at the rodeo carnival, mouths open, eyes wide; we look so happily terrified. She's written, *Today my best friend, the amazing Lucy Burgess, passed away. There are no words to tell you how I feel.*

I touch her face, desperate to comfort her. "I'm sorry, Mak," I whisper. I go to my page. My wall has turned into a book of condolences, but the last comment was months ago; it looks like everyone moved on pretty quickly. I'm not stupid. I know that even in death most of us only get our three minutes of fame before the next tragedy or celebrity scandal grabs people's attention. My heart sinks as I scroll down the messages.

RIP Lucy I'm sure you're smiling down on us. Charlotte
You're with the angels now, Lucy. Clare
So sorry you lost your battle, Lucy. Hannah ☹ ☹ ☹
Only the good die young, Lucy. Patty

Taken too soon. I wish I'd had a chance to get to know you. Ruth

Bailey Heights will miss you, Lucy. Tina ☺

Your brave fight against the cancer was an inspiration to all of us. Michelle

Praying for you, Lucy. Mary-Sue

We all miss you, Lucy. Love Angie

I'll never forget the precious time we spent together. You rocked my world. Josh

Apart from asshole Josh Dartmere, I only vaguely know the other girls. They're all from Bailey Heights. They probably thought it was the polite thing to do – leave a message to the dead girl from their grade. I wonder if I would have done the same in their position.

The comments go on but it's clear that they could be about anybody; they're all so bland. None of the messages actually say anything about me; everyone probably thinks that there's nothing *to* say and they're right. I didn't get a chance to achieve anything. If people remember me at all it's only as the poor little rich kid who got cancer when she was thirteen and then spent the rest of her short life trying, and failing, to survive it.

I don't know how I'm supposed to feel reading my own condolence page – it's not like there's any precedent for it. I should probably be wailing in distress at how twisted and screwed up it all is, but instead I'm just depressed and embarrassed at the confirmation of how unremarkable my life was.

I walk to the dressing table and pull back the shawl to

reveal a sliver of the mirror. I slip off Mak's jacket and make myself inspect the reflection. She looks so good. My new clothes suit this body. The sheer, floaty top reveals just a hint of cleavage; the skinny jeans look sprayed on to **her** long, shapely legs. I turn around and twist to inspect the back. I let out a laugh, half pleased and half jealous – she even looks good from behind. I find myself standing taller; running fingers through the strawberry-blonde wig so it flows prettily over **her** shoulders. This is the kind of body that gets you noticed.

As I stare at **her**, I realize that I can't fester in this house a minute longer. I need to start living. I need to get back to Bailey Heights and make myself into Mak's *new* best friend. Make her see that "Renee" is someone who can fill the hole left by Lucy. I know how dangerous it would be to tell anyone the truth about me, but she isn't just anyone, she's Mak. If I could befriend her then eventually ... maybe ... when the time is right, I could tell her what happened. My thoughts race wildly. What if I could convince her of who I was? Then there would be nothing to stop us being just like we used to be.

The thought of it sends excitement bubbling up in me. There's no reason why I can't go back to school. No one would know that I'm a freak. No one would know who I used to be. Maybe I could start being somebody for the first time in my life. With **her** body I've got a chance to be a girl to remember. I'd be stupid not to try.

I'm draping the shawl back over the mirror, deep in my beautiful daydream, as Mom comes in. Immediately her eyes fall on the laptop.

"What have you been looking at, Lucy?"

I rush over to shut the lid, but she holds it open.

"Oh, Lucy, you promised! This isn't good for you. You can't be looking at this stuff." She snatches the laptop from me.

"I want to go back to Bailey Heights!" I say emphatically.

"I'm sorry, honey; you know that's not possible." She puts her hands on her hip.

"Why not?" I demand.

"It'll be too stressful for you," she lectures.

"So what am I supposed to do? The homeschooling isn't working, so how am I ever supposed to pass my exams . . . get to college?" I point my finger at her, accusingly. "You know how depressed it's making me being stuck here like this."

Mom nervously twists her wedding ring around her finger. "Okay, I can understand that you need company; you want to be around kids your own age. I'll discuss it with Dad. Maybe we can find another school for you; one where you won't know people."

"But I *want* to be with people I know."

Mom tenses. "But they won't know *you*, so what's the point? If you return to your old school, we're running more of a chance that something will go wrong. I don't want people to get curious about you; start looking into things."

"I'll be careful," I plead.

"I know you will, but we can't take the risk. Anyway, your father will never agree to it," she says adamantly.

I raise my eyebrows like she doesn't know what she's talking about. "Really? We'll see." I'm all fired up and it feels good.

CHAPTER 14

PERSUASION

"I'm sorry, but it's a ridiculous idea." Dad's voice is rising. "We can't send you back to Bailey Heights. We made an agreement with Dr Radnor that we'd homeschool. You can't go back where you know everyone. You're bound to let something slip."

"I'm not a complete idiot," I protest across the kitchen table. "I'm not about to stroll into school and announce, 'Hey, guys, I'm Lucy Burgess, back from the dead, only now I'm a freak in another girl's body!' You think I want *anyone* to know the truth?"

"She's right, Lewis," Mom says calmly. "Lucy will be careful. No one will find out."

I try to suppress a smile. I knew that I could talk Mom around.

"You can't guarantee that," Dad scowls. "Renee won't know how she feels until she's actually there and then it will be too late. Say she's overwhelmed by seeing everyone? Say she can't control herself? The fallout would be catastrophic."

"Please call me Lucy, Dad," I plead. "You don't have to keep up the Renee stuff when it's just us."

"How can you call it 'the Renee stuff'?" he says, throwing his hands up. "This is exactly what I'm worried about. This isn't some kind of game. You can't pick and choose when you call yourself Lucy. You've been given a new identity and we *all* have to think of you as Renee. That's who you are now."

"Well, what was the point of keeping me alive if you can't even think of me as your daughter?" I snap.

Dad's face flushes. I know he feels guilty. It's been obvious from the start that the transplant wasn't his idea, but I won't let him stop me doing what I need to do.

I stand up to look him in the eyes. "*You* did this to me. You didn't even ask my permission. You can't even begin to imagine how I feel ... what it's like to be trapped inside a stranger's body with no one knowing who I am, no one to talk to; I can't even hug my own dog."

I watch with satisfaction as Dad squirms.

"If you don't let me go back to Bailey Heights then you can forget about my education because I won't go to another school or have tutors. I swear to you that I'll just lie in bed all day, every day, and you'll have to watch me getting more and more depressed, losing the will to live. Is that what you put me through this for? You had to drag me out of the pool, Dad. Have you forgotten already?" I say, not caring how manipulative I'm being.

Mom puts her arm on Dad's shoulder. "We should let her go, Lewis. I think it'll be good for her. We want Lucy to be happy, don't we?"

Dad shakes his head in defeat. "If anything goes wrong, it's your responsibility, Gemma," he says sternly. "This is your decision."

Mom nods solemnly.

"All right," Dad sighs, "but I'm warning you, the first sign that you're struggling or that people start asking too many questions and I'll pull you out of there. Do you understand?"

I suddenly feel strong ... exhilarated. After spending years being the powerless sick child, it feels great to be in control at last.

"Sure, stop stressing, Dad. I've got this." I smile triumphantly.

CHAPTER 15

BAILEY HEIGHTS

It's taken Mom two weeks but here we are, waiting outside Principal Sanderson's office. Mom is a very persuasive woman. When she practiced law she hardly ever lost a case, so convincing the school to enrol the "disadvantaged" girl that she's helping hasn't been so hard.

Mom seems more nervous than me. She fidgets, smoothing down the bangs on my wig.

"Stop fussing," I whisper. I feel the eyes of Mrs Andrews, the school receptionist, on us.

"Nice to see you again, Mrs Burgess," Mrs Andrews says from over the counter. She adjusts her glasses and peers at me. "We were all so sorry about your loss."

"Thank you," Mom replies uncomfortably.

It's strange how quickly I've gotten used to people talking about me being dead. It doesn't make me feel like throwing up any more. It doesn't make me want to grab hold of them and scream in their face that I'm alive and trapped in this body.

"You look very nice in your uniform, young lady," Mrs Andrews says approvingly.

I smile coyly. It feels weird to be in the Bailey Heights uniform in **her** body, but she looks so good that it gives me a confidence that I've never experienced in school before; it's like I'm playing a role and I've got all my backstory ready. The purple and black colors of the uniform look way better on **her** than they ever did on me, although I reckon she could wear a trash bag and still look good. Mom was delighted when she found me looking in a mirror this morning.

"Good girl, Lucy," she cooed. "You shouldn't start school without knowing how you look."

But the truth is, that each time I look at **her**, I feel less and less like me.

We're summoned into the principal's office. I wince as memories wash over me of the last time I sat in this office. I was with Mom when we told Principal Sanderson that the cancer had returned and I felt too weak to stay in school. Mom thanked her for all the support she'd given me during my years of erratic attendance, disturbed by hospital appointments and periods as an inpatient. Principal Sanderson had hugged me and said how much she looked forward to my return to Bailey Heights, but her watery eyes told me that she didn't believe that was ever going to happen.

Now she shakes Mom's hand warmly as we walk into her office.

"Thank you so much, Principal Sanderson, for allowing Renee to join Bailey Heights." Mom smiles sweetly.

"It's my pleasure," she replies, extending a hand to me. "Good to meet you, Renee."

"And you, Principal Sanderson," I say cheerfully.

"Do sit down." Principal Sanderson gestures to the two chairs in front of her desk. "Now, Renee, I understand that your schooling has been interrupted at times, but I am willing to place you in eleventh grade, as Mrs Burgess has requested. I appreciate that it's important to be with students your own age. If teachers report that you're struggling, then we'll review the situation." She smiles at me reassuringly.

"That sounds very fair," Mom says. "Renee has missed some of her education due to difficult circumstances, but she's very capable."

"I understand, Mrs Burgess." Principal Sanderson turns to me, her voice soft. "Renee, you need to know that at Bailey Heights we're not just concerned with academic achievement. Our students' welfare and happiness is paramount to us, and we have fantastic student counsellors should you ever wish to talk to them."

"Thank you," I mutter.

"I've looked at your request to be in classes with Makayla Walker."

"Well, I know what a great friend she was to Lucy. I just thought that being with her would help me to settle in," I say enthusiastically.

"Mrs Burgess did explain your reasons, so I *will* put

you with Makayla for now, but I have to think of Makayla's needs as well. She has taken Lucy's..." She pauses, looking over at Mom before continuing. "She's taken Lucy's passing very hard, so if I see that she's struggling, we'll have to think again."

"Thank you!" I'm so happy that I could hug her.

"Do you have any more questions?" Principal Sanderson asks.

"No, not from me," I say eagerly.

"Then I'll walk you to your classroom. Classes have started." Principal Sanderson gets up. "Goodbye, Mrs Burgess. Don't you worry about Renee. She'll be just fine here."

"I'm sure she will." Mom doesn't look convinced. "Now enjoy yourself, Renee, and work hard. I'll pick you up later."

"I don't need to be picked up!" I say it too harshly, forgetting myself. Principal Sanderson looks taken aback. "Sorry, Mrs Burgess, what I mean is that I don't want to inconvenience you when I can get the bus home."

"No, Renee. I'll pick you up." Mom gives me a hard stare.

Principal Sanderson walks me through the empty school corridors trying to orient me. "It's a big place but you'll get used to it soon. We're heading for room 11D."

I can't wait to see Mak. I find myself edging ahead of Principal Sanderson and turning right before stopping in front of the third door down the corridor.

I notice Mrs Sanderson looking at me oddly. She must be wondering how on earth I knew where to go. I quickly walk on, realizing my mistake.

"No, it's back here, Renee," she calls out

Principal Sanderson knocks and enters 11D, ushering me in. I scan the room for Mak. She's sitting in the front row. When I notice the teacher, I know why.

"Morning, Mr Kendrick. Sorry to disturb you. This is Renee Wodehouse. This is her first day at Bailey Heights and she'll be joining this class."

Everyone turns their heads to look at me. Hugh Grasso and his buddies start shoving each other and making kissing noises under their breath.

I feel myself blushing; they've never given me a second look before.

"Welcome, Renee." Mr Kendrick smiles. "Now let's see where we can put you."

There are spare seats dotted around the classroom, but I make towards Mak without hesitation.

"Would here be okay?" I ask boldly.

"I don't want anyone sitting there." Mak scowls at me.

"Oh, come on, Makayla. I know that a great girl like you would like to help out Renee," Mr Kendrick says.

His flattery sends Mak into a fluster. "Okay," she relents.

"I'll leave you to it," Principal Sanderson says.

I can't believe I'm here, sitting next to Mak. I give her a mile-wide smile, whispering, "Thanks."

She keeps her eyes straight ahead and doesn't respond.

I study her profile. She doesn't have her usual face full of make-up. Her skin is dull and her hair greasy. She wouldn't usually be caught dead looking like this in front of Mr Kendrick.

"Do you want a photo?" she hisses at me.

"What?" I say, confused.

"Well, you keep staring at me, just wondering whether it would be easier for you to take a freakin' photo!"

Now that's the Mak I know and love. I try to stop grinning, but I can't.

"Why are you smiling?"

"No reason, it's just good to be here."

She shakes her head. "Whatever."

Mr Kendrick hands me a book. "Renee, we're in the middle of studying Mary Shelley's *Frankenstein*. Do you know it?"

"Not really." I feel **her** fingers beginning to twitch; the tremors are starting. I grip the novel tightly. Oh God, please ... not now. Not in front of everyone!

"Don't worry, you'll be able to catch up," Mr Kendrick says, not seeming to notice. "Now, can anyone tell me what may have prompted the nineteen-year-old Mary Shelley to write such a disturbing story?" he asks.

"Was she high at the time?" Hugh Grasso shouts out from the back

The whole class bursts into laughter.

"Actually, Hugh, Mary was in the company of her lover Percy Shelley and the infamous Lord Bryon. They spent much of that summer in 1816 in villas on the banks of Lake Geneva drunk and high on opium, so your answer isn't as outrageous as you'd hoped."

"Hey, they sound like my kind of dudes," Hugh declares to more laughter.

"Yeah, thanks for that, Hugh," Mr Kendrick says drily. "Has anyone else got a theory?"

Mak's hand goes up. "Hadn't Mary recently lost a baby and had a nightmare about rubbing her child back to life?"

"Well, Makayla, it's good to see you've been doing some research. Yes, it's plausible that her subconscious desire to bring her child back from the dead may have been one of her inspirations for *Frankenstein*."

His words feel like being plunged in ice water – I think of Mom and what she's done to me in her desperation to keep me alive. My hands visibly quiver as the tremors build. I grip the book even tighter, breathing deeply, trying to appear calm, glancing around the classroom to make sure that no one is looking at me.

"So Mary Shelley's desire to bring her kid back to life meant she wrote about creating a monster from different body parts who goes around killing people?" Hugh protests.

"As with all the best works of literature, it's open to interpretation," Mr Kendrick replies. "The creature that Victor Frankenstein creates may have looked grotesque, but Mary Shelley also made it articulate, sensitive and intelligent. It's only when Victor, his creator, rejects him and then he's shunned by society that the creature turns to revenge and destruction. The creature says, 'When I looked around I saw and heard of none like me. Was I, then, a monster, a blot upon the earth from which all men fled and whom all men disowned?'"

"What are you doing?" Mak snaps at me in a whisper, staring at my hands.

I look down to see my white-knuckled hands twisting the spine of the book like I'm trying to choke the life out of it. I quickly hide my hands under the table. I grit my teeth behind closed lips as I strain to contain the shaking.

Mak shifts her chair away from me like I'm crazy.

"Anyway, that's enough Gothic horror for today. I'm sure you'll all have a nutritious, healthy lunch and I'll look forward to seeing you tomorrow," Mr Kendrick says playfully, speaking over the bell.

I stifle a sigh of relief as I feel the tremors calming, my tensed hands relaxing. I'm still trying to compose myself as Mak hurries away. Within moments the only people left in the classroom are me and Mr Kendrick.

"Don't you like the sound of the novel?" Mr Kendrick says, noticing my mangled copy of *Frankenstein* on the desk.

"I'm so sorry. I guess I'm just nervous. You know . . . being the new girl," I lie, hurrying out of the room.

The tremors, and the effort of trying to control them, has left me feeling drained and stressed out. I hide in a stall in the restroom, giving myself a few minutes to recover, and then I head to the packed dining hall, scanning around for Mak. The heat and the smell of food is making me queasy. There's a sea of heads bobbing up and down as people vacate and occupy seats. Nothing has changed; people are still territorial about their tables. Like every other school across the country you can map out the whole social structure of Bailey Heights by the different groups dotted around the cafeteria. Mak and me were never going to be part of any cool set, but we didn't care, as long as we had each other.

Mak is sitting at our corner table. I recognize girls from Christian Fellowship floating around her, but Mak has put her bag on the seat next to her – my seat. Looks like the CF girls are trying to befriend her, but their efforts aren't going down well. Mak shoos them away like flies. I'm glad she hasn't hooked up with anyone else; I suppose that's selfish of me, but I'm determined to be here for her now.

"Hi again!" I say cheerfully as I put my tray down next to her.

Anger flashes across her face. "Why are you following me?"

"I'm not," I stutter, nervously.

"I know who you are," Mak says accusingly.

I'm speechless. How can she know? She can't see *me*.

"You're the replacement for Lucy," Mak snaps, crossing her arms.

"Excuse me?" The collar of my blouse suddenly feels tight.

"You're the girl that Mr and Mrs Burgess have taken in. They didn't waste any time, did they? My best friend has only been dead a few months. What are you doing here?" she says bitterly.

"They're just helping me out," I reply apologetically.

"Yeah, I bet they are. I heard they've given you Lucy's room," she says, stabbing at the food on her plate.

"Who told you that?" I swallow hard.

"Lucy's grandma. She keeps in touch with me and my family. We're the ones who haven't forgotten about her; not like some people! You better not have touched any of Lucy's stuff," she says threateningly.

"No, of course not, but there's a denim jacket in her closet that Mrs Burgess says belongs to you."

Tears suddenly fill Mak's eyes. She looks away from me, chewing her lip.

"Do you want to come by the house to get it?" I ask hopefully. "I'm sure Mr and Mrs Burgess would love to see you."

"Get them to mail it to me," she barks. "And just so you don't go wasting your time, I should be clear that I don't care if you're the funniest, most talented, most wonderful person in the world, I don't want to be friends with you. Lucy's parents obviously think that she's replaceable, but I know that she isn't."

Mak leaves her food and walks away. I've lost my appetite too. I push my tray away and stare into space. I know it was stupid, but when I imagined seeing Mak again I thought that she'd recognize something in me; instantly feel some kind of connection. Her hostility feels like a punch in the belly.

A group of boys walk slowly past, their eyes on me. One winks.

I bow my head, flattered . . . embarrassed. I'm not used to this. Boys have never noticed me before. It's so strange to get this kind of attention, even if it's **her** and not me that they like the look of.

"Renee, we can't have you sitting on your own." Principal Sanderson strides towards the table. "Come with me. Let me introduce you to some students. Mrs Burgess told me that you're good at gymnastics. You'll have something in common with these young ladies." She takes me by the elbow and walks over to the table of chatting girls. I know who they are; everyone does.

"Afternoon, girls; this is Renee. It's her first day at Bailey Heights so I'd like you to make her welcome. Renee has an interest in gymnastics. You never know, she may be an asset to the cheer squad." Principal Sanderson sits me down among them and leaves. Why did Mom tell her I liked gymnastics? What's she trying to do to me? I feel sick.

I gawp at the six girls. I don't know what to say. I shouldn't be sitting here. These girls would never talk to people like me and Mak. The Airheads, that's what Mak calls them.

"So which school did you come from?" Ruby Garcia asks.

I've never been this close to her before. She really does look like a contestant on *America's Next Top Model* with her mesmerizing green eyes, golden brown hair and flawless olive skin.

I've got to stop staring and answer. "One in California."

Giggles fizz up from the group. I feel so self-conscious.

"Wow! That voice!" Ruby actually sounds impressed.

I'm laughing nervously. "I know it sounds like I smoke a pack a day, but I don't, honestly."

"No, I think it's cool." Laura Crompton gives a million-watt smile. I suddenly feel bad; me and Mak called her "Barbie Girl" but she seems nice.

"Why did your folks move to H-Town?" Tanya Queenan leans towards me, checking me out. Her deep red hair frames her delicate, ivory-skinned face. I notice how she's customized her uniform so it shows off her skinny, toned body.

"I'm not with my parents. I'm living with Mr and Mrs Burgess. I'm a friend of the family."

"Wasn't that girl who died named Burgess?" Ruby asks her friends.

"Yes," I jump in. "I'm staying with Lucy's parents."

"They're mega rich, aren't they? What's the house like?" Laura asks excitedly.

"It's nice . . . big," I reply.

"I don't care how big the house is, it must be weird living there," Tanya says. "The parents must be like crying all the time and going on about Lucinda. . ."

"Lucy," I correct her.

"I reckon my mom would actually kill herself if anything like that happened to me," Ruby declares.

"It's fine, you know. They're both sick about it but they try to keep the atmosphere okay around me." I squirm. This is awful. I have to think of a reason to excuse myself and get away from these girls. I wonder where Mak went to. Maybe I should go and find her.

"Well, I think it's nice that you're staying there. It's probably helping them having you around. It's like when couples lose a baby and then just go and get pregnant right away to make up for it," Laura suggests.

"Well, I don't know about that," I say uneasily, desperate to get away from this conversation.

"So, were you a cheerleader in your last school?" Ruby asks abruptly, obviously already bored of talking about "Lucinda" and her family.

"No, I never tried out."

"Why not?" Ruby says.

"I'm not good enough," I say adamantly.

"Are you being modest? Principal Sanderson said you do gymnastics. You might as well give it a try. I mean, you've got the right look already." Laura looks at me approvingly.

"What's the right look?" I ask, but I already know the answer.

"You know, long legs, pretty . . . pert," Ruby says, cupping her boobs and causing laughter around the table. "But I'm not sure about your nude look."

"What?" I blush.

"Your face; don't you wear make-up?" Ruby asks, disapprovingly.

"Sometimes." I knew that I should have put on make-up for my big return to school, but that requires mirror time and it messes with my head to look at **her** face for too long.

"Going out of the house without your make-up is announcing to people that you don't value yourself. And if you don't value yourself, how are you going to expect people to value you? Isn't that right, girls?" Ruby preaches.

There are enthusiastic nods around the table.

God, are those her words of wisdom? I wish I could tell Mak; it would crack her up.

"Listen," Ruby says. "I'm the captain of the team and if you want to try out for the squad, I'll let you."

Me, try out for the cheerleading squad? What a joke.

"Thanks, but I don't think so." I smile tightly.

"Well, maybe you just lack confidence," Laura Crompton says kindly. "Why don't you take some time to practice, then see how you feel?"

"Sure, thanks." No way. Not in a million years.

CHAPTER 16

GETTING TO
KNOW YOU

I'm surprised to see Dad waiting for me in the school parking lot. I can't believe he left work early to be here for me.

"Hey, Dad," I mouth at him as I near the Mercedes.

He ushers me in, wincing. "Close the door. You can't be calling me 'Dad' in public."

"No one heard. I didn't even say the words out loud. Stop being paranoid." I hate it when he talks like this; like he's disowning me. "Anyway, what are you doing here? I thought you'd be too busy to be playing chauffeur."

"Well, it's a big day, you going back to school. How was it? Any problems?" he asks casually.

I'm not going to tell him about the tremors. He'll just use them as an excuse to make me quit.

"Did you only come to get me to check whether I'd

screwed up? Don't worry, Dad, I didn't," I say coldly.

His face relaxes. "It must have been stressful for you, though. Can you see now that continuing to have tutors at home would make your life a whole lot easier?"

"No, Dad, that would make *your* life a whole lot easier. I admit it wasn't a great day. Mak doesn't want to get to know me, but I reckon she just needs time. She misses Lucy like crazy," I say, unable to stop my voice cracking with emotion.

For the first time since the transplant I feel like Dad looks at me for real. I see affection and sadness in his eyes.

"I'm so sorry, sweetheart. Listen, I can't change the fact that you have to be Renee now, but I'll always be your daddy. You know that, don't you?" he says softly.

Suddenly I'm five years old again, sitting on his shoulders, strolling through the woods on the lookout for the tree fairies that he swears live in the highest, thickest branches.

"Yes, I know, Daddy. Thank you," I reply quietly.

I see Mom waiting anxiously on the veranda as we drive up. She pounces as soon as I step out of the car, firing questions at me about my day. I tell her about Mak's frosty reception.

"Well, maybe it's best to get to know other girls instead," Mom says carefully. "It's going to put a lot of emotional stress on you if you're trying to be friends with Makayla."

"But she's the only friend I want. I can handle it," I say emphatically.

"Okay, honey." Mom doesn't sound convinced. "So what

else happened? How were the classes? Did you talk to anyone else?"

"Well, Principal Sanderson made me sit with the Airheads." I roll my eyes.

"The Airheads?"

"Yeah, the cheer girls."

"Hey, watch it, young lady. I was one of those 'airheads' in high school," she says playfully.

"How were they with you?"

I pause. "Actually, I suppose they were okay. They invited *me* to try out for the squad." I laugh at how ridiculous that is. "And by the way, why did you tell Principal Sanderson that I liked gymnastics?"

Mom ignores my question. She's excited all of a sudden. "That's fantastic! What a great idea – it'll be such a good way to make new friends."

"No, Mom, I'm not a cheerleader. All I want is to get Mak to like me."

"I understand, but it won't do any harm to practice a few moves with your old mom." She smiles enthusiastically. "You might actually enjoy it."

I don't particularly want to, but I know how happy it'll make her. "Okay," I groan, "but I want to see Arthur first."

I go into the utility room to attempt my daily charm offensive on Arthur. I've been trying to buy his approval with so many treats and toys. I've had my antihistamine pill – they seem to stop the allergic reaction. But nothing changes the way he reacts to me. I offer him a handful of snacks but, as usual, he turns his head, not wanting to accept anything from me. My old Bailey Heights sweatshirt is peeking out from under him. If I can only get it off him and actually squeeze into it, he'll be able to smell a trace of me and see past this body.

"Arthur, fetch!" I throw a rubber bone across the utility room. He raises his head to watch the bone in flight, then flops back down again. But I know how to make him move; after all, it's me who repels him. I begin to stroke along his shaggy back. It's terrible to feel his body quivering from my touch. He can't stand it for long. He stands and steps out of the basket but, as he turns to pick up the sweatshirt, I grab it and hold it tightly to me. He lets out a volley of ferocious barks, snarling and baring his teeth. I've never seen him behave like this. I edge towards the door, but he jumps up at the sweatshirt and clenches it between his teeth. As I try to pull it away from him, he snaps at me. I release it in fright. Arthur seizes upon it. I back out of the room and slam the door shut.

Dad and Mom rush into the kitchen.

"Did he bite you?" Dad asks, examining my arm.

"No, he just snapped at me. It was my own fault. I tried to take my sweatshirt from him." I try to sound like it was no big deal but inside I'm shaking.

They exchange a concerned look.

"Come on. Forget about Arthur for now. Come into the yard to practice," Mom says gently. "It's been years since my glory days, but I might remember something."

127

We walk past the pool and tennis court and through the landscaped gardens to the wide, open grounds.

Mom takes her jacket and heels off. She's in her element, calling out instructions as I attempt handstands and dive rolls. With every attempt my confidence is growing. Just like back in the clinic, I find that if I don't think about the movements, but just let the body take over, I can do them instinctively. There's a surge of adrenaline as I do handsprings and backflips one after the other down the lawn. I can't believe how good this feels. Mom is jumping up and down, punching the air.

"Way to go, Lucy!" She sprints towards me and twirls me around, making us both so giddy that we topple over in a heap, panting and laughing.

"What's going on?" Grandma's voice sails through the air.

We scramble to our feet. Mom dusts herself down, looking like a guilty schoolgirl.

"Hi, Mama," she pants. "I was just helping Renee with some gym moves."

Grandma takes hold of Mom's arm and pulls her away from me. She lowers her voice; she thinks that I can't hear what she's saying.

"What is happening to you, Gemma? Do you realize that you just called that young woman 'Lucy'?" Disgust is plain on Grandma's face.

Mom's face ripens tomato red. "Did I? Oh, God, how stupid of me."

"Hugging her? Rolling on the grass with her? You hardly know this girl."

"But I feel like I do, Mama. I feel like I've known Renee a long, long time," Mom says firmly.

Grandma's face softens as she smooths down Mom's ruffled hair. "My darling, I know how much you miss Lucy, but trying to replace her isn't the answer. This isn't healthy. And how much do you really know about this young woman? She comes from a difficult background. She may have all kind of problems and you've brought her into your home, lavishing money and affection on her."

"You know nothing about it," Mom replies hotly. "Renee is a good girl, and having her here is making me happy."

"What you need to do is get back to work, Gemma. You gave up your career to care for Lucy and I admired you for it. But now you need to fill that void. I guarantee that if you go back to law, you won't feel the need to invite a stranger into your life."

"Why don't you just try to get to know her? I'm sure that you two will get along well . . . more than well. Give Renee a chance, Mama."

"Okay, fine," she says coldly as she beckons me to her.

"Let's go sit by the pool, Renee."

The three of us walk in awkward silence across the lawns. Grandma reaches the swing chair next to the glistening water and pats the cushion. "Sit next to me, Renee. I don't bite."

Mom pulls up a lounger and sits straight-backed and tense. "Did you get the guest list that I emailed you, Mama?"

"Yes, thank you – better late than never. It's an impressive list; if all your lawyer friends and Lewis's finance colleagues open their hearts *and* wallets I think the charity auction could raise a small fortune. Now, Gemma, would you be a darling and bring us some lemonade?"

Mom hesitates. I know that she doesn't want to leave me alone with Grandma. "I'll call Lewis. He's just in the house. He won't mind making it."

"No, Gemma, I want you to make it; give me and Renee a chance to chat," Grandma says firmly.

"Okay then." There's a nervous flutter in her voice.

Grandma waits until Mom's gone in the house and then she gives me a tight smile. "Well, how are you enjoying your visit?"

"I'm having an awesome time, thank you." My voice sounds even more husky than usual. I should be excited to be alone with Grandma, but she's making me so anxious, I don't know how to feel.

She leaves an awkward silence hanging in the air. I feel compelled to fill it. I have to make a connection with her. "So, Mrs Kendal, Mrs Burgess has told me that you play bridge." I sound too enthusiastic; she'll think I'm patronizing her.

"Yes, I've played for years and I used to have a lot of fun trying to coach Lucy and her friend Makayla to play," she says, her voice heavy with melancholy.

I can't help smiling as I think of how terrible me and Mak were at the game, but it made Grandma so happy trying to teach us.

"Do you play bridge?" Grandma looks skeptical.

"A little and very badly," I say sweetly.

"Who on earth taught you? It's hardly a popular card game with young people."

"My grandma, but she passed away." God, that's an awful thing for me to say.

Grandma looks sympathetic. "I'm sorry for your loss."

"Thank you." The silence descends again. She's not going to make this easy.

"I believe Gemma has enrolled you in Bailey Heights, so she obviously thinks you're going to be here a while," she says abruptly.

"I guess so." I sound too apologetic . . . I've got to be more confident.

"And I gather that Lewis even went and picked you up from school today."

"Yeah, it was nice of him." I smile appreciatively.

"Nice? It's quite extraordinary. It's unheard of for Lewis to take time off work." Her voice sharpens.

"Oh, I didn't know that." God, she's annoyed. This is so awkward.

"No reason why you would, my dear. Now, Gemma insists that we should get to know each other, so why don't you tell me all about yourself?" It sounds more like an order than a request.

"Well, as you know, I'm originally from San Diego." It's going to be okay. I know my script by heart.

"Yes, but where exactly in San Diego? I know the city quite well. My late husband and I used to visit the yacht club at the marina."

131

"Well, me and Mom used to live in City Heights."

"I've heard of it, but it's not an area I've ever been to."

"No, it wouldn't be, Mrs Kendal. It's a world away from the yacht club," I say, knowing it will make her feel bad, but I need to take the sting out of her.

Grandma looks momentarily flustered with embarrassment.

"And what's your mother's name?"

"Maria."

"Maria Wodehouse?"

"Yes."

"Any brothers or sisters?"

"No, and I never knew my father. He didn't stick around."

"And your mother, she had problems?" she says, like I'm in a police interview.

"Yeah, drug addiction." I lower my eyes to the ground. I'm ashamed of lying to her.

"I'm so sorry. It must have been terrible for you." Grandma touches **her** hand. I can't resist. I put the other hand on top of hers. Her skin feels paper-thin. I search her aged face. She looks unnerved, but I see kindness in her eyes.

"And when were you taken into foster care?" she says gently.

"When I was eleven. I haven't seen my mom since."

"And were you all right? Did you feel looked after?" she says with genuine concern.

"It was okay. I coped." I blush.

She stares intently into my eyes. A strange look forms on her face. "You have Lucy's eyes," she whispers.

"Excuse me?" I gasp, frozen.

"You have Lucy's eyes. They're the exact same color – sky blue, like a beautiful cloudless day. Amazing! I bet my daughter noticed them the very first time you met. Perhaps that's why you caught her attention."

"I don't know. She hasn't mentioned it," I mumble, flustered.

"You met Gemma and Lewis at a charity event, I believe. Where was that?"

God! Where was it? I can't remember.

I make an apologetic face. "It wasn't so long ago, but my mind's gone blank."

"Oh, do try and remember," Grandma presses.

I start to prickle all over. I'm sweating.

"Are you feeling all right, dear?" Grandma asks.

"Yes, I just feel hot. It must be all the jumping around before."

"Well, don't worry, here's Gemma with our drinks. This should help."

I can't suppress a sigh of relief as I see Mom and Dad approaching.

"Mrs Kendal was just asking where the charity event was. The one we first met at. I can't remember," I garble at them.

"Well, let's think," Mom says casually as she puts the tray of drinks down. "Wasn't it at the town hall? It was a fundraiser for children and family services."

"Yes, that's right," Dad says, nodding too emphatically.

"Of course, I was invited as a representative; one of the young adults who'd benefited from the system." I take a gulp of the lemonade. Its sharpness makes me cough and splutter.

"Isn't it sweet enough?" Mom asks.

It's the first lemonade I've had since the transplant. It probably is sweet enough for me, but it's too sour for **her**. "No, it's fine. It just went down the wrong way."

"Lucy used to love her mom's lemonade. Didn't she, Gemma?" Grandma's face softens at the memory.

"Yes, Mama."

"The last time I saw Lucy we were sitting here on these very chairs, sipping lemonade. It was right before she went into the hospital." Grandma clears her throat as emotion chokes her.

"You must miss her," I say too earnestly.

Her cloudy eyes fill with tears. "Oh yes, I miss her. She was my beautiful granddaughter and she was so kind to me. When she was well enough, she'd come by with Arthur and we'd play for hours in the backyard, and when she was going through a bad patch, she'd always put a smile on her face; she didn't want to worry me. I miss her more than I could ever explain. There's been a constant sick feeling in my stomach since she died and I don't expect it will go away until the day I join her." Tears spill out of her eyes. Mom goes to embrace her but Grandma shoos her away.

"Don't fuss, Gemma," she says, producing a lace handkerchief from her bag and dabbing her cheeks as her face crumples.

I can't stand it. I want to stop Grandma's pain. The joy she'll feel when she knows that I'm alive. "But say Lucy isn't gone! Say she was still here with you, right now," I blurt out.

Dad and Mom look panic-stricken. Dad moves close to me, warningly.

"What are you talking about? How can she be here?" Anger sweeps across Grandma's face.

"I think Renee is talking about Lucy's spirit," Dad says, his eyes boring into me. "Have I got that right, Renee?"

My head drops. "Yes," I whisper.

Grandma nods solemnly as she pats a tear away. "You're right, of course. Lucy's spirit *is* with us. Maybe I just need to pray harder to feel it. I know that the good Lord will comfort me in my sorrow if I let him."

Mom puts her arm around Grandma as Dad says to me, "Let's give Mrs Burgess and her mother a moment together. Would you come help me in the kitchen?"

He swiftly maneuvers me into the house.

"What in God's name are you playing at?" He holds up his hands in disbelief.

"She needs to know. It's wrong not to tell her," I shout in anger and frustration.

"I know it's painful for you to hear Grandma talk like that, but you *can't* tell her!" Dad says, looking like he's going to explode with stress. "The truth could literally kill her – you can see how frail she has become – and even if it didn't, you can bet that she'll freak out and run and tell her pastor."

"She wouldn't do that." My voice is losing its conviction.

"Listen, Grandma won't understand what we've done. The afterlife is more important to her than the life we have on earth, and she'll think we've played God by what we've done to you. Once she tells her pastor, *everything* will be exposed. We'll get locked up. We'll lose you. You'll have no one to protect you. But you know all this, don't you?"

I nod my bowed head, tears of distress splashing on to the kitchen floor.

"You've got to keep your mouth shut. Can you keep your mouth shut? Can you, Renee?"

I raise my head and stare into his desperate face. "Yes, Da— Mr Burgess," I splutter.

I close my eyes as I realize that Grandma is lost to me. They've been telling me over and over since I had the transplant that I have to keep my mouth shut, but now it really hits me what this means. I'll never be able to be Lucy Burgess again.

CHAPTER 17

GETTING NOWHERE

In school, whenever I feel the tremors starting up, I head straight to the bathroom and lock myself in a stall until they pass. If it's in the middle of class, I clasp my hands under the table and focus on stopping the vibrations travelling up my arms. It's a real strain, and I can feel them getting worse, but it doesn't happen every day and no one has noticed ... yet. Anyway, the tremors aren't even my biggest problem at Bailey Heights; that honor goes to Mak.

Every morning for a month now I've been waking up and telling myself, "Today is the day I'm going to make a breakthrough with Mak." But it's getting harder and harder to believe it's going to happen. In class I try to sit next to her. I try and get her talking about stuff that I *know* she's into, but she's not interested if it's me asking. She huffs and groans and turns her back. She asks teachers whether she can change seats. Mr Kendrick even kept me behind after class last week to advise me to give Mak "a bit of space."

If she sees me coming in the dining hall she just walks out; leaves me standing there, feeling stupid. So, I eat my lunch in the courtyard, hoping no one will bother me, but the other week Josh Dartmere spotted me under the lilac tree and the next minute he's looming over me.

"Hi." His smile was more of a leer. "Remember me? We met a while back, in the mall. You were with Mrs Burgess."

I didn't raise my eyes to look at him. "Yeah, I remember."

"How are you settling in?"

"Just fine," I replied, coldly.

"Have you gotten to know people? You could always come to a football game if you want. I'm in the Bailey Bulls." He paused, expecting me to be impressed, but I remained silent. "You might not know, but I'm on the *varsity* football team."

"Oh." I sounded bored.

"If football isn't your thing, what about going to see a movie?" He really is a scumbag. He knows that I've already met *one* of his girlfriends.

"No, I'm good, thanks." I continued eating my sandwich.

"Suit yourself." His voice was tinged with resentment. I was relieved when he walked away.

And then, a few days later I thought I had a glimmer of hope for me and Mak. I pushed my way on to the school bus and grabbed the seat next to her. The bus filled up so quickly that she was trapped. She rolled her eyes and scowled at me. "It's my freakin' stalker," she hissed. I didn't say a word. I just got out my copy of *And Still I Rise* and made sure she could see the cover. She looked sideways at it as I read. I saw her mouth twitching as she tried to stop herself opening it.

"Do you like Maya Angelou?" I asked innocently.

"Yeah." She tried to sound casual.

Of course you do, I thought. *Last birthday I bought you a signed copy of* I Know Why the Caged Bird Sings. *You said it was the best present that you'd ever been given.*

"I love her poetry. *And Still I Rise* is *so* powerful." I mean it, but I also I know that she has a copy of it on her bedroom wall.

"Yeah, it sure is." She nodded, her voice softer.

"Hey, have you got plans, because maybe you'd like to come back to the Burgess place? I think they've got every book that Maya Angelou has ever written." I knew that I was oversmiling.

"No, thanks, I've already got every book that she's written," she replied.

"Well, I bet you'd like to see Arthur." I said it too abruptly. She started.

"Arthur? Lucy's dog?"

"Yeah, come and see him. You must have missed him, Mak. Mrs Burgess was telling me about the water polo game both of you used to play with him in the pool. It sounds hilarious."

Mak's face turned to thunder. "Firstly, only my friends call me Mak and secondly, yeah, me and Lucy had a blast playing that game with Arthur so I don't want to play it with you."

"We don't have to. There's plenty of other things we could do," I said, pathetically.

"Why are you so obsessed with trying to be friends with me?" she scowled.

"I'm not. I just thought it would be nice, seeing as you were Lucy's best friend and I'm living with the Burgesses."

She stood up as the bus bumped along. "So, you take Lucy's bedroom, her parents, her dog, so hey . . . why not take her best friend too? You are unbelievable," she seethed.

"No, that's not how it is, Makayla!"

She squeezed past me.

"But this isn't your stop," I said.

"How do you know which one is my stop?" she snapped.

I thought quickly. "We were passing the other day and Mrs Burgess pointed out your house," I lied.

"Oh, how kind of her," she said sarcastically. "Well, don't ever come knocking, because you're not welcome there."

Her venom poisons me. This isn't the way it's supposed to be.

Now I sit on the grass by the trash cans. It's quiet here. Not so many people pass by. I'm exhausted by Mak's rejections. I won't give up, but I'm struggling to think what else I can do to win her over. It's ridiculous, but the only thing that's making me happy is tumbling around the yard practicing moves with Mom. It's amazing to feel this well; to have this energy after all the sickness, all the exhaustion. **Her** body is the reason I can do all these things, and the tremors are her reminder that it will never really belong to me.

Laura Compton walks past, her platinum-blonde ponytail bobbing. I look down, but she sees me. This is the last thing I need. I've been avoiding the cheer girls since that first day when they invited me to try out.

"Well, hi, stranger. Where have you been hiding?" Laura asks cheerfully.

"Oh, I've just been busy," I mumble.

"What happened to you trying out, Renee?" I smile inside. She remembered my name.

I shrug. "I'm not good enough."

"Come on now, up you get." She's grinning as she hauls me off the grass. "Can you do a backflip?"

I nod shyly.

"Well, let's see it," she says brightly.

I hesitate. I shouldn't, but part of me would love to show off, and before I can think about it, I've done a round-off into a double back tuck.

"I knew it!" Laura trills, her brown eyes sparkling. "You're a natural. So, no more false modesty. Promise me that you'll try out?"

I'm blushing. I'm flattered, but it's not me who's the "natural"; it's my donor. I feel almost grateful.

Laura kicks a can out of her way. "Why are you sitting in this stinking corner all alone? Come sit with us. We don't bite," she says, pulling a vampire face.

I laugh ... a genuine laugh. It feels so good to have someone who actually wants me around.

CHAPTER 18

THE TRY-OUT

I've decided to take Mr Kendrick's advice and give Mak some space. I've been coming on way too strong. I've only been making things worse. Every time I'm within a hundred yards of her, she hisses like a rattlesnake. It feels odd, but the only people keeping me going are the cheer girls. They've made me feel so welcome. And it's not all pom-pom shaking and Airhead giggling like me and Mak used to think; I've been sitting in on their training, and they're real hard-core athletes.

At first I felt like an impostor who shouldn't be allowed to hang out with them, but each day I feel more confident in their company, as long as I remember to be "Renee". It's definitely fun being with them, and I haven't had fun in a very, very long time. In **her** body I'm discovering that people treat me differently ... better, as if I'm special. It's as if they think that being pretty is a talent worthy of their admiration. Even the teachers can't seem to help themselves; I've noticed that they smile more at me and they don't struggle to remember my name.

I know that I shouldn't laugh at the stuff Ruby says, because it's mostly bitchy, but she's so funny and she seems to know everything about everyone. She told me which boys in our grade are hung like donkeys and which ones look at the penis enlargement sites. She swears that Mike Hanson, the big-mouth homophobe in the football squad, secretly dresses up in women's clothes and that Principal Sanderson is dating a man half her age who works at Burger King. But sometimes when I'm laughing I suddenly feel sick as I imagine what Ruby would say if she knew the truth about me; even if she only discovered that my hair was a wig and my head was so scarred. She'd be horrified; she'd tell everyone. I have to be careful. I can't let my guard down.

When I woke up this morning I had butterflies in my belly at the thought of the try-outs today. I got up early and practiced my routine before breakfast. Mom said it was looking great. She insisted on twisting the long mane of my wig into a French braid. She kept adjusting me and wishing me good luck.

I feel bad for even thinking it, but it's a relief not to sit in class stressing about Mak. I see her across the room but all I'm thinking about is the try-out. All morning I count down the minutes until the lunchtime bell. As soon as it rings I race to the locker room and get into my tracksuit.

When I enter the gym my belly flips as I see half the cheer squad sitting in a row, waiting to audition me.

Ruby looks amused. "Don't look so scared, Renee. Come on, show us what you've got."

I try to remember the routine. I suddenly feel stupid as I begin clapping and dancing and trying to smile while chanting. "Go, Bailey, you're the best. So much better than all the rest. Go, Bailey, hit the Heights! Watch your back, 'cause Bailey bites!" I end with a half-hearted jumping jack.

Everyone stares at me, deeply unimpressed. Ruby rolls her eyes.

"Really? Is that your routine?"

"The dancing isn't my strong point. I'm better at the gymnastics," I say apologetically.

"Okay, let's see it," Ruby sighs.

I fight to block out the negative thoughts that are telling me I'm going to humiliate myself. I've got to remember that it was *my* body that was terrible at these things, but now I'm auditioning with **her** body and she can do this. I've just got to turn off my mind and let **her** do **her** thing.

As I walk to the back of the hall, I feel tingling in my fingers as **her** hands begin their tremor.

Not now, please not now!

"Wow, are you nervous!" Ruby exclaims. "Look at your hands!"

"Just relax, Renee. You're going to do great," Laura says kindly.

I close my eyes and plead with her. *Please stop. Don't you want to show them what you can do?*

"We haven't got all day," Ruby groans.

I try to clear my mind, think of nothing as I stretch upwards. I take a deep breath and bound forward into a sequence of one-handed springs and backwards tucks, ending with a full twisting layout. I open my eyes to the smiling row of cheerleaders.

"Way to go, Renee!" Laura whoops.

"That wasn't half bad," Ruby smirks. "I think we'd all agree that we need to work on your dance routines. But, if no one objects, as captain of Bailey Heights Cheerleading Team, I'd like to welcome you into the squad."

They all burst into applause. "Thank you, thank you so much." I'm ecstatic as Ruby hands me the cellophane-wrapped uniform.

I walk into the empty locker room and take my clothes out, but instead of getting back into my uniform I can't resist opening the new outfit. I peel off my tracksuit, then slip on the shiny blue-and-white skirt and top with BAILEY stitched across it. The sleeveless top comes to a V at the front but is high at the back, covering the nasty scar that runs down the back of the neck and top of the spine. I feel the silky material of the skirt. I get an overwhelming urge to see her.

My mouth is dry as I stand in front of the full-length mirror. I look **her** up and down. The flimsy short skirt shows off **her** long, lean legs. The top clings on to the contours of **her** boobs, flat belly and slim waist. **Her** shoulders and arms are toned, **her** neck long and elegant. The only evidence of me is the blue eyes shining out from **her** pretty face.

145

I step closer to the mirror, scrutinizing **her** image. The strawberry-blonde wig is pulled back behind delicate, small ears. There's a sprinkling of pale freckles on **her** cheeks and across **her** button nose. I hadn't noticed them before; the sun must have brought them out. I part **her** full lips and move them into a smile, dimples appearing in **her** cheeks and exposing a set of slightly snaggly white teeth. There's something attractively individual about them. They don't have the uniform look produced by years in braces.

I run a finger over the scar that cuts across her eyebrow. How did she get this? It's an old scar. She must have done it when she was little. Other than that tiny flaw, **her** face is perfect, so sweet. I bet she was popular. Maybe a gymnast or an athlete on the school team? Would she approve of being in the Bailey Heights squad? Maybe she used to be a cheerleader ... but what if she was just a very flexible goth who despised everything about cheerleaders and their plastered-on smiles?

I touch the reflection of her face in the mirror. She's not just a body; she's a girl with her own personality, **her** own family and history. I'm suddenly filled with curiosity. Did she leave behind brothers and sisters, friends, a broken-hearted boy? All **her** dreams and plans for the future gone in a split second. I know that Dr Leo said I couldn't be told anything about **her**, but I'm gripped by a desperate need to learn about who I've been made part of. I owe **her** everything. I wouldn't be alive without **her**. Together we could be someone; she just needs to let me be in complete control.

By the time I arrive home Mom has literally put the flag out
for me. I chuckle as I see the stars and stripes fluttering at
the top of the pole by the electric gates. She comes skipping
all the way down the drive to greet me.

"Hey, Cheer Girl! Principal Sanderson called to tell me
the good news." She high-fives me like *she's* the teenager. "I'm
so proud of you."

I'm glad that Mom is proud, but I wonder who she's proud
of really – me or **her**?

"Thanks, but I nearly blew it with the hand tremors. They
started when I was auditioning." I only realize what I've said
seconds after Mom hears it.

"What? They haven't settled down?" she says, her eyes
widening. "We need to get you back to Dr Radnor right away."

"No! Don't make me go back there." I'm so annoyed with
myself. I've been doing so well keeping the tremors hidden
and now I've messed up.

"You won't need to be there for long. We have to take care
of you; you're still adjusting."

"I know something that might help me 'adjust'," I say
pointedly. "I've been thinking, Mom; I want to know about
the donor. I figure that if I found out her name, what she
was like ... then she won't feel like a stranger, an impostor.
Maybe I could even accept what's happened to me. Isn't that
what you want?"

"Of course." Mom looks choked up. "But Dr Radnor said
it's confidential. It can't happen."

"But you can explain to him that it will help me get my head around what you've all done to me." I look at her accusingly. "He wants to help my mental health, doesn't he?"

"Of course he does, but it's not that simple, Lucy."

"Please ask him, Mom, and I'll think about going back to the clinic."

"Okay, I'll ask," she says reluctantly.

CHAPTER 19

THE STABLES

Mom chats happily with the cheer girls as we walk over to the stable block. At Mom's request, I've invited them over to ride and have some lunch so that she can meet my new friends.

I dared to speak to Mak in history to invite her too, but I knew that she wouldn't come and anyway, she doesn't like the cheer crowd; she'd be all uptight around them and probably ruin the day.

"I am just thrilled that Renee made the squad," Mom beams. "I don't tell many people this but, back in the day, I was a flyer for my senior team."

"No way?" Ruby looks genuinely impressed. "Which school?"

"Stepton High."

"Wow, you know that they were the best in the county last year," Tanya says.

"Yep, we actually won the Nationals when I was on the team, but that was a *long* time ago," Mom says, waving her hand dismissively.

"I bet you still got it, Mrs Burgess," Ruby says, looking her up and down.

"Oh, I wish! Though it's been fun doing all the routines with Renee."

"Why don't you come to a practice? You might be able to give us some old-style moves," Laura smiles.

"No," I jump in nervously. "Mrs Burgess is a busy woman. She doesn't have the time."

"It's okay, Renee, I wouldn't embarrass you in front of your friends," she chuckles.

Jim is waiting for us. He's got four of the horses out of the stalls, all saddled up. I shoot a look of alarm at Mom.

"Hey, Mrs Burgess, you know that I don't ride. I'm just here to watch," I say, panicking.

"I thought that you might want to give it a try today, seeing as your friends are here. Nothing too hard. Just get up in the saddle and see how it feels. Jim's here to help you."

"Oh, come on, Renee! I remember the first time I got on a horse. I was terrified, but once I got used to it, I loved it," Laura says.

Jim looks nervous. He has seen how the horses behave when I visit the stables.

"Don't be a baby, Renee. Get up on that horse. What's the point of living somewhere with stables if you won't even ride?" Tanya says.

"I really don't want to," I reply firmly.

"Well, I'm not going to ride unless you give it a try," Ruby says, crossing her arms.

"Renee, you can't ruin the girls' day. Please try. You'll feel so much better once you've done this," Mom says. She's so convinced that I can overcome the problem with the animals.

I sigh, my insides starting to churn. They're not going to leave me alone. I'm going to have to try it. Maybe once I'm actually on Moonshine's back she'll be able to connect with me.

The girls watch as Jim pulls the reluctant Moonshine towards me and I walk around to her side. The sleek chestnut mare snorts in protest as I grab a hold of her saddle.

"Come on, Renee, up you go. Jim's got a tight hold on her, don't you, Jim?" Mom smiles reassuringly.

"Sure do, Mrs Burgess," Jim replies, his strong hands straining to keep a grip on the reins. "But Moonshine seems a bit spooked today."

"She's scared of me," I say flatly.

Mom laughs nervously. "Don't be silly, Renee. Come on, jump up."

As I put my foot in the stirrup Moonshine jerks away, shaking her head violently.

"Calm down, girl," Jim whispers in Moonshine's ear, stroking her forehead.

Moonshine stills, but her wide eye watches me. Her muscular flanks quiver as I pull myself up and into the saddle.

"There you go. I knew that you could do it." Mom looks thrilled.

Laura and Ruby give a gentle round of applause. Tanya is holding her phone up, filming me. I grip the horse's flanks with my thighs.

As I sit astride her I can feel Moonshine's fear passing directly into me. I hold on tight to the reins.

"You can let go now, Jim. Let Renee take her for a walk around the yard."

Jim looks concerned. "Best give it a minute. Let them get used to each other."

"She looks fine to me. Let her go," Mom insists.

"No!" I gasp, but it's too late. As soon as Jim steps away, Moonshine throws her head back, ears flickering, nostrils flared. I shriek and grip on to the saddle as she rears up on her hind legs, trying to throw me off, as if she has the devil on her back.

The girls scatter and the horses in the yard start to squeal and pull at their tethers like a stampede is about to break out.

"Help her, Jim," Mom shouts.

But Jim can't get near Moonshine's nine hundred pounds of pumping flesh and muscle. I'm jolted back and forth as she rears up and crashes down, again and again, dust rising from the ground.

"Jump off this way!" Jim is shouting, standing at the front of my wild horse. "Throw yourself clear. I'll catch you."

Terror makes me grip the saddle even harder. My legs

squeeze even tighter around Moonshine. The thought of throwing myself off goes against every instinct in my body.

"Come on, Renee!" Jim's arms are stretched out towards me. "As soon as she comes down, let go of the saddle and jump this way."

I've got to think straight – if I don't jump, I'm going to be thrown off any second. I'll land on the ground and break my back, split my head open – I've got to try to reach Jim.

I clutch on to the saddle and reins as Moonshine rears up again; as she descends, her front hooves jar against the ground and I let go. I'm catapulted forward, flying over her bowed head and landing in Jim's arms with such force that I knock him clean off his feet. I'm lying on top of him. We stare at each other and exchange a smile of utter relief. Mom runs over and peels me off him. She gathers me to her, gently dusting down my Bailey Heights hoodie and jeans.

"Are you okay? Have you broken anything?"

"No, I'm okay . . . I think," I say, trembling.

Jim gets up unsteadily and approaches the horse. Moonshine stands as docile as a dormouse; the other horses have all calmed down; silence descends on the yard. He strokes Moonshine's neck, saying softly, "Everything's all right, girl."

"Thanks, Jim," I say quietly, biting my lip to stop myself from crying.

"Don't mention it." His weather-beaten face crinkles into a smile, but he's looking at me with curiosity. He knows that the horses are terrified of me, he just doesn't know why.

"Oh my freakin' God," whispers Tanya, her knuckles white around her phone. "What the hell happened there?"

Laura rushes over and hugs me. "That horse is dangerous. It could have killed you," she splutters.

"With all due respect, I know Moonshine; she isn't dangerous. She was always as gentle as a lamb with Lucy," Jim says defensively.

"Well, it wasn't Renee's fault. All she did was sit on it," Ruby protests.

Jim casts his eyes to the ground, kicking up dirt with the toe of his boots. "Some folk just aren't horse people. I guess Miss Renee is one of them."

"That's not so, Jim. One day Renee will be galloping around this paddock. We just need to find her the right horse." It's clear that Mom is in denial.

"No, no more horses," I whimper.

"Mrs Burgess, I think that we'd better go home and let you look after Renee," Laura says, concerned.

No! I can't have their first ever visit ending like this; they might never come back. "I'm fine, really. Just a little shaken up. There's no need to go. Did you bring your swimsuits like I told you?" I sound desperate, but I don't care. I can't lose them.

"Yep," Tanya replies enthusiastically.

"Well then, why don't you all use the pool and I'll take some painkillers and sit on one of the loungers. Mrs Burgess has made you a big lunch, haven't you?"

"Well, yes I have, but are you sure that you're okay, Renee?"

"Don't fuss. I'm fine. Listen, you've got to stay; Mrs Burgess has this new 'miracle juice' that she wants you to try. Apparently, it's amazing for your skin. All the Hollywood A-listers are going crazy for it."

"Okay then, if you're sure," Tanya says, already heading in the direction of the pool.

Laura and Ruby link arms with me as we walk back towards the house. They pick bits of straw and grit out of my wig. I'm so relieved that it has stayed tightly glued to my scalp. It's weird, but I actually feel happy; I know that I made Moonshine crazy and my whole body is aching, but Laura is telling me how awesome and brave I am and Ruby is saying that this has been way more exciting than her usual Saturdays of shopping and listening to her boyfriend's football stories and suddenly, I'm feeling like this may not turn out so bad after all.

I've had all weekend to recover but my legs and arms still feel stiff as I walk up the school steps. Everyone's swarming in, like bees returning to a hive, but over the buzz of the crowd I hear the sound of whistling as someone shouts out, "Yee-haw!"

I look around to see what's going on and notice the expression on faces as they pass me. People seem to be grinning at me, knowingly.

"Hey, you entering the rodeo this year, Renee?" A girl giggles and walks on by.

"Respect, stunt girl!" A boy hollers to me.

What the hell is happening? What do they know?

Hugh Grasso skips towards me, holding his phone up. I feel the blood drain from my face as I watch the chaotic video of Moonshine bucking me up and down as I cling on to him.

"Renee, I just want you to know that you can be my buckaroo babe any day," he says.

Oh my God. This can't be happening. What will everyone think of me?

Principal Sanderson stops me as I enter through the doors. "I'm glad to see you in one piece, Renee. That was quite some tumble you took."

What? Has everyone on the planet seen it?

"Yes, Principal Sanderson, but I'm fine." I hurry away, trying not to catch anyone's eye.

"You look good even in mid-air." From behind me, Josh Dartmere whispers in my ear. His voice sends me scurrying down the corridor.

"Renee!" It's Laura. She's with Ruby and Tanya. Tanya is looking pleased with herself.

"What the hell, Tanya? Why did you film it and then post it for everyone to see?" I think I'm going to burst into tears.

"What's your problem, Renee? You should read all the comments. People think it's awesome. I've made you into a freakin' celebrity." She slaps me on the back.

"'Buckaroo Babe', *that's* what you called the video! You made me sound like a porn star," I splutter.

"Yeah, no wonder it's had so many hits." Ruby's face creases with laughter.

"Look, it was too good not to share. It's not like you were hurt or anything. I wouldn't have posted it if you'd broken your neck," Tanya says.

"Well, that sure is thoughtful of you," I seethe.

"Listen, Renee, I know that Tanya should have asked you first, but you've got to admit it's a very cool video . . . everyone thinks so." Laura widens her eyes as she tries to charm me into submission.

"But Tanya didn't know what people would think. For all she knew it could have given every student in this school an excuse to make my life hell."

"Hey, Renee, tell that old guy who caught you that we need him as goalkeeper on our soccer team." I turn around and see Dan Woods, the best-looking guy at Bailey Heights, smiling at me. I'm completely tongue-tied. A ridiculous giggle is the only response that I can manage.

"See!" Tanya says smugly. "No need to thank me."

Part of me wants to slap her, but with all these people loving it . . . thinking I'm something special, making such a fuss over me, I'm buzzing. I try to look annoyed as I say to her, "Okay, but swear that you'll take it down . . . NOW! I don't want anyone else seeing it."

Tanya waggles her little finger in front of me. "I pinky swear."

CHAPTER 20

THE CLIP

The boy clicks the YouTube link that he'd been sent entitled "Buckaroo Babe". The video shows a girl sitting atop a chestnut horse that's going crazy – trying to buck her off. A woman can be heard shrieking in the background, and an older cowboy-type is desperately trying to get close to the raging animal. Dust rises from the ground as the horse's hooves stamp up and down. It's difficult to make out the girl's features as the horse jolts her back and forth, but she's putting up a good fight as she clings on like a rodeo rider. The man shouts "Renee!" and urges her to jump forward. Seconds later she sails over the horse's head and is caught in the cowboy's arms, sending them both crashing to the ground.

As the dust settles it's clear that she's a teenager with long strawberry-blonde hair, but as the camera zooms in, the boy freezes the footage, his eyes wide, his mouth open. The girl's eyes are blue but he recognizes the freckles on the heart-shaped face, the smile that's showing off white, uneven teeth and causing dimples in her cheeks, the button nose, hooded eyelids and thick, long lashes. The boy draws closer to the screen peering at the girl; he gasps as he sees it: a faint, diagonal scar cutting across her thick right eyebrow.

His shaking finger touches the frozen face on the screen as he whispers, "Hayley."

CHAPTER 21

THE FUNDRAISER

I sit at the table smiling at Ruby as she makes jokes about how she had to lie on the floor so that her mom could squeeze her into the skintight dress she's wearing, but all the while I recite the letter in my head. Dr Leo passed it on to Mom a few days ago. It's handwritten using old-fashioned ink. The lettering is elegant and refined and the light blue writing paper is thick and smooth. It feels like a treasure. I've read it so many times that I've memorized every word:

> *Hello,*
>
> *When Dr Radnor informed us that you wanted to know more about our daughter, Amy, we were delighted. We want to share with you what a wonderful young woman she was and how proud we were of her. She was loved by so many and lived life to the fullest.*

Amy enjoyed going out with her many friends, but she also spent time helping the less privileged in our community. She had such a big heart and hated to see anyone suffer. She was always organizing bake sales and sponsored events to raise funds for charities.

Amy was happy and popular at school and worked hard. She was a valued member of her high school cheer squad and never missed a practice. Her favorite classes were the arts, and she hoped to major in history at college. Mike and I always said that, one day, she'd make a great teacher. She was kind and patient and had a maturity beyond her years.

Of course, we are devastated that our baby has gone, but it brings us such comfort to know that our only child didn't die in vain; that because of Amy you have been given a second chance at life. We know that to help others, even in death, is what she would have wanted, and we're sure that you will make the most of this most precious gift in honor of our beloved daughter.

Our prayers and thoughts are always with you.
God bless,
Hazel and Mike

The letter makes me feel more at peace with her, closer to her, and I think she feels it too. It can't be a coincidence that I haven't had a tremor since I received it. To now know her name is so wonderful. It's weird, but little things have made me happier, like knowing that she'd approve of me being in the cheer squad and the fact that, even though she was popular and pretty, I bet that Amy would still say hi to girls like the old me. And it's obvious just how much donating her body has helped her mom and dad with their grief. I feel like I have Amy's approval as well. It makes me feel less guilty that I've gained from her death. I feel like we can make this work. I feel good.

I watch as Mom walks over to our table. She's so glamorous, all dressed up with a glass of champagne in hand.

"Hello, girls, it's lovely to see you again. You all look gorgeous!" She goes to touch my bare shoulder but checks herself. I know how delighted she is that I'm wearing a figure-hugging cocktail dress and heels that I can hardly walk in. I've helped transform Amy from a pretty high school girl into a sophisticated young woman – but I like to think that Amy would be okay with it. No one looking at me would have a clue about us.

"Are you enjoying yourselves?" Mom asks the cheer girls.

"Yes, thanks, Mrs Burgess. It was so nice of you to get us a table. The food is delicious and this is such a cool place," Laura says, looking around at the sparkling ballroom full of guests in tuxedos and sequined dresses.

"Well, it's my pleasure. It's just a little thank-you for being so welcoming to Renee. It's hard when you're new."

"Oh, we just about put up with her," Ruby jokes, smiling at me.

"I hope you make a lot of money for the foundation tonight, Mrs Burgess," Laura says politely.

"Thank you, Laura. That's what it's all about, of course, but I want this to be an uplifting occasion as well, so I look forward to seeing you up on the dance floor later." Mom smiles.

I watch her glide to the next table, chatting with her guests. Her party mood is making me nervous. I guess it's because she's loving seeing me with my new friends, but this is still supposed to be a fundraiser for her dead daughter's foundation. She should try being more subdued.

Mak is sitting with her parents at a table across the room. I knew that they'd be here for Lucy. She looks over, but as I wave at her, she quickly looks away.

"Hey, your foster mom is cool *and* she's in good shape," Ruby declares admiringly.

"She's not officially my foster mom," I say swiftly.

"Her daughter didn't look anything like her, did she?" Tanya says disapprovingly, nodding towards the massive photo displayed above the stage.

I cringe at my old image. My mousy hair sits limply around my pale, plain face and weak chin, and I'm wearing a horrendous flowery dress with a velvet trim on the collar.

Laura stares at the photo, deep in thought. "It doesn't make any sense; why would someone as stylish as Mrs Burgess dress her daughter like *that*?" she muses.

Suddenly I get it. After all this time I understand Mom. I feel myself welling up. "Once Lucy got sick Mrs Burgess tried to make her stay a little girl, so she dressed her like one," I whisper. "Maybe she thought that she could hold on to her that way."

"Ahh, did Mrs Burgess tell you that?" Laura replies. "That's so sad."

"I'll tell you what's sad," Ruby says, "the fact that this room is full of old people. The average age must be fifty!"

"It's a fundraiser. They invited people with money," I say defensively.

"Well, we're not going to get through this without a little help." Ruby opens her purse under the table and pulls out a small bottle of vodka. "Pass your glasses, girls."

I hesitate, looking around at all my parents' friends and Houston dignitaries.

"Hurry up, Renee. You have had vodka before, haven't you?"

"Sure I have," I lie, "but Mr and Mrs Burgess wouldn't like me drinking."

"So what!" Tanya says. "They're not your parents; they can't tell you what to do. Come on, loosen up. You seem kind of tense."

"No, really I can't, but you go ahead." The only alcohol I've ever had was a glass of wine at Thanksgiving. I want the cheer girls to like me, but I can't risk losing control when I have so much to hide.

I see Grandma heading up onstage to the podium. God, she's going to give a speech. This is going to be unbearable.

"Ladies and gentlemen." Grandma's voices echoes around the ballroom. "Thank you so much for coming here tonight.

I hope that you're all enjoying the delicious food, and later there'll be plenty of time to dance to Houston's finest big band."

A round of applause rises as Grandma gestures to the musicians behind her.

"However, in a minute we'll be coming to the most important part of the night – our charity auction in aid of the Lucy Burgess Foundation. All monies raised tonight will go towards research to beat cancer – the despicable disease that took the life of my granddaughter. Money will also be given to cancer hospices around the county, and eventually, I'd like to build a hospice of our own, dedicated to the care and support of young people and their families."

The audience claps in approval.

"I'd like to tell you just a little about my granddaughter, Lucy." She points to the photograph, her voice breaking. "She was a dear, sweet child who never got a chance to live a full life. Her youth and future was stolen by cancer. But in the years that she had, Lucy was the loveliest, kindest of granddaughters and daughter to Gemma and Lewis. I remember one day Lucy overheard me telling Gemma that I was having to cancel a luncheon at the church for the homeless because a volunteer had dropped out. The next minute I see Lucy with her coat on and her scarf around her head saying, 'Come on, Grandma, I'll help out.' That child was so fragile ... so exhausted, yet there she was, willing to help."

I bow my head. Blocking out the room. I remember that afternoon. I hadn't realized it meant so much to Grandma.

"Lucy's courage and dignity throughout her illness was an inspiration to me and it is in her honor that I have set up this foundation to help others. So please, be as generous as you can tonight, so that one day we won't have to see any more young lives lost to cancer."

People stand to applaud Grandma as she leaves the stage. I shrink into my seat, fighting back tears. Laura turns to me, fanning her face with her hands, like she's overcome with emotion.

"Weren't the grandma's words just beautiful? Lucy sounds so brave." Her voice strains.

I feel like such a fraud. I can't listen to her sympathy. "I'll be back in a minute," I say, getting up.

I walk towards Mak's table, passing Dad, who stands brooding, holding a large scotch.

"How are you doing, Mr Burgess?" I ask, concerned.

"Not great, but at least Mrs Burgess seems to be having a good time," he says bitterly. "How about you, Renee?"

"I'm doing okay."

He lowers his voice. "You shouldn't have come. It's not right that you have to sit through this."

"I needed to. I want to support Gran ... Mrs Kendal. This is helping her. It's getting her through the grief. She's doing a good thing."

"Yeah, all in the memory of her granddaughter," he says grimly, knocking back his drink.

As I approach Mak's table I see her looking for an escape route.

"Hi, Makayla," I say, plastering a smile on my face.

"Hi," she mumbles.

"Are these your folks?" I beam at her mama and dad. It's so good to see them.

"Yeah. Mama, Daddy, this is Renee. She's the girl who's staying with Lucy's parents."

"Hello, young lady," Mr Walker says, offering me his hand. I clasp it tightly, then, without thinking, I lean across and kiss Mak's startled mama on the cheek.

"It's great to meet you," I gush. "Makayla and I are in the same class. It's awesome to be with her."

Makayla rolls her eyes.

"You look lovely in that dress, Makayla."

"Thanks," she replies coolly. Can't she even bear to take a compliment from me?

"Are you enjoying your visit with Lucy's parents?" Mrs Walker asks.

"Yes, they're such kind people."

"It's more than a visit, Mama. They've moved her in. You know that she sleeps in Lucy's room," Mak says in disgust.

"That's none of our business, Makayla," Mr Walker says sternly.

Mom's laughter sails across the room.

"I suppose having a young person around is helping Gemma," Mrs Walker says, looking across at her doubtfully.

"You're not kidding. I don't think I've ever seen her so happy," Mak replies bitingly.

"You're wrong. Mrs Burgess is always talking to me about Lucy. She misses her daughter *so* much. She just puts on a brave face in public," I lie.

"Well, we all loved Lucy. We're glad that her grandma has set up this foundation in her memory," Mrs Walker says.

"Shouldn't you get back to your friends?" Mak says coldly.

"Sure. Catch you later?"

Mak doesn't reply.

As I approach my table my belly starts to cramp. I breathe deeply and sit down. From the noise level, it seems like Ruby, Laura and Tanya have been getting through the vodka.

"What's wrong? You don't look so good," Laura says.

"I'm fine, it's just a bit of belly ache. It's probably something I ate."

"Hey, I saw you talking to that Makayla. I've seen you in school, trying to be nice to her. Why do you bother? She obviously doesn't want to know you," Tanya says, brutally.

"She was best friends with Lucy, so I thought it would be good to be friendly," I reply as if it's no big deal.

Ruby looks across to Mak's table before announcing, "You know, that girl could be cute if she'd just lose forty pounds."

"What, Makayla? But she's curvy ... voluptuous," I say defensively.

"Oh, please," Ruby replies. "You're just using polite words for 'fat'. You don't do fat people any favors by not telling the truth. I swear, if that girl shows some self-control, does some exercise and loses the weight, her life could be transformed."

"Maybe she's happy with how she is?" I say it more like a question, but why? Mak has never been hung up about her weight, has she?

"Renee, people who say that they're happy being fat are the ones who are too lazy to do anything about it," Ruby lectures.

No, Ruby can't be right! Mak has always seemed confident in the way she looks. She wouldn't be happier if she had a body like the cheer girls . . . like me . . . would she?

"Quick, look at her . . . she's stuffing another piece of cake in that chubby face of hers," Tanya exclaims.

Laura slaps her on the arm. "Stop that, Tanya!"

"Yeah, shut up, Tanya," I say sharply, but I can't stop myself cringing as I watch Mak. I find myself saying over and over in my mind, *Stop eating the cake, Mak. Stop eating!*

What's happening to me? I can't believe that I actually feel embarrassed by my best friend.

There's a big cheer as the auctioneer takes the stage. He's some kind of celebrity radio host, but I haven't heard of him; I think he works on one of the stations that Grandma listens to. Anyhow, he gets the auction under way and there's some pretty impressive things on offer. We watch in awe as people bid thousands of dollars for the lots. It brings a smile to my face to see Grandma looking so delighted as the money rolls in.

Ruby keeps offering around the vodka under the table but I refuse; I don't know why, but my belly keeps cramping. I sit at the table trying my hardest to look like everything is fine. I don't want to get up in the middle of the auction.

I'm so relieved when the auctioneer announces, "And that concludes our auction, folks. Thanks for your amazing generosity. Enjoy the dancing."

The big band strikes up and people flood on to the dance floor. I feel lousy but Tanya is up on her feet.

"Let's hit the dance floor, ladies," Tanya insists.

"But it's all that old-fashioned stuff. We don't know how to dance to this," Laura replies nervously.

"Just feel the rhythm, honey," Tanya says, clicking her fingers.

Ruby drags me up. She makes a path through the dancers as they waltz. She puts one hand on my shoulder and the other on my waist.

"I'll lead," she says, putting on a Southern-belle voice.

She starts whisking me around the dance floor, excusing us every time we bump into other couples.

Tanya appears at our side. She's dancing with the auctioneer guy. She keeps standing on his toes and bursting into laughter.

I catch Grandma glaring at me as we spin around.

I suddenly feel something warm trickling down my legs. I look down in panic. There are drops of red at my feet. I twist around, gasping as I see a crimson patch spreading across my ivory dress.

"What is it? What's the matter?" Ruby asks.

I clutch the back of my dress, trying to hide the stained material. "Nothing . . . I just need to pee. I . . . I won't be long."

I put my head down and try and get off the dance floor, but every way I turn there are couples waltzing, hemming me in. The panic is choking me. I start to push through. As I emerge from the crowd I come face-to-face with Mak, standing on the edge of the dance floor. I push past her in distress as I scuttle towards the restroom.

I head into the nearest stall and lock the door. I hear a couple of women leave. It's all quiet. I'm alone. I pull up my dress. There are blood streaks down my legs and my underwear looks like a red rag. *This can't be happening.*

I reach for the toilet paper but there's only a couple of sheets left. I look in alarm at my hands as I feel them tingling. My eyes widen as the fingers flutter. Within seconds they're shaking uncontrollably, worse than ever before.

I ball them up into fists and bang on the stall wall, fighting back tears, whispering to this traitorous body. "Stop it! Don't do this to me!"

There's a creak as a door opens.

"Renee, are you in there?" It's Mak!

I don't answer. I don't want anyone to see me like this.

"Renee, I saw the blood on your dress."

"Oh God, did everyone see?" The words burst out of me.

"No. No one noticed. Do you want me to get your friends in here to help you?"

"No!" I say. *Tanya would tell the whole school. People will laugh at me, make gross jokes about me. Forget being pretty, forget "Buckaroo Babe", this is all I'd be remembered for.* "I can't come out. I'm a mess."

171

Mak passes damp paper towels over the top of the stall. "Clean yourself up. I'll get you pads. Have you got a ticket for the coat check? I could go get your coat so you can cover up."

I open the stall door and see my friend standing there. I burst into tears, mascara tracks down my face. "This can't be happening. I don't want this."

"Well, who does?" she says as her eyes flash to my shaking hands. "If it makes you feel any better, it happened to me once, only it was on the school bus in eighth grade! Me and Lucy Burgess ducked down and stayed on until it reached the depot and then we ran past the driver, hiding our faces."

"Yeah, it was terrible," I say without thinking.

"What do you mean?'" She looks confused.

"I . . . I . . . mean it must have been terrible."

The restroom door opens and a woman in a floor-length dress starts to walk in.

"Sorry, lady, this restroom is closed," Mak says, ushering her out. Mak keeps glancing at my shaking hands. "Do you need a doctor? Maybe I should get Mrs Burgess."

"No. I just want this to stop," I plead. "I thought we were at peace with each other, but she's taking control. I've never had a period before. Do you see what it means? She showing that me that this body can make *new* life." Distress is making me forget myself; I'm talking to Mak like she can see Lucy.

Mak holds up her hands, shaking her head. "Wow, that's all a little heavy for me. If you want to have some kind of philosophical debate with Mother Nature about your menstrual cycle then please do it when I'm not around."

"Sorry, ignore me. I'm upset. I don't know what I'm saying," I garble, clutching my shaking hands together.

"Listen, I'm going to get your coat and then I'll get Mrs Burgess to take you back to her house, okay?" She's staring at me like I'm completely unstable.

"You won't tell anyone about this, will you?" I beg.

"No, of course not! I may not like you, Renee, but I wouldn't do that."

CHAPTER 22

AMY'S CHILD

I'm lying on a table in the ballroom. My stretched belly rises up in front of me like a boulder. Sweat plasters the wig to my face. Men and women dressed in tuxedos and ball dresses hold me down. I shout at them. I try to bite them, but their grip gets stronger. Dr Radnor steps to the side of me. He's in pristine white scrubs; a mask covers his mouth and nose. His brown eyes smile as he holds up the cold steel scalpel.

The scalpel makes an incision below my belly. It feels like he's cut me in two. I howl as Dr Radnor tugs and pulls, forcing my belly apart. His brow furrows as he struggles. There's a sickening noise as he pulls it out of me. A mouth suddenly appears as the thing lets out an inhuman sound. It begins to squirm and shriek. It's monstrous.

"Get it away from me!" I scream as Dr Radnor forces it into my arms.

"It's a miracle," he says, ecstatically. "It's Amy's child!"

CHAPTER 23

THE VISITOR

Mom sighs deeply as she dishes out supper in the dining room. "Lucy, I've listened to you all day and we're going around in circles. As I've told you a hundred times, getting your period is the most natural thing in the world, and frankly, I think you're whipping yourself up into hysteria, giving yourself that horrendous nightmare."

I put my head in my hands. Mom is treating me like a child. She's refusing to even acknowledge what this means ... the implications. I know that if this body has periods it means it's fertile, which means it has the potential to reproduce. And I can't stop thinking about *what* it would reproduce. What kind of creature would it be when nature has been screwed up like this? The thought horrifies me. Why can't Mom understand why I'm so freaked out by this? Can't she see why this is proof that Amy's body will never really belong to me?

Dad pushes his plate of food away. "I've lost my appetite. I'm going to my study," he says.

"It's a bit late for you to get squeamish, Dad," I scowl.

"Listen," Mom says calmly. "We need to see Dr Radnor about the tremors anyway. He has all the tests results back from your last visit and he wants to discuss them with us. While we're at the clinic you can talk to him about your ... worries. I'm sure that he'll be able to put your mind at rest, Lucy."

Before I can protest I'm disturbed by Arthur barking from out in the hallway.

"It's the buzzer. Someone's at the gate," I say, walking to look at the video intercom. I jolt back when I see a policewoman leaning out the window of her patrol car.

"It's a police officer!" I whisper.

"Why's a police officer coming here?" Dad says, hurriedly getting up from the table.

"She's buzzing again. What do I do?" I feel my pulse quickening.

"Let her in," Mom says, twisting her wedding ring around her finger. "It won't be anything to do with you. There's probably been break-ins or something around the neighborhood." She gestures at me to respond to the buzzer.

"Hello. Can I help you?" I say nervously into the intercom.

"Evening, I'm Officer Jane Parnell from Houston Police Department. I'm here to see Mr and Mrs Burgess. May I drive up to the house?"

"Yes, of course, officer."

I press the button to open the gates. I wait outside. My belly twists with anxiety as I watch the car swing into sight up the driveway.

"Hello, miss." Officer Parnell hoists herself out of the car. She stands tall and broad as she readjusts her gun belt around her hips. "Wow, it's been a hot one today." She smiles, flashing her badge. "As I said, I'm here to have a chat with your folks. May I come in?" She steps into the house before I even answer, her eyes roaming everywhere.

"Mr Burgess, Mrs Burgess, there's a police officer here to see you," I call out, trying to sound casual.

Long seconds pass and there's no sign of them.

"It's a big place you've got here; perhaps you need to shout a little louder," she suggests.

"Mr and Mrs Burgess, there's a policewoman here to see you!" I holler.

They appear from the kitchen, Mom wearing a sickly smile.

"Hello, officer. How can we help?" Mom asks.

"If you don't mind, ma'am, I'd like to talk to your daughter in private and then I'll have a word with you and your husband. I just need to clear a matter up."

"Renee isn't our daughter," Dad says quickly. "She's a friend of the family. You could say that we've unofficially fostered her."

"Is that so?" Officer Parnell, says looking at me. I nod too enthusiastically.

"Is there a problem, officer?" Mom asks in her best lawyer voice.

"It's just about clarifying this young lady's identity. Let me talk to Renee first. Is there a room we can use?"

A look of panic crosses Mom's face. She masks it with a smile, pointing to the kitchen. "By all means. Renee, offer the officer a drink."

As Officer Parnell heads to the kitchen, Mom glares at me with a look that says *Just stick to your story.*

I pour us both some iced tea from the fridge and sit down at the table, fidgeting with my glass.

"So, tell me all about yourself, young lady," Officer Parnell says warmly.

"Okay, well, my name is Renee Wodehouse. I'm nearly seventeen. I was born in San Diego, California."

"Well, I haven't travelled much but that sure don't sound like a California accent." She gives a fleeting smile.

"Yeah, everyone says that." I shrug and begin the story I know so well. "I moved around *a lot.* My accent is pretty strange. You see, I was put in foster care when I was eleven ... my mom was a little messed up. I met Mr and Mrs Burgess a while back, at a fundraiser for children and family services. They were lovely ... we just got along. They were going through a hard time; their daughter, Lucy, had died of cancer and a while after Lucy's passing, they invited me to come live with them."

"That was nice of them," she says, taking a sip of the iced tea. "And are you happy living here?" Her eyes are searching my face.

"Yeah, who wouldn't be? They're wonderful people." My fingers tighten around my glass.

"Well, that's good to know. Now, if you don't mind, I'll just need to see some official documentation to confirm your identity."

Mom and Dad sweep into the kitchen; they've obviously been listening at the door. Mom hands a passport to Officer Parnell.

"I thought you might ask for this. It's Renee's passport."

Officer Parnell scrutinizes the document. "Thank you, ma'am, this all looks in order. Can I ask if you color your hair, Renee?" she asks abruptly.

My eyes widen. I fight to stop my fingers touching the wig. Can she see that it isn't my real hair? Maybe she's wondering why my hair is blonde when my eyebrows and lashes are so dark. What the hell should I say?

"Yeah, I like to play around with the color. I'm natural dark but I thought the strawberry blonde kind of suited me," I reply, my mouth suddenly dry.

"It does," she nods, writing in her notepad. "I've just got one more question, if that's okay – do you wear colored contacts at all?"

"No ... no, I don't," I answer hesitantly.

"Renee, why don't you let the officer look in your eyes," Mom says, maneuvering me face-to-face with Officer Parnell. "It's quite obvious she's not wearing contacts." Mom's voice rises. She needs to back off. She's coming across way too anxious.

Officer Parnell stares into my eyes for a moment. "Fine, I'll leave you folks in peace. I'm satisfied that everything is okay here. Thanks for your cooperation. I won't need to bother you again."

She walks into the hallway and Mom swiftly opens the front door to usher her out, closing the door on me when I try and follow them.

I'm burning with questions but Dad reads my face and shakes his head. "Just let her go," he whispers in my ear.

I pace around the hall, waiting for Mom.

"Go and finish your meal," Dad says tensely, stroking Arthur as he sits on the bottom stair.

I ignore him. Seconds later I hear a car starting up and driving away. There's a delay before the door opens and Mom appears. Her face is drained of color. Her eyes seem unfocused.

She steps inside, wobbling slightly as one of her heels slides on the marble floor. She regains her composure, clasping her hands together.

"Well? What did she say?" I ask anxiously.

"She didn't say anything," Mom replies, matter-of-fact.

"But she must have. You were with her for long enough," I protest.

"I was just passing pleasantries with the officer. Telling her what a great girl you are. We want her to think everything is okay, don't we?" she says commandingly.

"But don't you want to know why she needed to check my identity?"

"Of course I do, but I couldn't seem too interested. The last thing we want to do is arouse suspicion."

I look over at Dad anxiously. "But it could be to do with

Amy, or maybe it's the fake ID Dr Leo sorted out."

"Possibly," Dad replies, looking deep in thought.

"There's no point worrying about it," Mom says, sharply. "You heard what the police officer said; she's satisfied that everything is okay, so whatever it *was*, it's not a problem *now*."

I don't understand how Mom can just brush this off. Officer Parnell asked me about my eyes ... my hair. They must know something.

I search her deathly pale face. "If it's nothing, then why do you look like you've seen a ghost, Mom?"

"Maybe because I've just had to lie to an officer of the law," she snaps. "Now, let's all go back to the table and remember that we are a *regular* family, having a *regular* family supper."

CHAPTER 24

IN CONTROL

Dr Leo is waiting at the entrance of his clinic. He hurries to greet us as Mom and I step out of the cab.

"Renee," he says warmly. "Welcome back."

He walks us to his office, offering us seats.

"Do you know that a policewoman came to the house yesterday to check my identity?" I ask him.

"Yes, your mom phoned me last night to let me know what happened. We've established that there's nothing to worry about," he answers coolly.

"But she was asking whether I wore colored contacts ... whether I dye my hair. Could it be about Amy?"

"Amy?" Dr Leo echoes, looking puzzled.

"Yes, Amy," Mom interrupts. "In her parents' letter, that you very kindly passed on to us, they told Renee their daughter's name and a little about her. They didn't disclose their last name, of course, but we really appreciate you asking them to write Renee. It's been such a comfort to her to learn more about the donor and to know how much it has meant to Amy's parents."

"Yeah, I should have contacted you to thank you for the letter," I say guiltily. "It was great of you, really." I smile at him but his eyes are locked on Mom's. I look from one to the other. Why does he look so annoyed with her? "Dr Leo?" I say, trying to get his attention.

He turns a cold smile on me. "That's all right, Renee. I was prepared to break with protocol on this occasion and I'm delighted to hear it's helped."

"So could the police visit be connected with Amy?" I ask again.

"No," he replies emphatically. "The only people who know that Amy was used for the transplant are her parents and they wouldn't have got the police involved, would they? You have their letter. You know that donating her body has been a positive experience for them."

"Then it must have been about the fake identity," I insist. "About Renee Wodehouse. Someone could have tipped them off."

"How can the police have been tipped off when no one knows?" Mom asks, as if I'm being stupid.

A thought suddenly hits me. "What if someone who doesn't like me asked the police to check my ID to make trouble?" I say.

"Who would do that?" Mom asks incredulous.

"Grandma ... or Mak even? Maybe they did it together,"

I reply bitterly. "They'd be happy to uncover something bad about me to get me out of your life."

Mom is silent, as if weighing up what I've said. "Look, I don't believe that either of them would do that but, if they did, then their plan failed, so let's stop worrying."

"I agree with your mom. The police have no reason to suspect anything. We just need to concentrate on what's important, and that's you and your health," Dr Leo says with such kindness in his voice.

He perches on the side of his desk, wiping his glasses with a cloth before placing them back on his nose. I can't help wondering whether he still has his gun; it unsettles me to think of it in that bottom drawer.

"I've got all your test results from your last visit, but before we discuss them I think I need to put your mind at rest about the issue of your periods."

I cringe and sink back into the chair.

"Your mom has told me how distressed you are, and I want to reassure you that the start of your menstrual cycle is something to celebrate, not fear. It shows that you and your donor body are working in perfect harmony. It's an incredible development." His smile is so broad; he can hardly contain his delight.

His attitude enrages me. "Dr Leo, you, of all people, understand that if this body can have periods, then it means that it's fertile; I can get pregnant, have a baby."

Dr Leo nods. "And if it does mean that you're fertile, isn't that amazing? You'd have the option of having a child. I know

184

that it's the last thing you would want right now, but think of when you're in your twenties . . . thirties."

"Are you joking? I don't want to reproduce a freak," I say in disgust.

"You shouldn't call any baby a freak," Mom says sharply.

"What else will it be? Any baby that grows in this body wouldn't be mine, it would be Amy's. Any baby I gave birth to would look like **her**, not me; that's if it doesn't come out with some horrible deformity because of what's been done to me."

"There's absolutely no reason to think that your baby would be deformed," Dr Leo says adamantly.

"But you've messed around with nature; with me, you've created something unnatural, untested. You don't know what the consequences will be. It can't be my baby when it'll have Amy's nature, Amy's DNA. There'll be nothing of me in it. What would I be to it? Not its mother . . . not even a surrogate mother." I hear my voice straining with stress.

"I understand your confusion, but you're wrong," Dr Leo says firmly. "I'd consider any baby you gave birth to as one hundred per cent yours and, once the baby was born, you'd be able to nurture and shape it as any mother would. The way you bring it up, the environment that surrounds it, the opportunities you give it, will have more influence on the child than its DNA."

I can't stand the thought of it. I won't listen to him. "No!" I shout. "It wouldn't be fair to me or a kid to bring it into the world. This freakishness stops with me!"

"But given time I believe that you'll come to think differently," Dr Leo says gently.

I cross my arms. "Listen, I'm freaked out by it all, but there's no point talking about it because it's never going to happen. For starters, I'll never have a boyfriend! Who's going to want to be with me... have sex with me once they know about the transplant?" A wave of sadness hits me. My head drops. There's been so much else to stress about that I hadn't had the space to work through the whole boyfriend thing before now.

Dr Leo bends down to me, staring deep into my eyes. "The solution to that is simple: you don't tell them about the transplant – as we've been telling you, you can't. No one must ever know."

"So you're saying that any relationship I might have has to be based on a lie about who I am ... what I am," I protest.

"Every relationship has secrets, and this would have to be yours," Mom says, taking my hand. "It won't mean that your partner doesn't really know you. It won't mean that the love he feels for you isn't real. You'll just be protecting yourself and making things easier for both of you."

I pull away, scowling at her. *She can always make bad things sound acceptable. But how can she be right? It would be despicable to do that to someone, but if it's my only way of finding love, could I really go through with it? I'd be living a lie, but if you keep up a lie for long enough I bet, eventually, you can convince yourself that it's the truth.*

"Look, Renee, your periods and fertility are not something

to be distressed about. If, in time, you do start a sexual relationship, then we'll make sure you have the most effective form of contraception," Dr Leo says, making me squirm. "You need never have a child. Do you understand? You have no need to even think about pregnancy or its implications."

Hearing his logic suddenly calms me. I know he's right. I've just been so horrified by the thought of being able to have Amy's baby that I've been going crazy ... lost perspective. Why should I let these thoughts ruin my new life when it need never be a problem?

I jolt as Dr Leo's cell goes off.

"Excuse me," he says apologetically to me and Mom as he answers it.

"Hello ... yes. Take her through. I'll be along shortly." He ends the call and turns his attention back to me.

"So what do you think, Renee? Can you see why you have no need to worry?" he says with a reassuring smile.

"Maybe." I nod, subdued.

Mom rubs my hand, looking relieved. "Good girl. I knew that Dr Radnor would help you to see sense about this."

He rises from his chair. "I think that we could all do with a short break before we go through Renee's results. Mrs Burgess, would you go to the cafeteria and get some refreshments for you and Renee? And Renee, you look like you could do with some fresh air. Why don't you go and sit in the garden for five minutes?"

He's right. I need to clear my head. I thank him and head out into the walled desert garden.

I sit on a bench, closing my eyes to the harsh sunshine as I listen to the water trickling from the fountain, but my calmness is disturbed by a creeping sense that I'm being watched. I open my eyes and look around.

Inside the clinic I see Dr Leo with an old woman leaning on a walker. They're staring at me through a large picture window. No one is even supposed to know that I'm here. Who is she? Why is she looking at me like that? Impulsively, I run inside to confront them.

"Renee!" Dr Leo's voice flutters guiltily.

"Who's this?" I nod towards the stooped old woman. She has the stretched look of someone who has had too many facelifts. Her lips are alarmingly plump and her eyes too wide, like they're pinned open. Her smiling mouth reveals perfect teeth as her eyes seem to drink me in.

"Hello, dear." She offers a wrinkled hand. "It's an honor to meet you. I've seen the videos of you, but it's not the same as seeing you in the flesh."

"What?" Has Dr Leo invited her here to gawp at me, like someone visiting a freak show?

"This lady is a visitor of mine," he says. "She was just leaving."

He tries to maneuver her away but the woman touches my face, looking awestruck.

"Dr Radnor has told me about all your wonderful progress. It's just incredible that your menstrual cycle has started."

I gasp. My flesh crawls. "That's my business. I thought all this was supposed to be confidential?" I splutter at Dr Leo.

188

"I'm sorry. I didn't mean to upset you." The old woman looks flustered. "It's just so exciting to meet you and to know that, if I'm as lucky as you with my donor, I might be able to have a child. It's what I've always longed for: a baby of my own."

My mouth slackens. This old woman is going to have a transplant . . . she wants a baby?

"It's lovely to see you, Elizabeth, but I must go now." Dr Leo ushers her down the corridor, calling to me, "I'll be back in a minute."

I'm still standing, dumbfounded, when he returns.

"Renee, I'm so sorry about that. She got carried away. You weren't supposed to meet."

"You're going to give *her* a body transplant?" I say, outraged.

"Possibly."

"But why? She's so old!" I hear the disgust in my voice.

"And that's exactly why she needs one. Her body isn't going to last much longer."

"But I thought the transplants were about saving young people. What about all those teenagers you've got files on? Why would you be offering the surgery to a rich old woman when you've got kids waiting?" I feel sick; is it really just about the money for him?

"Those teenagers will remain my priority but Elizabeth still has a lot to give the world. If she lives another lifetime, think about how much she can achieve."

"But those kids need the donors, not a woman who has already lived her life. It's going to be hard enough for you to find parents like Amy's who'll donate their child's body for this. If a donor's family knew that their loved one was going to be used for an eighty-year-old, they wouldn't want you to have it." My voice is getting louder.

"Listen, Renee, who are you to judge which people are *worthy* of a transplant and which aren't? Elizabeth has come to me for help and I'm going to help her if I can," he says firmly.

"Yeah, and she's going to be paying you millions of dollars for that 'help'," I reply scathingly.

"Just like your parents did," he shoots back. "It's a shame that I can only offer the surgery to the privileged few like you but hopefully, one day, that won't have to be the case."

His words stop me in my tracks. I blush with shame. He's right. If I didn't have such rich parents I'd be dead by now. They were able to buy me a new life – but what about all those people who can't afford to cheat death?

"Now, Renee." He places a hand on my shoulder, taking control. "I think that you'll agree that there's no need to continue this discussion. Let's go back to the office and discuss your test results with your mom."

Dr Leo shuffles through his papers as Mom and I sit opposite him in nervous silence. I'll tell Mom about the old woman later, when we're alone. I need to hear what she thinks without Dr Leo putting his spin on it.

"I've had time to assess all the test results and I'm glad to say that most of the results are well above average," Dr Leo says. "I'm really happy with your progress. However, there are a few issues. As we know, the allergy to animals is unfortunate but the antihistamines are allowing you to have contact with them."

"Yes, but the problem is that they don't want to have contact with me," I tell him. "They're scared of me."

"I don't believe that for a second," he says dismissively. "They're picking up on your anxiety. If you can just learn to be more at ease with them, you'll see how differently they respond to you."

I roll my eyes. He doesn't want to hear the truth.

"And what about the tremors?" Mom asks anxiously.

"Okay," he says gently, "this is the not-so-good news."

Oh God, I know that tone. That's the one the doctors used with me every time they told me that the cancer had spread. What's he going to say?

"I've discovered that the tremors appear to have a neurological cause. Dopamine levels in Renee's brain's motor cortex are low and some of her neurotransmitters aren't functioning properly."

What? I thought it was Amy making the tremors happen, showing me that she still has some control, but is he saying that it's neurological, that my own brain is causing them? I can't believe it.

"What exactly do you mean?" I ask in dread.

"In layman's terms, it means that your brain isn't sending the correct signals to your limbs, which is resulting in the tremors," he answers.

"So can you fix it?" I ask in trepidation.

"I have to be straight with you; if not managed correctly

this has the potential to become a lot worse. It has the markings of a serious condition that could degenerate if you aren't given the correct medication."

"No!" Mom gasps. I take her hand as my belly flips.

"But there's no need to be alarmed. I can control it. Once I sort out the correct combination of medication the tremors should stop, allowing you to live as a completely healthy person." He says it with such confidence, smiling reassuringly.

"So it can be controlled but not cured?" Mom asks, her voice quivering.

"Exactly. But remember that millions of people live with conditions that, if controlled properly, don't adversely affect their lives. I will keep monitoring Renee and make sure you have the right medication to stop any deterioration."

"So will I have to take the meds for the rest of my life?" I ask, grimly.

"Yes, if you don't take them the symptoms will escalate and the consequences could be devastating but I'd say that taking medication for the rest of your life is a minor inconvenience given the huge success of the transplant," he says brightly.

Mom hugs me tightly. "Don't worry, honey. It can be controlled. You're going to be okay." She's trying to convince herself as much as me.

Anxiety wells up in me. "But say you can't find the right meds, Dr Leo? Say it gets worse?"

"I won't let it." He sounds supremely confident. "Just trust me, Renee. Your good health means everything to me."

CHAPTER 25

THE CUCKOO IN
THE NEST

I get Dad to drive me to school early. It's the first chance I've had to be alone with him since I got back from the clinic. He's giving me a pep talk; telling me how I shouldn't worry about the tremors because Dr Radnor will keep them under control. I guess I have no option but to put my faith in Dr Leo, but there are other things that happened at the clinic that I just can't get out of my head: I'm trying not to be paranoid, but I can't stop thinking about how puzzled Dr Leo seemed when I mentioned Amy's name. And then there was that look between him and Mom. He looked *mad* at her. But what had she done wrong? And I know that Dr Leo and Mom tried to convince me that Officer Parnell's visit was nothing to worry about, but surely it has to have been Mak or Grandma who asked the cops to check my ID.

The last time I saw Mak she was helping me in the restroom at the charity auction, so it's painful to believe that she still hates me enough to be behind the police visit. It makes me even more determined to tackle her head-on today.

As we approach the school parking lot, I tell Dad about the other incident that's been plaguing me – meeting Elizabeth at Dr Leo's clinic. When I tried to discuss it with Mom, she just said that it was none of our business who Dr Radnor decided to operate on.

"You think the same thing I do, don't you, Dad? Dr Leo told me not to be judgemental, but it's not right. The operation should be about saving young people," I say fervently.

"Yes, it should be," he replies solemnly. I'm relieved. I knew Dad would agree with me.

"Anyway, I reckon Elizabeth's transplant will never happen. No family is going to donate a body to be used for an old person, are they?" I say.

As I look over, I watch the color drain from Dad's face.

"What is it, Dad? Do you think Dr Leo won't tell the families? Do you think he'll tell them it's for a kid? He wouldn't do that, would he?" I say, outraged.

"I don't know," Dad mutters to the floor. "Listen, you just go and have a good day at school. Don't worry about Radnor."

"Are you around tonight? Do you want to catch a movie or something?" I say, hopefully.

"I'm sorry, Renee. I'm going to be away for a couple of days on business."

"But I only just got back from the clinic. Don't you want to spend time with me?"

"Sure I do. But it'll have to be another day."

His words kill me. "You hardly ever look at me," I say sadly. "You think I'm a freak, don't you?" I hold my breath, waiting for his answer.

"No, of course I don't! I love you." His voice cracks. "It's just . . . it's just every time I look at you I feel ashamed of what we've put you through, the constant stress that you're under."

My face crumples with relief. "I thought it was me . . . I thought that you *couldn't* love me now that I'm like this."

"Don't ever think that," he says, looking pained.

"Then please just start being my dad again. You said the other week that you'll always be my daddy, so let's go to the movies, take me to a Springsteen gig . . . just stop running away and *be* with me."

He nods his head, holding back tears.

I kiss him on the cheek and get out of the car feeling stronger, convincing myself that I've got my dad back.

I hang around the stone steps to the entrance of Bailey Heights. I don't have to wait long before I see Mak walking through the parking lot alone, her head down.

"Morning, Makayla!" I say cheerfully, walking next to her.

"Morning," she mumbles, giving me a sideways glance.

"I've been wanting to say thanks for helping me out at the fundraiser last week. Sorry if I was a little. . ."

"Weird?" she suggests.

"I was stressed."

"Sure, I understand." She shrugs.

"I brought your denim jacket, the one I found in Lucy's closet. I know you wanted it back." I pull the jacket out of my bag and hand it to her.

"Thanks." She half smiles, but keeps walking.

"Hang on, Mak."

"I've told you, don't call me Mak," she warns.

"Sorry, it's just that I wanted to ask you something," I fix my eyes on her face.

She grimaces, impatiently. "What is it?"

"Do you know anything about the police coming by the Burgess place the other day, asking to see my ID?" I scrutinize her face for any signs of guilt, but all I see is curiosity.

"No," she answers, obviously wanting to know more. "What happened?"

"Nothing. I showed them ID and they were fine about it," I answer coolly.

"So why would you think it had anything to do with me?" she scowls.

I feel embarrassed. I shouldn't have doubted her.

"No reason. I'm sorry I asked. Listen, Makayla," I say quickly, "I know that you don't like me but I wish that you'd just give me a chance. I think that if you got to know me we could be friends . . . really good friends."

Mak gives a melodramatic shudder. "I don't know what your game is, but I'll never be friends with you; you're nothing but a cuckoo!" she says with disdain.

"What do you mean?"

She puts her hands on her hips. "I *mean* that you're a cuckoo in the nest. Getting yourself all comfortable in Lucy's home, taking her room, her things, her parents. Making Lucy's mom and dad buy you stuff, treat you like their *daughter*. It makes me feel sick!" Mak spits.

She marches away. I feel my top lip start to quiver and curl. I don't know how I can ever make her like "Renee", and I can't take all her rejections and anger any more. I'm beginning to think it would be better for both of us if I just let her go.

I try to banish her from my thoughts. I can't just stand here feeling sorry for myself. I've got to be focused. I've got fifteen minutes before the bell. I head to the computer room. It's already busy with seniors working on assignments. I find a free computer in the corner and log on. I know what I want to check first, even though it's a long shot. I put in different combinations of the words into the search engine: *Amy. Sixteen, America, brain aneurysm, Mike, Hazel*. I'm not surprised when nothing useful shows up. I just haven't got enough information; no last name, no location. I look over my shoulder to check no one is watching and then I add two other words to my search: *body transplant*. Nothing appears that tells me about Amy. I didn't really expect it to; after all, I'm sure Dr Leo would have made sure there would be no record of the transplant.

The links that do come up are mostly articles about "rogue" scientists claiming that body transplants could be a reality within years. The articles all seem to end with comments from other scientists dismissing the claims as "science fiction". It's a horrible reminder of what a worldwide freak show I'd become if anyone found out the truth about me.

But what's weird about all these links for body transplants is that Dr Leo isn't even mentioned, and yet he's been researching and attempting the operation for years.

I puff my cheeks out, confused. I wonder what the internet knows about Dr Leonard Radnor. I type his name and press search. I get a rush of excitement as the page fills with links to articles. I click on one after another. I'm able to read about his exceptional academic ability, which saw him fast-tracked through high school. I learn that he was top of his class in med school and has won numerous awards for neurosurgery. I can access his publications on stem cell research and watch his conference speeches on brain injuries. One of the articles even mentions his clinic in El Paso, where, it says, he performs the majority of his neurosurgery and there's a reference to a grant he received to set up a clinic in Yorkshire in the UK to look into how teenage health affects neurological development. On the personal side, I discover that he's divorced, has no children and likes to compete in triathlons in his leisure time, but what I can't find on the internet is any information about what he *really* does. No mention of his research into body transplants, of his failed attempts and, of course, no mention of his success.

However, one article from six years ago captures my attention. It's a short report buried in the depths of a medical journal. It says that Dr Radnor was cleared of unethical conduct by a disciplinary committee after concerns were raised by nursing staff that he was witnessed putting undue pressure on the parents of a patient who had suffered a brain aneurysm to donate his body for medical research. The committee concluded that "while Dr Radnor was overzealous in his attempts to persuade the parents, he acted within the bounds of ethical behavior but must take a softer, more sensitive approach in the future."

I sit back in my chair, deep in thought. Is that what happened to Amy? Did he pressurize her parents into donating her body? I massage my temples, my head throbbing as the bell rings out shrilly. Everyone gets up and files out of the room. I've got to get to class. *Think straight, Lucy*, I tell myself. Don't jump to conclusions. There's no information here that proves that Dr Leo is anything other than what I've seen: an incredibly talented surgeon who was willing to break the rules to save my life.

Thanks to Laura and the cheer girls, I get through the day, going to practice with them in the gym at lunchtime. I haven't had time to dwell on Mak or Dr Leo.

As the final bell rings, Laura links arms with me and we join everyone pouring out of Bailey Heights and heading home.

"So are you going to have a party for your birthday?" she asks excitedly as we walk down the path.

I shrug. I'm regretting telling them that it's my birthday soon.

"Come on, Renee, you could have the best party ever at the Burgess house," Tanya says, nudging me.

"You'd be a legend!" Ruby declares. "You could hire that DJ who plays all hottest clubs in Texas. And I could help you with the guest list. It's going to be awesome, Renee!" she says, dancing in front of me.

"Hey, hang on. I haven't even asked Mrs Burgess," I say, trying to calm them down.

"Yeah, she's cool. She'll be up for it. Anyway, I think she'd give you anything you asked for," Tanya says, raising her eyebrows.

"Why do you think that?" I'm feeling uncomfortable.

"Well, I've seen how she treats you: like a daughter. She'd do anything for you."

My cheeks burn; I wonder how many other people are thinking the same as Tanya.

Students squeeze through the school gates. As we're taken along on the wave of bodies, I catch a glimpse of a tall, good-looking boy with thick black hair and deep brown eyes, standing at the side of the lawn. He seems to spot me in the crowd and his voice rises above the noise. His face is full of desperation as he shouts in my direction, "Hayley! Hayley! Please stop!"

The sea of students keeps flowing as we reach the sidewalk. I crane my neck to look back, but I can't see him above the crowd. If he's still calling out, then I can't hear him. My insides churn. I stop in my tracks. Who is he? Was he really shouting at me?

People curse as they bump into me. Laura grabs my arm, dragging me onwards.

"What are you doing, Renee? You're going to get trampled to death," she says, pushing me on to the bus.

I sit between them in an unsettled silence as the girls continue to plan my party. By the time we get off near the shopping mall I've convinced myself that I probably got it wrong. I'm not sure that the boy was even speaking to me. He could have been calling out to anyone in that crowd. I've got to stop getting so paranoid about everything and everyone. I need to calm down or I'll make my tremors worse.

CHAPTER 26

BIRTHDAY GIRL

I pop the assortment of pills into my mouth and wash them down with water. The combination of drugs from Dr Leo is definitely working. As long as I take them every six hours they keep the tremors away. It's such a relief not to have to stress about them, especially today. Nothing is going to spoil my party. I don't want to think about anything but having a good time.

I can't contain a squeak of delight as I look out of my bedroom window at the metallic-blue BMW in the driveway. It was obvious when Mom handed me the keys this morning that Dad didn't approve of her purchase. But he kept his lip buttoned, trying to be supportive.

I check the reflection in my dressing-table mirror. I've gone for the "vamp" look, as recommended by Ruby. She said that for the party, we should both go for smoky eyes, false lashes, blood-red lips and matching fake nails.

I stare in the mirror, blocking out any negative thoughts. I feel sexy, confident ... happy. "I can do this," I say, blowing a kiss at my reflection.

I walk downstairs and into the balloon-filled hallway. Mom is running around shouting orders at the catering team.

"Put all the food in the dining room. Drinks go on the table by the Jacuzzi. Where's the ice? We need buckets of ice!"

"Calm down, Mrs Burgess," I call to her.

Mom's face lights up. "You look beautiful, young lady!"

"Thanks, but would you stop stressing about this party?" I smile gratefully. It's so nice that she's excited for me.

"Your guests will start arriving any minute and things aren't ready," she worries.

"Listen, we've got the pool, the biggest bounce house I've ever seen and one of the coolest DJs in Texas, so I don't think people are going to be worried about the ice," I try to reassure her.

"I just want everything to be perfect for your birthday," she stresses.

"But it's not my birthday, it's Renee's," I whisper.

"Sure, but when it's your real seventeenth we'll celebrate too – just me, you and Dad – but today is a great excuse to have all your new friends around." She gives me a squeeze.

Dad appears from the kitchen with a drink in his hand and Arthur at his heels.

"Hello, Arthur!" I bend down to him as he cowers behind Dad.

"Lewis, why don't you take Arthur for a walk? Get him out the house?" Mom says.

"No, I'm staying around for this party," he says stiffly, taking a sip of his bourbon.

"There's no need to get worked up." Mom straightens his tie. "Everything is going to be great. Have you even looked at your daughter? Doesn't she look beautiful?"

His face creases with stress. "For God's sake, Gemma. Watch what you're saying! Don't you think we should be keeping a low profile instead of presenting Renee to the world?"

"No! I want her to enjoy herself," Mom retorts.

"How many kids have you invited to this thing?" Dad asks me.

"Um . . . a lot?" I reply.

"Is Makayla coming?" Dad asks.

"I didn't invite her."

"What? You didn't invite your best friend?" Dad says.

"I've tried, I really have, but she was *Lucy's* best friend; she doesn't want to know Renee and to be honest I'm tired of her telling me to get lost." It hurts so much to admit that I've lost Mak, but for the sake of my sanity, I've got to accept it and concentrate on my new friends.

Dad shakes his head sadly.

"Well, *I* completely understand, honey. Makayla will learn to move on, just like you have." Mom takes my hand.

"I'm so proud of you. I know it's been unbelievably hard, but look where you are now. Principal Sanderson says that you've settled in so well. She's pleased with your grades and she's delighted that you got involved in the cheerleading squad. She called you a real asset to the school. Isn't that wonderful?"

"I suppose," I say, unable to stop grinning.

"Tell me that you're not still angry with me. Tell me that I did the right thing," Mom pleads.

"I don't know, Mom; all I know is that right now, I'm happy, really happy." I beam at her.

Mom throws her arms around me. "That's all I needed to hear."

The doorbell rings.

"Go greet your guests," Mom trills.

I rush to open the door. It's Grandma! I haven't seen her since the charity auction. I'm so pleased that she wants to be here for my party.

"Hi, Mrs Kendal! I'm so glad you came." I move in to kiss her but she turns her head and my puckered lips land on her ear.

"Gemma was very insistent I came," she says. "Happy birthday, Renee. Is today your actual birthday?"

"Yes, today is my actual birthday." I smile.

She gives an unnerving smile and hands me an envelope.

"Thanks, Mrs Kendal." I slice it open with my sharp fake nails and pull out a bland card of a flower. Inside it says, *To Renee, Happy Birthday from Mrs Kendal*.

"I didn't think that you'd need a gift. You're getting so

much already. Dare I ask, is that new car outside a birthday present?" she says, looking like she's sucking lemons.

I struggle for words. This must look so bad to her. "Yeah ... it's crazy, isn't it? Mr Burgess let me drive around an empty parking lot this morning. It was awesome."

Her face can't hide her disdain.

"Honestly, Mrs Kendal, I've never asked Mr and Mrs Burgess for anything. They're just so unbelievably generous to me," I say apologetically.

"Renee." She leans towards me, her tone almost threatening. "I can see how happy you make my daughter and for that I'm grateful to you. But she's been through so much. She's still grieving for Lucy. She's vulnerable right now so I have to look out for her. I'd hate for Gemma to be hurt; you understand, don't you?"

I nod dumbly as she pulls away.

"Gemma," she calls out to Mom. "Did you write that piece for Lucy's foundation website? We need to thank everyone for their generosity at the auction the other week."

Mom blows a kiss at Grandma. "I haven't finished it yet, Mama. I'm working on it," she says distractedly.

"Well, maybe I could see what you've written so far."

"Not now, Mama, I'm busy. It's Renee's party – why don't you relax and have a drink?" Mom hurries towards the kitchen and Dad takes over.

"Welcome, Charlotte. Let me get you a drink."

Arthur lollops over to greet Grandma, making sure he keeps his distance from me.

"Lucy's dog doesn't seem to like you, Renee," she says. "It's most unusual for him. Arthur is friendly towards nearly everyone. I wonder what it is about you he doesn't like?"

She watches with satisfaction as I blush with embarrassment. I always knew Grandma was no pushover, but I never knew that she could be so bitchy! Dad gulps down his drink nervously and steers Grandma towards the bar.

I try to compose myself as the bell rings again. I am not going to let her or anyone else ruin my party. I plaster on a smile and open the door. There's a crowd on the doorstep and, by the noise and the fumes, they've all been getting pre-loaded with alcohol. A tsunami of kisses and hugs rains down on me as the cheer and football teams swarm in. Gifts are piling up faster than I can put them down.

Ruby sashays towards me with her arm firmly around her boyfriend, Neil Cooper, the captain of the Bailey Bulls.

"Happy birthday, babe. We are rockin' this look!" She plants a sticky red kiss on my cheek. "Thanks for inviting all the boys. It wouldn't be a party without them."

I scowl as Josh Dartmere rolls in behind them. I didn't mind inviting the football team. I knew it would keep the girls happy, but I hate that Dartmere is in my house. I didn't have a good enough reason to stop Ruby inviting him, though. What could I say – by the way, I know he's a jerk because I used to date the guy?

Josh leans towards me for a kiss; his breath reeks of liquor. I turn my back on him, pretending to be sorting out my gifts.

"Later!" he shouts at me as he heads to the pool.

The doorbell doesn't stop ringing. It looks like almost everyone that I invited has turned up: all the cool, popular kids that I would never have dared speak to when I was the old me.

Ruby gets ahold of me as I greet everyone. "Well, I'm glad that you've stuck to our guest list. This has real potential," she grins.

My heart sinks as I spot Grandma leaving. She's been here less than an hour. She hasn't even come to say goodbye. I tell myself that she didn't want to disturb me, but who am I kidding – she can't stand me.

Mom is in the middle of the cheer squad, laughing and joking. They seem to love her and she's in her element surrounded by giggling, glamorous girls.

"Do you have any photos of you and the Stepton High squad?" Laura asks.

"Well, as a matter of fact I do have one or two," Mom beams, "but let's leave them for another time, this is Renee's party, not mine."

I sidle up to her, suggesting quietly, "Why don't you and Mr Burgess go out? Have a nice time. I'll keep an eye on everything."

She wags her finger at me. "No way, young lady. I remember the parties *I* used to go to. I don't want our house trashed."

"Well then, why don't you at least go upstairs? Watch a movie?"

"Okay, I know that you want me out of the way. I understand," she laughs.

I take Mom over to where Dad is lying on a sun lounger, sipping another bourbon.

I crouch down next to him. "Mrs Burgess is going upstairs to give us some space. Why don't you go with her?"

"You need supervision," he says as I roll my eyes.

"Loosen up, Lewis. Can't you remember being young and having *fun*? Come upstairs with me." Mom drags him off the lounger.

"Thanks," I say to her.

"You just make sure y'all have a great time. You know where we are if you need us," Mom says, hugging me and planting a kiss on my cheek.

Tanya's staring over at us. "I told you, didn't I? Mrs Burgess found herself a new daughter pretty quick," she stage-whispers to Ruby.

I cringe as I usher Mom away.

As darkness falls, the strings of lights hanging from the trees start to twinkle. The pool is alive with a riotous game of volleyball and the yard is filled with squeals and shrieks coming from the bounce house as people try to catapult each other off it. A throbbing beat sails over from the tent. I double take as, in the distance, back by the house, I see a familiar figure. Her long curly hair frames her face; her denim jacket clashes with her stonewashed skirt. Mak! Yes, it's definitely Mak. I can't believe that she's here. I thought that she didn't want to have anything to do with me.

She's standing in front of a boy I can't quite see. They seem deep in conversation. I go on my tiptoes to get a better look; a shudder ripples through me. It's the boy at the school gates. The boy who shouted "Hayley".

I've got to get over there and talk to them but a hand grabs me before I can move. "Hey, birthday girl," Laura trills, "the music has started. How about we get in the dancing mood?" She produces a bottle of vodka from her handbag.

"You go ahead but I'd better not. I've got to stay sober, make sure no one pukes in the pool," I say, keeping an eye on Mak. "Anyway, I just need to see someone."

Laura pouts. "Oh, come on Renee, don't run off on me. I've hardly seen you. You've got plenty of time to mingle, but now is the time to *dance*!"

I look back at Mak. She and the boy have sat down by the pool. They don't look like they'll be leaving anytime soon. I'll dance for a few minutes to keep Laura happy and then head straight over to them.

Laura has poured out two large shots. "Come on! Just a little one. It's such a great party. I want you to relax and enjoy it." She raises the glasses. "Cheers?" she says hopefully.

I stare at the glass of clear liquid. It's so tempting. Yeah . . . why not? This is my night, my party! This is the new me! I'm no longer the poor little rich girl with cancer who was too sick and afraid to enjoy herself.

"Okay, but just this one." I take a swig of the burning liquid, screwing up my face. It's disgusting!

Laura giggles, rubbing my back. She pulls me towards

the tent, collecting most of the cheer squad en route. Inside, the dance floor is already filling up.

The DJ salutes me as he announces, "This one's for Renee, the birthday girl!"

A heavy bass line kicks in, followed by a funky guitar solo. The music brings people flooding into the tent, but I don't see Mak or the boy. Everyone is whooping, arms aloft. It seems I'm the only one who's never heard the tune before, but it doesn't matter. I'm in the middle of a mass of dancing bodies and it feels great ... exhilarating. Ruby grabs me around the waist.

"Come on, Renee, get those hips moving," she shouts, circling her hips with mine. We're clinging on to each other, gyrating and howling with laughter. The floor's getting more crowded as people squeeze on.

"Mind if I cut in?" Josh Dartmere maneuvers Ruby out of the way and stands in front of me. "It's hot in here. I brought you a drink." He passes me a large glass of orange juice.

Despite myself, I'm grateful to him. My throat is feeling raw.

"Thanks," I say, gulping the whole thing down before it even hits me that it tastes funny. "What the ... ? What's in it?" I gasp.

"Just orange juice and some vodka to give it a kick," he says, smirking at me innocently.

"Get lost, will you," I splutter, fighting my way through the crowd.

I need some air. My body feels like someone's lit a fire

in it. It's taking forever to get out of the tent. People keep grabbing me for a dance, telling me what a cool party this is, saying I look pretty. I know that most of their words are fuelled by liquor but it doesn't matter; even though my head is spinning it still makes me feel fantastic.

As I step outside, the cool night breeze makes my head ache. Goosebumps erupt over my arms and bare legs. I hug myself as I head towards the house to look for Mak.

I don't know whether it's my heels or the drink Dartmere gave me, but I'm unsteady on my feet. I take my shoes off and walk barefoot through the yard. As I pass the bounce house, a voice calls out to me.

"Hey, Renee, come bounce with me!" Hugh Grasso is shouting.

Did he gate crash? I don't suppose it matters; tonight I want *everyone* to have a good time.

I wave at him. "Later." God, I'm slurring.

Hugh and a girl that I don't even recognize jump down from the bounce house and drag me on to it as I cry out in protest, half laughing.

It's like standing on Jell-O. I try to make it to the side but I'm swaying like a boat in a storm. The girl bounces and I fall flat on my back, looking up at the stars. Panic starts to creep over me as I feel myself being sucked into the rubbery surface of the bounce house.

"Don't let me sink!" I shout.

"You're not sinking," Hugh laughs.

"I am. I'm sinking into the bounce house!" I cry.

Raucous laughter fills my ears.

"Quick! You'd better stand up, then." Hugh hauls me up and holds my arms as he bounces, making my feet lift off the ground. I let go of him and fall on to my butt, bouncing straight back up.

"Don't let your feet touch the ground or the bounce house will swallow you up," Hugh says in a spooky voice.

They're laughing hysterically, bouncing off the sides. I feel dizzy, sick. I need to get off.

"Renee, do one of your cheer routines for us," the girl is saying.

What's wrong with her? Doesn't she even know my name?

"My name's Lucy," I tell her, annoyed.

"What? Your real name is Lucy?"

"Yeah, of course it is. Whose party do you think you're at? I'm Lucy Burgess."

All the bouncing stops; the surface is becalmed. I lean against the side, relieved.

They're staring at me.

"Hey, why would you say that?"

Why does the girl sound angry with me?

"What?" I put my head in my hands to stop the spinning.

"Was that some kind of joke? 'Cause it's just freakin' weird," Hugh says, screwing up his face.

"What if Lucy's mom and dad heard you say shit like that?" the girl snaps.

Oh my God, what did I say? I can't think straight. "I didn't mean it. I had a drink. I'm not used to it."

"But saying you're the dead girl?" Hugh shakes his head.

"It's because I'm here, living with Lucy's parents, surrounded by all her things. She's on my mind. It just came out. I'm sorry. You won't tell anyone, will you?" I plead.

"Whatever," Hugh says coldly. "You ought to just sit here for a while. Get ahold of yourself. We're going to check out the DJ."

I nod, mortified. I can't believe I've been so stupid.

I watch the two of them walk into the distance. They're talking about me. I'm sure of it. They're going to tell people what I said. I've got to drink some water, stop my head from spinning. Maybe I should ask Mom to keep an eye on things. I could just go and lie down; try phoning Mak tomorrow, thank her for coming. Everyone's having a good time, no one will miss me. If Hugh tells people, I'll think of a way to laugh it off. People say all kinds of weird crap when they've had something to drink.

I try to lever myself up but slump back in the corner. Out the corner of my eye I see that boy who was with Mak. He's standing under a tree nearby, looking over at me.

"Hey, Renee. You okay?"

I jump at the sound of the voice. Oh crap, it's Dartmere again. He's the last person I want to see.

"Yeah, fine, thanks," I say icily.

"You look like you need a hand."

"No!" I wave him away. "I'm just having some quiet time before I get back to the dancing."

"Mind if I join you?" He hops on to the inflatable without waiting for my answer.

He plonks down next to me, our shoulders touching. He opens his jacket and pulls out a small bottle of tequila, knocking it back. "Want a drink?"

"No."

"You don't look great. Not that you look bad or anything. You're the kind of girl who could never look bad." He gives me a dazzling, perfect-toothed smile and my belly churns.

"I'm not feeling well. I really need to get off here," I say, attempting to stand up.

He takes my hand. I think he's going to help, but instead he pulls me back down.

"You're so pretty, Renee. You *must* know that I like you." He brushes my hair away from my face.

"What do you think you're doing?" I swat his fingers away.

"Just getting to know you, that's all."

He puts a hand on my cheek and the other moves towards the back of my neck. He'll feel my scars. He'll tell everyone! I panic, jerking my head away and lashing out at his face with my long, fake nails.

He cries out. His hand flies to his bleeding cheek.

"I don't want you to touch me," I splutter.

His shock turns to anger as he grabs my shoulders, shaking me. "Why did you do that, you crazy bitch?"

"Get off her!"

It's the boy from the school gates. He pulls Josh off

me, looming over him. He's bigger than Dartmere, more powerfully built.

"This is none of your business?" Dartmere doesn't sound so sure of himself.

"Leave her alone or I'll bust your nose all over your face."

His voice. He has a strange accent. Is he British? I try to concentrate on him but I'm not really seeing straight.

Dartmere climbs off the bounce house and walks away shouting threats at the boy. "I'll be back real soon, and unless you want the crap beaten out of you, you'd better be gone."

The boy is staring deep into my face, his brown eyes wide and wild. "Hayley! Hayley! Is it you?"

What's he saying? My head is spinning. Why is he calling me Hayley?

"Hayley!"

Oh God, I have to get off here before I puke.

"Hayley!" His voice is pure anguish. His handsome face is pale and washed out.

He's some kind of crazy. I can't mess up again. *Think straight, Lucy.*

"I'm Renee Wodehouse. I'm sorry, I don't know Hayley." My words run together like liquid.

"Your voice? Whose voice is that?" he demands. "Come on, Hayley, who am I? Who am I?"

I can taste puke rising in my throat. "I don't know who you are," I mumble.

"I'm your brother!"

I gasp as he takes my face between his hands. He's

searching my eyes like he's desperate for some sign of recognition.

"What are you doing?" I whisper, but I don't pull away. There's something about this crazy boy that draws me in.

His hands drop down. He looks like he's going to cry.

He backs off, shaking his head despairingly. "I'm sorry. I've made a mistake. I'm sorry." He seems to just disappear as if he was never here in the first place.

I try to stand up to look for him. My belly heaves and yellow vomit spews out on to the bounce house.

I'm still sitting in a pool of my own puke when the crowd starts to gather. Josh is at the center, pointing at me.

"I should call the cops," he's shouting. "Get you charged with assault."

The cheer squad are flapping around him, inspecting his inflamed cheek. There are too many people. I'm so confused. What did that boy want? Where did he go?

"Why, Renee?" Ruby shouts.

I don't want to deal with this, now or ever. "He touched me. I didn't want him to touch me," I whimper.

Laura climbs next to me, skirting around the puke. "Where did he touch you? Was it somewhere private?" she whispers.

"He touched my face and he was going to touch my neck."

There's giggling from the crowd.

"What's your problem?" Neil Cooper yells.

"He was going to kiss me," I say.

"No I wasn't. I just touched your face and you attacked

217

me, isn't that right?" Josh rages. "If you don't tell the truth then I'm calling the cops right now and I'll take this thing all the way to court."

"Okay, yes, I overreacted. I'm sorry, I'm not feeling well." I just want them all to go away. I can't handle this.

A rumble of disapproval rises from the crowd.

"Let's get you to the house and clean you up," Laura says gently.

"No, Laura. Don't you dare help her," Neil Cooper says. "She attacked Josh."

"Hugh Grasso is going around telling everyone that you said you're Lucy Burgess!" Ruby sounds freaked out. "Is that true?"

"I can explain," I whimper. "I'm not used to alcohol."

"No, no, no!" Ruby wags her finger at me. "I don't care. That is not cool, Renee."

"I'm sorry," I mumble. "Why don't you just leave me alone to get straightened out and everyone can go back to the tent and keep dancing."

"No way!" Neil Cooper puts two fingers in his mouth and produces a piercing whistle that sails around the garden. "Go home, y'all," he hollers, "this party is OVER!"

CHAPTER 27

THE BOY

"Lucy! Lucy!" Mom's irate voice pierces my throbbing head. I don't even have time to sit up in bed before she's on me like a vulture.

"What's the problem?" I try to sound innocent.

"The 'problem' is that I've just had Josh Dartmere's mother on the phone saying that he has scratches on his face from where *you* attacked him last night," she says, her hands on her hips.

"Oh." I cringe. I'd been hoping that I'd dreamt it all.

"You lied to us; telling us that you called a halt to it because it was getting a little wild? Look at you! I had no idea you were in such a state." She's fuming.

"Please can we do this later," I groan, putting the pillow over my head.

She snatches the pillow off me. "I haven't dared to tell your father. He'd only blame me for having the party in the first place. Why did you scratch Josh? His mom is demanding that we discipline you or she'll take matters further."

"He was touching me when I didn't want him to. He was about to touch my neck scars. I didn't want him telling people and having all their questions."

Mom seems to soften. "Okay, but wouldn't it have been less trouble just to tell him to go away?"

"I tried that, Mom." I put my head in my hands. "Oh God, I really can't go to school next week."

I'm not going to tell Mom that I announced I was Lucy Burgess at the party. She'll go ballistic. I don't know how I'm going to face people. Please, God, I hope by Monday, this will be old news and there'll be other disasters to talk about.

"Look, I'll tell Josh's mom that we punished you. You can't *not* go to school because of that jerk," Mom says.

As I massage my temples to relieve the throbbing, an image of the boy from last night comes to me.

"Did he say his name?" I'm thinking aloud.

"Who?"

"The boy from last night. I think he came with Mak. He was so strange," I say, vaguely.

"Mak came? I didn't even see her. She must have arrived after your dad and I went upstairs," Mom says, picking up my party clothes from the bedroom floor.

"He kept calling me Hayley."

All the noise seems to get sucked out of the room as Mom stands, statue still.

"Mom? Are you even listening to me?"

She lets out a puff of air like someone has breathed life back into her. "Of course I'm listening." Her voice flutters.

"The whole night got so weird and I'd had a drink," I say, guiltily.

I get up and open the balcony doors, hoping the fresh air will help clear my head.

"What did he say?" I ask myself, trawling through my addled brain. "Come on ... remember." I try to conjure up words ... his face. I get a powerful echo of his desperation. "He thought that I was Hayley and said he was my brother? But then he got upset, said he'd made a mistake and just disappeared."

Mom has her back to me as she fiddles with my perfume bottles on the dressing table. "Okay, well, that *is* a little strange. Maybe he'd been drinking." She sounds stressed out.

"But why would he mistake me for his sister? Why did he get so upset?"

She turns to me, her cheek muscles twitching. "I don't know," she says impatiently. "Maybe he hadn't seen her in a while. Maybe they'd lost contact."

"It can't be anything to do with the donor, can it?" I whisper my half-formed thought.

"You really are hungover, young lady." Mom shakes her head, disapprovingly. "How can it be anything to do with Amy? He called you Hayley, didn't he, and anyway, Mike and Hazel wrote that Amy was an only child; she doesn't have a brother. He was obviously just drunk and confused."

I groan. Oh God, it's too complicated. My head is spinning.

"I'll call Mak later," I say. "She might be able to tell me about him."

"I thought Mak wasn't your friend any more," Mom says harshly. "You shouldn't call her. You'll make her suspicious. How do you know that she'll even want to talk to you?"

"She came to my party, didn't she?" I reply hopefully, but then I have a flashback of myself on the bounce house last night, claiming to be Lucy Burgess. I screw up my eyes, trying to make the image disappear. I hope that Mak hasn't heard, or any last chance I have with her is gone.

"Hi Makayla, it's Renee here." I'm using my most upbeat voice.

There's a moment's silence and I'm wondering whether her phone has cut out.

"How did you get my number?" Her tone could freeze hell over. She's definitely heard.

"Mrs Burgess gave it to me. Thanks so much for coming to my party. It meant a lot to me. I'm just so sorry I didn't get to talk to you, but maybe you'd like to hang out tomorrow?" I hold my breath.

"No, we won't be hanging out tomorrow or ever," she replies with disgust.

"Okay, I guess that you've heard that I said and *did* some weird stuff, but I was drunk. I was being ridiculous. I'm sorry. I hope that we can get over that."

"What's with all this *we* crap. There is no *we*. Now get lost!"

"No! Please, I won't hassle you. Could you just tell me if you know anything about that boy you were talking to at the party? I think he may be British? Jet-black hair . . . good-looking. You'd remember him."

"You want *me* to tell *you* about him? But he's your friend, not mine!"

Is she trying to mess with me? "No he's not. He was at the school gates the other day and then he turned up at my party, but I don't know who he is."

"What? You don't know him?" She sounds confused . . . angry.

"Well, no."

There's silence again, but this time she's cut me off.

CHAPTER 28

FACING IT

The news of what happened at the party is all over Bailey Heights. All morning people have been looking at me strangely in the corridor. I hear them whisper as they go past.

I walk into English and everyone stares. I quickly grab a seat at the back and pretend to be reading but Hugh Grasso shouts over, "Hey, Renee, or is it Lucy, or maybe we should call you tiger?" He swipes the air with a clawed hand.

Toxic laughter fills the room. Mak isn't joining in, but she turns and looks at me, contempt written all over her face. What the hell must she be thinking? I can't face this. I turn to run but Mr Kendrick comes in behind me, closing the door.

"Hey, guys, there's a terrible vibe in this room today. Lighten up, everybody." Mr Kendrick claps his hands to break the atmosphere.

I'm trapped. Sweat patches bloom on my blouse. A thousand needles prick my fingers, crawling up my arms. The sensation is unbearable. I need to scratch. I try to do it subtly, my nails delivering tiny scratches in the crook of my arm, but once I start, the relief is so great that I can't stop. I scratch more and more furiously until blood streaks the sleeve of the blouse and relief is replaced by the hot sting of the torn skin.

People are staring. Mr Kendrick kneels down and gently takes my arm. "That looks sore, Renee. Something must be irritating your skin. Why don't you take yourself to the nurse? I'll write you a hall pass."

"It's not a nurse she needs, it's a psychiatrist," Hugh says, creating a wall of laughter.

"You've just earned yourself a detention, Hugh." Mr Kendrick glares at him.

I grab my bag and keep my head bowed as I hurry out of the room.

I head to the bathroom. I'm not going to the nurse. She might phone Mom. I'm already in enough trouble with her and Dad.

I wince as the running water washes over my bleeding arm. There's still forty minutes of class left, but there's no way I'm going back into that room. I lock myself inside one of the stinking stalls. I slump down on the toilet seat, wanting to stay here for the rest of the day, but a voice in my head starts bugging me ... lecturing me. It's ordering me to pull myself together, to stop being a wimp. It tells me to get out there and rescue the situation.

The ring of the lunchtime bell startles me – it feels like I've only been here five minutes. I stand up, shaking myself, jumping up and down like a pumped fighter. Whatever this voice is, it's right – sitting around here isn't helping me.

I've got to get out there and face them all.

In the dining room I walk confidently towards Ruby's table. I should just act normal, take my seat and ask about the next training session. My heart lifts as Laura gives me the tiniest wave. I go to sit down but Tanya puts her legs up on the chair.

"Sorry, this seat is taken," Tanya says with an icy glare.

"What are we working on at training tonight?" I sound casual though my insides are quaking.

There's an unbearable pause as the girls exchange glances. I feel my fragile confidence crumbling.

Ruby takes a deep breath. "Listen, Renee, people are a little freaked out by your behavior at the party."

"But I only said that crazy thing because of the drink," I say desperately. "Obviously I wasn't being serious."

"Yeah, well, there's been a discussion and we've decided that it would be best for everyone if you weren't on the squad. Neil is really pissed at what you did to Josh and Josh is threatening to quit the football team if I don't drop you. You're a great gymnast, but you've got some personal issues you need to work on," she says, looking at me with distaste.

"I'm sorry, it was a one-time thing. I'll never behave like that again. I love being on the squad. It's the best thing in my life. Please, Ruby, please give me another chance," I plead, leaning in too close to her.

"Don't beg. Have some dignity, will you," she cringes. "Just go away. You can leave your uniform by my locker."

"Laura?" I look desperately at her, praying that she'll speak up for me, but she flushes and looks down at the floor, ignoring me.

I straighten up, looking for the nearest exit. As I rush towards the door to the yard, someone sticks out their leg directly into my path. I see it too late. I trip, grabbing for the table to break my fall, but I send a plate full of food crashing to the floor with me. The whole dining room comes to a standstill. People are craning their necks to get a better look.

Josh Dartmere pulls his leg back under the table and looks down at me. "Oops, clumsy you," he sneers.

There's a ripple of nervous laughter around the room. My hands start to tingle and then they're shaking violently for everyone to see. Some people look away, embarrassed for me. I must look pathetic. I close my eyes as tears start to roll down my face. I want the earth to open and swallow me up, but hands suddenly grip me and start to pull.

"Come on, get up."

It's Mak! That's Mak's voice!

Her face is hard as she hauls me off the floor. She walks me out of the dining room, flicking the finger at Dartmere.

"Thank you," I whisper as she takes me into the courtyard.

"Don't get the wrong idea. I still don't like you; you're creepy and crazy, but I happen to *hate* Dartmere even more. What you did to him at your party; he probably deserved it."

"Yeah, yeah." I'm nodding manically. I fumble in my bag and take out the bottles of pills from Dr Leo.

I tip one from each bottle on to my palm. The pills oscillate like there's an earthquake.

"That's a lot of medication," Mak says, handing me a bottle of water.

"I know, but they stop it. I'll be okay in a minute." I swallow them down. She watches, then turns, looking like she's going to leave. I blurt out the first thing that comes into my head. "Who is that boy that I asked you about on the phone? How did you meet him?"

Mak sways from side to side, looking uncomfortable. "He said his name was Ben. I met him when he was hanging around the school the other day. He said ..." She gives an exasperated sigh. "Well, he *said* that he was a friend of yours. To be honest, I only took him to your party because he said he wanted to persuade you to leave town with him."

I frown at her. "But he thought I was his sister. He kept calling me Hayley and then he said he'd made a mistake and ran off."

"Whatever." Mak waves her hand dismissively. "The boy wasted my time ... it looks like those shakes of yours are under control, so I'm out of here."

"But what about your classes?"

"What about them?" She shrugs. "I need to get away from this place. It's full of assholes!"

She heads across the courtyard without a backwards glance. I wait until she's almost out of sight to start following her. I can't let this chance pass. She's just proved that she doesn't hate me; there's hope for us.

She walks to the far end of the playing field and looks around before prying open a gap in the wire fencing and squeezing through. I watch to see which direction she takes and sprint after her.

CHAPTER 29

ASK ME ANYTHING

I follow at a distance as Mak walks towards the Museum District. She heads into a florist's. I wait across the street, keeping an eye on the entrance. Minutes later, she emerges with a big bunch of mauve and pink freesia. They're beautiful.

She makes her way to a tram stop and I loiter at the newspaper kiosk as she gets a ticket from the machine. A tram glides to a halt, the doors slide open and she steps inside one of the cars. Maybe I should call out to her, but something holds me back. I want to see where she's going; I want to see if Mak has secrets now that I don't know about. Maybe she's even going to meet that boy, Ben.

I haven't got time to buy a ticket. I slip into the car behind a guy the size of a house. He shields me from Mak, who's only feet away, but focused on keeping her flowers from getting crushed by the other passengers. I catch glimpses of her as people shift in the car. She looks deep in thought, ignoring the trickles of sweat running down her forehead as the sun beats through the glass. We ride seven stops before I see her making for the opening doors, holding the bunch of flowers aloft like a tour guide trying to keep her group together.

I excuse myself as I start to push past people. I don't want to get stuck on this thing and lose her. I don't really know this area; it's not somewhere we used to go together.

She crosses the street and heads purposefully up a steep road. I watch from a distance as she enters through the massive wrought-iron gates of a park. I jog after her, but I'm stopped in my tracks by the ornate lettering on the entrance sign. My warm body shudders. I know why she's here. I should turn around and go home. But as I watch Mak striding into the distance, I have to follow her. I take a deep breath and step through the gateway.

Mak crunches along a gravel path, ignoring the endless rows of headstones on either side; so many that, even in death, it seems like people end up like cramped commuters. I can't chance following her along the noisy path; it's safer to pick my way through the graves. I need to keep track of her, but my eyes are drawn to an oversized headstone in the shape of a teddy bear. It's the grave of a four-year-old girl called Lily. I read the inscription.

Our beautiful angel, taken from us too soon, but always in our hearts.

I didn't know this little girl, but anger bubbles up in me, thinking of her life being over when it had barely started. If Lily's mom and dad could have saved her with a body transplant, would they have done it? I understand why Mom asked Dr Leo to do this to me. No parent wants their child to die before them. Dr Leo could stop that from happening. He needs to concentrate on helping kids. If he makes more transplant people like me, maybe we won't be thought of as freaks; maybe one day the world will be in awe of us, jealous that we've been able to cheat death.

I stroke the cool surface of Lily's headstone as I walk on.

The cemetery continues to slope gently upwards as I weave between the sycamore and oak trees that are dotted around the acres of graves. The sprawling trees are a relief from the overwhelming landscape of death, but I can see where their roots have spread under the coffins, making the graves so unsettled it looks like the dead have been trying to break their way out.

The sun is too strong. It beats down on my thick wig, making my head itch. I'm starting to wish Mak would slow up when she suddenly veers off the path and across the grass. She's stopped in front of a shiny white marble headstone. I need to get closer. There's a mausoleum opposite, which could give me cover. I make a run for it, looping around Mak. I creep down the side of the ivy-clad walls and peer around the corner. Mak has her back to me. She's obscuring the headstone as she crouches down and replaces the wilting flowers in the vases with her own. The grave is tidy and well kept; the mound of soil is still curved, not flat like on the older graves.

She sits back on her heels and the headstone comes into view.

Lucy Burgess 2002–2018. Beloved daughter of Gemma and Lewis. Rest in peace, our darling.

Seeing my own grave feels like being punched in the belly. I grab on to the wall. I'd never asked Mom where they'd buried me. I didn't want to know. I stare at my headstone. There's a small, golden-framed photo set into the marble. It's another one of the dorky photos of me that I didn't want Mom to use. Droplets of condensation have pooled at the bottom of the frame; the photo is already starting to curl and discolor, but I bet Mom has never even been back to check; why would she, when what she wants is alive and well? Bile rises up into my throat.

Mak kisses her fingers and presses them on the framed photo, whispering, "I miss you so much, Lucy. Everything's so bad without you." Her whole body starts shaking with sobs. "I can't imagine ever feeling happy again."

I can't stand it. How can I let her go on suffering when I'm right here in front of her? I know that she's not ready to hear it, but she'll never be ready. I've just got to do it. I bolt over and wrap my arms around her. "It's all right, Mak. I'm here. It's me, Lucy. Everything's going to be all right."

She lets out a shriek and throws me off, scrambling to her feet. "What's wrong with you?" she bawls. "You're completely insane. How dare you say you're Lucy!"

I hold up my hands to calm her down. "Mak, I want you to listen very carefully. I'm going to tell you something that you won't believe, but I swear it's true." My voice shakes.

"I don't want to hear anything you've got to say, and *stop* calling me Mak! I knew that I shouldn't have helped you out. Now you're never going to leave me alone."

"I heard what you just said. I can't let you suffer like this." I'm desperate now.

"You're spying on me. Get lost or I'll call the cops."

I hesitate; it feels like I'm about to jump out of a plane without a parachute, but I've got to put my faith in her. "Lucy Burgess's body is in that grave, but her brain isn't," I blurt out.

"What the f—"

"No, listen, please just listen. Lucy *didn't* die. She was terminal, you know that, you saw her in the clinic, but they didn't let her die. They did an operation, the kind everyone thinks is only in sci-fi movies. They took her brain out of her dying body and they put it inside another girl's body – this body!" I beat my hands on my chest.

Mak is frozen, her face contorted in disgust.

"I'm Lucy Burgess even though this body isn't mine. But my brain, my eyes – they're my own. Look at my eyes, Mak. Can't you see I'm telling the truth?"

Mak stares at me like she's looking on the face of evil, but I've got to continue. I've got to convince her.

"Why do you think Mr and Mrs Burgess took me into their home just months after the death of their daughter? They had it all planned, but I knew nothing about it until I woke up in her body."

Mak is looking around for help. She's slowly backing away.

"Don't go! I can prove it. Ask me anything: things that only Lucy would know."

"Stay away from me." Mak's voice quivers.

"Do you remember when you texted me all the answers to the algebra paper in Mrs Hopkins' class? She kept walking past your desk while you were doing it and she never even guessed."

Confusion floods Mak's face.

"And when I was sick and you visited me, you'd never say goodbye when you left. It was always *arrivederci* because you thought it would keep me alive."

Mak's mouth goes slack.

"Your jacket, the one that was in my closet, you gave it to me when we went to the planetarium. I got cold and you wrapped it around me and we got bored with all the science stuff and went to the multiplex instead. And the first-ever time we met was the first day of Bailey Heights and I'd tripped getting out of Mom's car and you helped me up, just like you helped me up in the dining room today. You've always been there for me, Mak. You're the best friend anyone ever had." Tears cloud my eyes. I'm desperate to hug her; to hear her say that she believes me.

"Who told you this stuff?" she stutters.

"No one told me. What else do you want to know? Ask me, ask me anything!"

She bends down and grabs a granite vase from a grave. "Don't take another step or I swear I'll hit you with this."

"Okay." I try to calm my quaking voice. "I understand. It's too much to take in, but you need to hear it. You need to know the truth. I can't let you keep thinking I'm dead. It's destroying you. Just stay calm, Mak, and tell me what you want to know. How about your crush on Mr Kendrick?" I say, sounding manic again.

"What are you talking about?" Mak gasps.

"You've been in love with our English teacher since we started Bailey Heights. You wrote him a love sonnet and you made me stick it under the windshield wiper of his car. It was in the school parking lot. I was terrified someone would see me and think I'd written the stupid thing. We hid at the side of the bike shelter because you wanted to see his reaction when he found it. He stayed late and we waited forever. When he eventually came out he found it, opened it and went bright red. You whispered to me that if he didn't crumple it up and throw it away it meant he liked it; that he'd know deep down who it was from. When you saw him put it in his pocket you nearly peed yourself with joy, but I said to you, 'He's not keeping it because he likes it, he's keeping it as evidence for the police when they come and charge you with being a stalker.'" I gasp for breath.

"How do you know all that?" Mak whispers.

"Because I was there. Because I'm Lucy Burgess, your best friend," I declare, my face ecstatic.

"No! Get away from me. Lucy must have told her mom all this stuff and then Mrs Burgess went and told you. What did you do, pump her for every last bit of information about Lucy so you could do this to me? Do you get off on this?" she roars.

"How could you even think that I'd tell my mom about Mr Kendrick? It was our secret. You made me swear on Arthur's life that I wouldn't tell anyone. It would have been social suicide if it had gotten out."

Mak shakes her head violently. "No, this is bullshit. I've seen things like this on the TV. You're like one of those mentalists, messing with strangers' minds by coming up with all kinds of private stuff that you think they can't possibly know. Why are you doing this to me? Is it because I didn't want to be friends with you? Is this some kind of payback?"

"I'm not trying to hurt you, Mak. I'm telling you the truth. If you dig up my body you'll see that there's no brain, no eyes, because they're here and here!" I point to my head. I point to my eyes. "I can show you what they did to me. Watch."

I take tight hold of the wig and start to drag it off. I grit my teeth in pain as the glue rips out tufts of the hair underneath, but I keep pulling until it comes away. I throw the wig on the ground and undo the buttons on my blouse as my friend watches in horror. I strip the blouse off and turn my back to her.

"Look at me, Mak. Look at the scar down my neck and the top of my spine. Look at the ridge where they cut the donor's skull open, removed her brain and eyes and replaced them with mine. This is what they did to me. I was ready to die but they trapped me inside her because they couldn't stand to let me go." Unstoppable tears run down my face.

There's a thud as the granite vase falls from Mak's limp hands. She bends forward, unable to stop herself puking. She wipes her mouth with shaking hands, tears swimming in her eyes.

I stretch my arms out to her but she backs away, her whole body trembling. "You're in shock, Mak. You need to come sit down."

Her breathing is getting louder and faster; her pupils are huge. I take a step towards her but she turns and runs, stumbling over tree roots and knocking into headstones as she flees the cemetery in terror.

CHAPTER 30

LIAR

Mom gasps as she opens the door. "Lucy! What's happened to you? Your hair! Your blouse is half undone. Did someone hurt you?"

"No, it's okay, Mom." I step into the hallway, straightening the wig that I'd thrown back on my head.

Mom cups my face between her hands. "You've been crying. What happened, honey? Has Josh Dartmere done something to you at school?"

I gnaw on my lip. "I told Mak."

Her hands drop from my face.

"What have you told Mak?" She asks me the question but she already knows the answer.

"About the transplant. About who I really am."

Mom pales.

"I had to. We were at my grave. She's depressed ... seriously depressed. I had to tell her the truth."

"What did she say?" Her hands flutter by her mouth.

"She looked horrified. She ran off," I sob. I step towards Mom, needing her arms around me, but instead she grabs her cell.

"I need to call your father. I need him here, now. You get upstairs and clean yourself up. Don't contact Mak, don't answer your phone. I need time to think."

Dad must have broken every speed limit. It's only been half an hour and I hear his car roaring up the drive.

"Where is she?" His voice echoes around the house. Arthur starts barking from the kitchen. "Gemma, go shut that dog up!"

I look in my dressing-table mirror and make sure the brushed wig is secured back on my sore scalp. I've changed out of my crumpled uniform. I don't want to make Dad any more stressed than he's going to be. I go to face him. His eyes bore into me as I walk down the stairs.

"Why, Lucy? Why?" His voice judders. "They'll take you away from us! You had to be Renee so we could protect you."

"I don't think she believed me," I whimper. "I tried to convince her. Showed her my scars; told her a ton of things that only I'd know, but she thought I was some kind of mentalist or that I'd gotten all the information from you two."

Dad heads to the cabinet and pours himself a drink.

"That isn't going to help, Lewis. We need to keep our heads clear." Mom's voice is brittle.

Dad looks her straight in the eye and gulps it down.

Mom's cell rings. Mak's mom's name flashes up.

"Don't answer it," Dad orders.

"We need to face this. It's not just going to go away," Mom says.

"Hi, Monica, what's wrong? You sound upset... Yes, Renee is at home... Of course ... if it's something you feel that you need to tell us face-to-face then please do stop by, but could you give me an hour? I'm in the middle of something very important... Yes, I'll make sure Lewis is here as well. Okay then, I'll see you all later."

Mom turns off her cell and turns to us. She straightens her back and clasps her hands together to reassure us that she has this under control.

"Okay," she announces calmly. "Makayla and her parents are coming over. Lewis, please stay clear-headed. Lucy, you need to tell us every single word that you said to Makayla and then you need to agree to *everything* I tell you to do. We have an hour to get our story straight. We can do this."

Dad answers the gate buzzer. "Hi, Barry, drive right up."

"Go to your room, Lucy. Only come down when I call you. You can't afford to make *any* mistakes. Do you understand?" she says intimidatingly.

I nod meekly and disappear up the stairs, leaving Dad hovering anxiously by the front door.

I leave my bedroom door wide open so I can hear them arrive. The greetings between them are strained. Dad sounds so stiff and formal; usually there'd be manly handshakes and pats on the back between him and Mak's dad.

"Come straight through to the living room. Lewis and I are anxious to hear what's going on." Mom's voice floats up to me.

As soon as the living room door closes, their conversation is lost to me. I pace my room, playing their imagined conversation through my head, but I can't stand not knowing what's being said. I can't wait up here. I have to know.

Slipping off my shoes, I creep downstairs and out the front door, leaving it on the latch. I walk down the side of the house until I reach the living room. The voices in the room sail through one of the open windows. I get down on my knees and peer in. Everyone is standing stiffly; Mak and her parents are on one side of the coffee table and Mom and Dad are on the other. Even from outside I can feel the tension in the room, like the oppressive heat just before a summer storm breaks.

"She even said that if you dig up Lucy's body you'd see it had no brain or eyes because *she* had them." Mak's mama sounds outraged. "Isn't that right, Makayla?"

Mak nods silently. She looks shattered. Her eyes are puffy, her skin blotchy.

Dad runs his hands down his face, letting out a long sigh. "I told Renee that we'd donated certain organs of Lucy's to medical research. We'd lost Lucy, but we wanted to do anything we could to help fight this disease for others. I can't believe that she went and used that in some warped fantasy."

"But what about the scars she showed me? How did she get them?" Mak asks, her voice subdued, like she's still in shock.

"Apparently, they're from a car accident when she was still in the care of her mom. Her mom was high on some drug or other and crashed. Renee went through the windshield. She nearly died," Dad says, undoing his top button as sweat patches appear on his shirt.

"I don't know what to say." A single tear runs down Mom's cheek. "It's so shocking to hear the perverse lies Renee has told Makayla. We knew that the girl had been through a lot in her life, but Lewis and I had no idea how damaged she was."

I study Mom, astounded at how well she lies; she sounds and looks so convincing, as if she believes every word coming out of her mouth.

"When she first came on the scene, Monica and I didn't want to judge this girl. We hoped that she was genuine, but it must be clear now that she's been exploiting you," Barry says, looking at them pityingly.

"Exploiting us?" Mom echoes.

"Sure, Gemma," Mak's mama says solemnly. "This young woman is clearly manipulative. When you met her she would have seen how distraught you were over Lucy and she's targeted you; exploited your grief to worm her way into your affections, your life. Look how quickly she got her feet under the table, got herself invited to move in. She's had you buying things for her, throwing big parties for her birthday. She knew that Lucy left a massive hole in your lives; she knew that you'd be hungry to make sense of your loss by helping another young woman. She's been using you."

Mom shakes her head in disbelief, twisting her wedding ring around and around.

"But how did she know all those things about me and Lucy?" Mak says quietly, wrapping her arms around herself.

"What does Renee know about?" Dad asks.

Mak looks down at the floor, embarrassed. "Stuff about Mr Kendrick."

"About your crush on Mr Kendrick?" Mom asks gently, her face full of sympathy.

"You know about that?" Mak's cheeks heats up.

"Yes, and about the poem you asked Lucy to put under his windshield?" Mom says softly.

"Lucy told you about that?" Tears pool in Mak's eyes.

"Yes. Lucy and I used to talk about everything."

"But she swore she wouldn't tell anyone." Her lips quiver.

This is torture! I want to shout out to her, to tell her that I never betrayed her secrets.

Mom leans across and strokes Mak's arm. "She wasn't making fun of you, Makayla. She loved you. She just loved talking about what you and she got up to."

"And you told Renee all these stories about Makayla and Lucy?" Monica asks Mom.

"I'm afraid I did." Mom looks ashamed. "Renee was always so interested in Lucy and I needed to talk about her. I loved telling someone all her stories. It gave me comfort. It made me feel close to Lucy."

Dad puts his arm around Mom. "It's okay, Gemma. You didn't do anything wrong."

"Well, I don't care how tough this Renee's life has been — it's no excuse. This girl may be mentally disturbed or maybe she's just plain bad, but either way, Gemma, you need to get her out of your lives!" Mak's dad blusters.

Mak walks over to the display cabinet that Dad put together. She's staring at photos of me in disbelief. "I trusted Lucy. We told each other everything. I can't believe that she'd tell you all my private stuff."

Mak's eyes glaze over.

"Makayla, you can't think for one second that this girl is telling the truth. I know how much you'd love to have Lucy back and this Renee knows that too. This is her sick game. She's wicked!" her mama blazes.

"I want to see her," Mak says calmly.

Her dad puts his hand up in protest. "That's not a good idea, Makayla. We shouldn't give that girl another opportunity to distress you."

"I *want* to see her!"

"Monica, Barry, let's get Renee down here," Mom says, taking control. "If Makayla needs to talk to her to be absolutely sure, then it's best to do it now."

They nod reluctantly.

"Okay, she's in her room. I'll go get her," Dad says.

I'm so transfixed by the scene that Dad has left the room before I register that I need to get back in the house. I sprint to the front door and into the hallway, but Dad is already halfway up the stairs.

"Dad," I whisper to him.

His face contorts. "For God's sake, can't you do anything that you're told? Get in the living room, now!"

As he escorts me in, it feels like I'm about to face a firing squad.

Mak's mama looks at me like she's got a bad taste in her mouth. Her dad huffs disapprovingly, but Mak looks me square in the eyes.

"The very last time I saw Lucy she pleaded with me to do something for her. If you're Lucy, you'll be able to tell me what it was." Her stare is almost pleading.

I begged you to tell my parents to stop the treatment and let me die. My mind, my body, my soul couldn't take any more. I was ready to die. But you wouldn't help me. You couldn't let me go either. I needed your support more than any other time in our lives and I felt that you were letting me down. I tried to make you say a real goodbye, but you wouldn't. You walked out of the room and your last memory of us together is me being angry with you. But I'm not angry with you, Mak. I love you and it's killing me to see you like this. I want to be here for you. I want you to know that Lucy is here for you.

"I'm waiting. Tell me what it was," Mak demands.

If I tell her now then there's no going back. The truth will be out there. Mom and Dad will go to prison and everyone will know what I am.

"Tell me!" Mak implores.

"I can't. I wasn't there. I'm not Lucy," I whisper, my heart breaking.

Mak's face crumples.

"See, Makayla. The girl has admitted it. She's a liar. A sick liar," her mama shouts, jabbing her finger at me.

"Why, Renee?" Mom asks. "Why would you hurt us all like this?"

I fight to hold it together. I have to play my part. "I'm sorry. I can't explain it. Maybe I want to be Lucy. I want what she had: awesome parents, a great best friend. I'm so sorry, Makayla. What I did to you is unforgivable. And Mr and Mrs Burgess, after all you've done for me ... I'm so ashamed. I'm going to go and pack and you'll never have to see me again."

"Good!" Mak erupts. "I hope you die on the streets, you twisted bitch."

I scuttle out of the room with Mak's rage raining down on me.

CHAPTER 31

CHOOSE

I'm six feet under but I hear Mak's voice, like she's shouting at me from behind a thick wall. She's on her knees, shoveling handfuls of soil from my grave as she pleads. "Hang on, Lucy."

"Keep going, Mak. You're nearly there!" I shout, my heart pounding.

Joy spreads through me as her muffled voice becomes clearer. There's the thud of her shoes standing on the coffin lid, followed by a frenzy of scratching on the mahogany wood. She's trying to pry the lid open!

"I can't move it, Lucy. I'm going to climb out and I want you to push the lid off from inside. Can you do that?"

I won't let her down. I don't know where my strength comes from, but it pulsates around the cushioned coffin as I press my hands and feet against the lid. Shafts of brilliant sunlight start to shoot into the blackness as the wood creaks and splinters and nails rise out of their holes. I hear gasps of excitement as I kick the lid again and again, sending it flying into the air.

My head feels like a boulder on my shoulders. I can't seem to hold it up. I struggle to my feet, clinging on to the surrounding walls of earth for support. Mak's arms reach down, ready to haul me up. I grip them and she leans in, peering into the grave.

Her arms shoot away from mine as she lets out a scream. Suddenly, ten, twenty, thirty people surround the open grave. I recognize kids from school, from my party; there's Mak's parents, Mr Kendrick, Principal Sanderson, Grandma. There's the girls from cheer with Dartmere and the football squad. They all look terrified ... appalled.

"What is that?" Ruby is pointing at me, her face twisted in horror.

"It's me, Lucy," I shout, but no words come out.

"It's disgusting," Dartmere says.

"No, can't you see? It's me, Lucy Burgess." I hold my arms up pleadingly and see the thick black stitching on my wrists where hands have been sewn on to my arms. I feel the tightness around my throat and trace the rough zigzag of thread connecting my head to my neck. I stagger back, flailing against the walls of earth.

The crowd parts as a figure steps forward and looms over me. He's dressed in the vestments of a priest, but he has Dr Radnor's face. He turns to the mounds of soil and, scooping up a handful, he throws it down on me.

"Mak, please help me!" I scream.

She stares, petrified. The doctor takes her hand and places soil into her palm.

Her hand shakes; the soil falls through her fingers.

"Do it! Do it!" the crowd goads her.

"Do it, Makayla," her mama bellows.

I try to shake my head. I need to make her understand. "No, Mak. NO!"

She can't look at me as she lets the soil slide from her hand, into the grave. The crowd surges forward, swallowing her up. A storm of inky black earth rains down on me. I try to shield myself, screaming at them to stop, but the soil fills my mouth, choking me. I fall back into the open coffin. I hear my moans as I try to get up, but the soil is weighing down on me; every second, more layers cover my body, until I can't hear the baying crowd any more. My fingers claw at the earth, desperately trying to uncover my face, my mouth, but I can't stop the darkness. Please ... please, help me. I can't breathe! I can't breathe...

"I can't breathe! I can't breathe!"

"Lucy! It's okay, calm down."

Mom is standing over me, pulling sweat-soaked blankets off my bed.

"What have you done to yourself?" she cries, holding my hands.

My mouth feels enormous; it stings, like it's filled with hundreds of paper cuts. I raise my hand to touch it.

"No, don't!" Mom says. "I need to clean it up."

I'm still dazed as she leads me to the bathroom. She tries to block the mirror but I see my bloated lips. All around my mouth it looks like I've been feasting on blood. I wince as I slowly part my lips and reveal the mess inside. White teeth stained red, gums shredded by nails, a swollen tongue oozing blood from claw marks.

"Soil in my mouth. I had to get it out. They were burying me alive," I whimper.

Mom wraps her arms around me. Her body quivers as she whispers in my ear, "Everything's going to be okay. I'll fix it. I promise."

Mom won't stop fussing over me. She's got me down in the sunlit kitchen, drinking milk through a straw, but it hurts every time I part my lips.

"Dad will be back with the ice cream soon. It'll soothe your mouth." She strokes my wig as if it's my real hair but I can't feel any calming sensation.

Dad was speechless when he saw what I'd done to myself. He looked so distressed. He couldn't get out of the house quick enough.

"It'll heal soon. Mouths are good at repairing themselves. You'll look fine in a day or two," Mom says, her eyes full of anguish.

We turn our heads as we hear the front door open.

"Hey, here's the ice cream man back!" Mom shouts out cheerfully.

"What's that, Gemma? Were you expecting someone with ice cream?"

It's Grandma! I don't want her to see me like this. I look around frantically to escape.

"Utility room, now!" Mom hisses to me as she goes into the hall to stall Grandma.

I disturb the sleeping Arthur as I rush into the room. It takes him a second to realize that it's me, but then the barking starts.

"What's wrong with Arthur?" I hear Grandma say. "He sounds upset. Let's get him out of there."

"No! He's fine, Mama. Ignore him, he'll settle in a minute."

I move away from Arthur. He stops barking and cowers in the far corner, his eyes trained on me.

"Where's Renee?" Grandma asks coldly.

"She's just gone out."

"Isn't she going to school today?"

"No ... actually, we've decided Bailey Heights isn't the right environment for her. We're looking into other options," Mom says, trying to sound matter-of-fact.

"But I thought she was doing well; getting into the cheer squad, making new friends."

"Yeah, she was, but I don't think Bailey was pushing her enough ... academically."

I can hear the strain in Mom's voice as she tries to deflect Grandma's questions. I shift closer to the glass door, trying to hear over Arthur's whimpering.

"Oh, really? Anything else you need to tell me about? Any other problems?" Grandma's voice is stern.

"No, I don't think so," Mom says casually.

"Not even that she went and told Makayla that she was Lucy?"

My heart thumps as I peer through the glass, into the kitchen.

"Who told you that?" Mom snaps.

"Monica, she told me everything. I know they came by here yesterday." Grandma looks ready to do battle.

"Well, there's no need to be concerned, thank you, Mama. The matter has been dealt with."

"If the matter had been dealt with, then that young woman would no longer be living here. Monica was under the impression that she was leaving." Grandma wags a finger at Mom.

Mom narrows her eyes, defiantly. "Renee was willing to leave, she's so ashamed about the terrible lies that she told, but Lewis and I thought long and hard about it and we decided we want her to stay. We're going to get her the help she needs ... psychiatric help from professionals. She can't be held responsible for being so messed up after the life she's led," Mom replies fervently.

Grandma sighs so deeply that I see her whole body slump. "Darling, I need you to listen to me: those perverted lies she's told aren't your only problem. I believe that young woman may be a danger to you."

"What are you talking about?" Mom laughs nervously.

"You'll have to forgive me, Gemma. What I did, I did to safeguard you. A grieving mother is so vulnerable and I was alarmed how quickly you'd made her part of your family, so I hired a private investigator to look into Renee's story."

"You did what?" Mom's voice rumbles with anger.

"Hear me out, Gemma. The investigator found records of a Renee Wodehouse with the same date of birth, born in the state of California. There are also records of Renee Wodehouse being taken into foster care there."

"See! I hope that you're ashamed of yourself for doubting the girl." Mom puts her hands on her hips.

"No! This girl you have let into your house has been lying to you. She's not Renee Wodehouse. The records show that the real Renee Wodehouse *died* when she was twelve years old!" Grandma's voice rings out triumphantly.

I clasp a hand over my swollen mouth to stifle a gasp.

Mom's eyes flicker. She twists her wedding ring around and around on her finger. "That's just ridiculous!"

"The information is correct. He showed me a copy of the death certificate. This ... *demon* that you've brought into your home is impersonating a dead girl."

I can't take my eyes off Mom. Her face is rigid. What's she thinking?

My heart thumps out of my chest as I realize that *now* is the time! Now she'll have to come clean to Grandma – tell her the truth about me. Mom can't risk her going to the police with proof that I use a false identity; they'd investigate and everything would be exposed. Mom has got to trust her. She'll finally know who I am and she *will* accept it ... *she will* accept what they've done to me and I'll have my grandma back. I hug my knees with my arms, overjoyed by the thought of it.

"Gemma, sit down," Grandma says. "Have some water. I'm sorry to be the one to tell you all this, but I've had my suspicions about that girl since the first time we met. She was so overfamiliar. Do you remember how she threw her arms around me? There was something about her that didn't feel right. She was trying to get under your skin. She's been trying to replace Lucy."

"I would never let anyone replace Lucy." Mom bristles.

"I know that, darling. We need to call the police; let them deal with her. If we call them now, they could be here waiting for when she gets back."

Mom looks panicked. She sits up, her voice urgent. "No. There's no need for the police."

Oh my God, Mom is going to tell her the truth! I edge even closer to the glass, holding my breath.

"Renee needs help, not punishment," Mom says.

No, Mom. Please don't keep up the lie. Tell Grandma who I am!

"I agree, Mama." Mom speaks slowly. "The girl is obviously disturbed and she's done bad things, but the easy option would be for me to abandon her and that's why I can't. She's the kind of young woman who needs our help most. She has such potential and I'm going to make it my mission to make sure she reaches it."

"You can't be serious, Gemma," Grandma snaps. "Surely Lewis won't agree with you."

"He'll agree, one hundred per cent. This new information doesn't change the way we feel. We're going to help Renee."

"This is madness. If you won't call the police, then I will."

"No! I'll handle this my way."

"But you can't, my darling. You're not thinking straight. It's best to let the authorities deal with her," Grandma pleads.

"Mama, I love you, but you need to understand that Renee is staying. We're going to help her through her problems, and if you had any compassion, then you'd accept her. Aren't you supposed to be the Christian one? Didn't Jesus come to help the sinners? Would he abandon her?" Mom's voice is hard.

"This is entirely different," Grandma says, flustered. "You don't know what this girl is capable of. She could stab you both in your sleep."

"You're being ridiculous! At the end of the day Renee may have done wrong, but she makes me happy; she makes me forget my grief."

"Gemma, you don't need this girl to fill the void in your life. You can go back to work, and we have Lucy's foundation now. Look at all the good we can do. I need your help with it," she begs.

"Enough!" Mom holds up her hand to silence Grandma. "This is my decision, not yours. You need to stay out of my business, and if you involve the police or tell another soul about what you've found out, then I'll never speak to you again."

Grandma's mouth falls open.

"I mean it, Mama!"

"You don't know what you're saying." Grandma is trembling. "Would you really choose this girl – this disturbed, manipulative stranger – over your own mother?"

"I shouldn't have to choose. You're the one putting me in this position."

Grandma grips the back of the chair. "I'm going to go now, Gemma. You've had a shock. I don't want you to say anything else that you're going to regret."

Mom holds out her hand. "You need to give me the house keys, please. I don't want you letting yourself into my home when you're just coming around to cause trouble."

"What's happened to you?" Grandma gasps.

"Give them to me, please!" Mom orders, her face as hard as ice.

I hug my knees tightly to stop myself rushing out to tell Grandma the truth. I can't stand to watch Mom do this to her, but I know that Grandma won't believe what I say without Mom backing me up. If I tried to tell Grandma that I was Lucy, all she'd see is Renee, the twisted, manipulative girl who's exploiting her daughter.

I watch helplessly as Grandma fights back tears and drops the keys into Mom's hand. "Gemma, please don't do this," she says, her voice suddenly frail.

Mom folds her arms across her chest. "Goodbye, Mama," she says coldly.

Grandma seems to age before my eyes as she turns and walks unsteadily out of the kitchen and out of our house.

CHAPTER 32

SOLUTIONS

It's been four days since Mom watched Grandma walk out of our house and she hasn't spoken to her since. I know that Grandma called Dad, pleading with him to make Mom see sense, but Dad told her that he agreed with his wife and that Renee would be staying.

Mom is pretending to be fine by being manically upbeat. She's carrying tension around with her like an unexploded bomb.

I haven't been back to school; I haven't even been out. I've spent days in limbo, wandering around the house and grounds, not knowing what's going to happen next. I don't want to bump into anyone. I dread to think what Mak and Grandma have been telling people about me: the evil psychopath who has her claws in Lucy's parents and turned Mrs Burgess against her own mother? What can I say to them? How would I explain myself?

As I stand in the hallway I hear the sound of a laughing child coming from the basement. I walk down the steps into my darkened den. The only light is from the sliver of frosted, sealed windows, high up on the outside wall. Projected on the huge screen at the far end of the room, I see me, as a toddler, being chased around the yard by Dad.

"Mom?" I call out into the dark.

"It's me," Dad replies, getting up unsteadily from the couch.

"Hey, are you all alone down here?" I ask.

"Yep, I put on some old home movies a while ago and I don't seem to have moved." He gives a lopsided smile and raises the glass to his mouth to take a sip of bourbon.

He's unshaven, grubby-looking. His thinning sandy hair needs a wash. His shirt is crumpled. He hasn't been to work all week. I've never seen him like this before.

"Come and sit next to me." He beckons me over. "There are some great videos of you."

I sit down and he wraps his arm around me. I snuggle into him. I know that he's a little drunk, the liquor fumes are overpowering, but it doesn't matter; it feels so good.

"Do you remember this?" He points to the screen excitedly. "You were in second grade. Look at you go in that pool. You won that race by a mile."

"Of course I remember it. It was the first and last time that I ever won anything," I laugh.

"We were so proud of you," he says, kissing my head.

"Hey, what are you two doing down here?" Mom shouts

from the top of the stairs, switching on the lights. "Turn the video off. Lewis, we have things to discuss."

"Not now, Gemma. My daughter and I are having a nice time," he grunts.

My daughter; his words send joy through me. I kiss his scratchy cheek.

Mom ignores his comment and stands in front of us with her laptop as if she's about to give a lecture. "Listen, I've been looking into what's best to do, given our changed circumstances, and I've come up with a great solution."

"But, Mom, I've already told you the solution; you tell Grandma the truth. You missed your chance the other day, but it's still not too late. She loves me; she'll keep our secret," I say confidently.

Mom gives an exasperated sigh. "I'm not going through this again with you, Lucy. You don't know Grandma like I do. Of course she loves you, but that won't be enough to keep her mouth shut. She'll be horrified; she'll think we've played God by keeping you alive like this. She'll believe she has some kind of moral duty to tell her pastor, and before we know it, we'll have the police knocking on our door again."

"Well, she already knows that I'm using the identity of a dead girl; she'll want to tell the police about that, won't she?" I stare Mom down.

"But she won't. She doesn't want to lose me. She still thinks I'll 'come to my senses'." Mom looks agitated.

"If 'Renee' stays, you know that Makayla's family and your mother won't let this drop," Dad warns as he struggles to sit up straight. "You're the one who pushed for all this, Gemma. I told you we shouldn't send her back to Bailey Heights, surrounded by everyone she knows. You think you're so smart, setting everything up, getting stories straight, but this was never going to work. You weren't dealing with a robot that you could program to play the role; this is our daughter who you've traumatized and then brought home, expecting her to go along with all these lies." His face twists as he spits out the bitter words.

"Shut up, Lewis! I'm not wasting my breath arguing with you. I'm too busy figuring things out. We're going to make a fresh start. This is what I came to talk about. We're going to move." Mom's face is lit up with determination.

"No way! I want to stay here with people I know," I panic. The thought of running away is too much.

"How can you stay here?" Mom snaps at me. "You need a reality check, young lady – Makayla despises you and will never talk to you again. You can't go back to Bailey Heights, and even if you could, the kids at school have turned on you and Grandma thinks that you're some kind of evil con artist who's going to kill us in our beds. There's no reason for you to stay here. There's no one here for you now."

I know that she's right. Her words make me feel sick.

"I can't move from Houston," Dad says angrily. "What do you expect me to do about my work?"

"You don't need to live here to be able to do your work. You can manage the firm with a laptop and Skype. If you have essential meetings, then you can fly out for them."

Mom's eyes are bugging out, she's speaking too fast ... she could crack any second.

"Stop pretending it's that easy, Gemma. My HQ is here. Most of my staff are here," Dad protests.

"Are you determined to undermine me, Lewis? Think positive. I've found us the most glorious house in New York State and a wonderful school for you, Lucy. It's very prestigious. They get the most astounding results." She thrusts the laptop under our noses.

"What? You'd leave Grandma?" I ask incredulously.

Mom's sparkle vanishes; her pitch rises. "There's no other way. I'd stay in touch; come visit, of course. She'll forgive me ... eventually."

"And what am I supposed to do? Be the new girl again. Try to make a bunch of new people like me?"

"Don't worry about it, honey; it's easy for someone like you." She cups my face in her hands.

Someone like you; I know what she means and it hurts.

"Lucy, you've just done it once so you can do it again. You'll join the cheer squad, make lots of great friends." Her expression is manic.

I pull away from her, swallowing the lump in my throat. "I don't know whether I want that."

"Well, of course you do. Who wouldn't?" Mom gives a confused smile.

"Mom, I know that you prefer Renee to me," I say, sadly, "but I don't think that I can be the person you want me to be."

"What on earth are you talking about?"

"You've been so different with me since the transplant; you've been happier, more fun, because the surgery gave you what you always wanted: a beautiful daughter, a cheerleader, someone that you could be proud of and show off to the world."

"Lucy! How could you even think that? I don't ever want to hear such talk from you again." Mom flushes with anger, or is it shame?

"Don't you miss me at all?" I say quietly.

She lets out an exasperated sigh. "Why would I miss you when you're right here?"

"I mean the daughter you gave birth to, that you watched grow up." I scrutinize her expression.

She hesitates for a second before gathering herself. "Listen, if I want to remember you as a little girl then I can sit watching home videos like your father." She gestures at him dismissively. "But I'm more interested in the here and now and our future."

"But what about the girl I was less than a year ago?"

"You're still that girl, Lucy, but if you're asking me if I miss the torture of watching you dying, wishing I could swap places with you to take the agony away, then no, I don't miss *that* girl. Do you understand? I don't miss the body that failed you. I'm glad it's gone and you should be too."

I bite my lip. I will not cry. This is typical of my mother the lawyer; she's so good at making everything sound right.

"We can't move anyway," I fight back. "You know that Arthur can't travel."

Mom starts fiddling with the laptop. She's not looking at me. "Let's not get sidetracked by Arthur."

"No," I say. "We talk about him, now!"

Mom puts the laptop down, avoiding my eyes. "It may be for the best if Arthur stays here, anyway. He has been so unhappy. He doesn't know you, Lucy. It's not your fault, but you know that he's scared of you. It's not fair to him. Living with us . . . with you, distresses him. Now that we're moving, it's the right time to let him go."

"What do you mean 'let him go'?" I rasp.

"I mean that we'll find him a good home. With people that he can live out his days with in happiness. I know it's hard for you, but it's what's best for Arthur. It would be cruel to take him with us."

"No! You're not getting rid of my dog. He's the only thing I've got left. I can make him understand who I am. He'll learn to love me again," I say desperately.

She shakes her head and says softly, "Lucy, you've been trying for so long. It's not going to happen, but I promise you that once we're settled in the new place you can choose the cutest pup ever born."

"Do you think that everyone can be replaced?" I spit.

"How can you say that to me when I've risked everything to keep you alive?" She looks at me, disgusted that I'm so ungrateful.

"You did that for yourself, not me!" I cry. "I'm not moving. You're not taking me away from everything I grew up with and you're not getting rid of my dog or you'll wake up one morning and me and Arthur will be gone and you'll never see us again."

"Don't threaten me, young lady," Mom says, her anger boiling over. "I'm the only one in this family who is thinking straight. I'm not talking to you while you're being so irrational." She picks up her laptop and marches up the steps. As soon as she's clear of the basement, she must get a signal because her cell rings immediately. I hear her grumble, "God, I bet this is Mama again."

I race out of the basement and into the hallway with Dad following unsteadily behind.

"Mom, if it's Grandma you should talk to her. She's worried about you. Tell her the truth," I plead.

"I know how to handle your grandma." Mom lifts the cell out of her pocket, rolling her eyes at the screen. "It's Monica. I wish that she'd just leave me alone. Keep quiet, I don't want her hearing your voice. . . Monica," she says too cheerfully, "lovely to hear from you."

I see Mom's body go rigid as she listens. "No!" Her voice rises. "She's been fine. That can't be right." Her eyes are like saucers. "Let me speak to her! Let me speak to her," she whimpers into the cell.

"Gemma, give me the phone." Dad prics it from her iron grip. "Monica, what happened?"

Mom stands, frozen, whispering into the air in disbelief, "She says that my mama is dead."

CHAPTER 33

THE FUNERAL

From my bedroom balcony I see the funeral car coming up the driveway. I run downstairs to beg Mom and Dad again.

"*Please* let me go with you. I'll hide at the back of the chapel, out of the way. People won't even notice that I'm there."

"You've got to stop asking, Lucy. Your mom is in a bad way. Don't make it even worse for her," Dad says grimly. He looks washed out; dark rings circle his eyes. "You know we can't turn up to the funeral with you."

"I know that people blame me," I say tearfully. "They see that Mom chose Renee over her own mother and they think Grandma died of a broken heart."

"Don't be so melodramatic. She was an old woman who had a heart attack; there's nothing else to it," Dad replies unconvincingly.

Mom appears in the hallway. She looks frail; her black funeral clothes have drained any color from her face.

"Mom, you've got to let me say goodbye to Grandma," I plead.

"You can't, honey . . . not today. In a few days we'll visit her grave together. I promise." Her face crumples but she hurries into the limousine, not wanting me to see her cry.

"We'll be back by six." Dad kisses my cheek. "None of this is your fault . . . none of it."

I wait until the car disappears down the driveway before going upstairs and rifling through Mom's closet.

There's no way I'm going to stay at home. She's my grandma; I'm not going to let them stop me being there for her. I have to see her one last time – to tell her how sorry I am.

I pick out one of Mom's dark pantsuits that she used to wear for work. It's only slightly too long for me, but not so people would notice. On the shelf I find a wide-brimmed black hat. I pin my wig up to conceal it. I look in Mom's full-length mirror and pull the hat's brim down to shield my eyes. No one will look twice at me; I'm just another mourner.

I go down into my den and find a pack of playing cards. I pull out four aces, four kings and one jack. All those times Grandma tried to teach me and Mak to play bridge she'd laugh and say that if she ever got this exact hand, she could die happy. It was her little joke, but I want her to know that I remembered and that I'll *always* remember the times we spent together.

I call a cab and wait outside the gates.

The cab drops me a little way from the chapel on the

265

hill. A crowd of people are making their way inside. I slide in behind them and take a seat at the back of the flower-filled chapel. It's hot outside, but in the stone church, there's a chill in the air. The place is full. It fills me with warmth to see how many people are here; to see how many lives Grandma touched. I crane my neck to look over the rows of heads and hats. I glimpse the raised, open coffin in front of the altar. Knowing that Grandma's body is lying in there makes me shiver, but the thought of her being put in the ground without me seeing her is unbearable.

The elderly ladies next to me are speaking in hushed voices.

"Poor Charlotte never got over young Lucy's death," one says, looking tearful.

"But what was Gemma thinking, bringing that girl into her home? That didn't help. That didn't help one bit," the other replies. I want to scream at them to shut up. My guilt is already suffocating.

"Come on now, Amelia, we've got to be understanding of Gemma. I can't imagine how she feels losing her daughter and now her mama within a year of each other."

"Shush now, they're here," the other lady says.

I look over my shoulder and see the pastor process solemnly down the aisle with Mom and Dad following. Everyone watches as they take their places in the front row. Rousing hymns are belted out by the congregation and friend after friend takes to the pulpit to read out Grandma's favorite scripture with passion and conviction – Grandma would approve. The pastor delivers a heartfelt eulogy about his friend and her great faith.

"But there is no doubt in my mind," the pastor continues, "that Charlotte will be blissfully happy and at peace, now that she is reunited with her beloved granddaughter in God's mighty kingdom."

I screw up my face to hold back the tears but they come like a dam bursting. The old lady next to me wraps her arm around my waist.

"It's all right," she whispers. "You just let it all out." She hands me a handkerchief and I nod my thanks, bowing my head.

As the pastor invites us to say a last goodbye to Grandma I watch as, row by row, the congregation process in front of the coffin. Some people start to cry, some just silently pray, others lean in and touch her. I see Mak and her family linger at the coffin, arms linked, before slowly returning to their seats. As my row is ushered down the aisle, I keep my head bowed. I don't know whether I'm being paranoid but, as I pass Mak, I feel her eyes burning into me. I brush past Mom but she's too engrossed in grief to notice and Dad just stares straight ahead as if he's in a trance.

I stand mesmerized by Grandma's body. Her wispy hair is like a spider's nest, gathered in a bun above her head. Thick make-up emphasizes every wrinkle and line on her gaunt face. Her eye sockets are sunken and even her nose appears thinner and pinched. A line of bright lipstick sits mockingly where her lips should be. She's wearing a long silk dress and high heels, as if she's intending to go to a ball. Her arms are crossed over her collapsed chest. A creeping blackness is spreading up her fingernails. With all life gone from her, this isn't my grandma any more.

I hear a polite cough from the person behind me. I've been standing here too long; people are noticing. I slide the playing cards out of my pocket and slip them down the inside of the coffin. I gently kiss her stone-cold forehead and move away.

As I walk back to my place Mak stands up, fury in her eyes. I panic as I see her rejoin the line and slip her hand into the coffin to look at the cards. She replaces them and turns to find me, her face covered in confusion. I've got to get out of here. I can't handle Mak's anger and accusations today. As Mom and Dad stand up to say goodbye to Grandma before the coffin lid is sealed, I slip out of the chapel. I call a cab as I scurry down the drive. My skin prickles with nerves as the minutes pass too slowly.

The sight of my cab turning into the cemetery calms me. I jump in, telling the driver my address. Only when we start to pull away do I feel safe from Mak. I peer out of the cab window to take a last look at the chapel on the hill and I see her again. Mak is walking down the cemetery drive, her face serious and animated, her arms gesticulating as she talks to a boy by her side. His head is bowed towards the ground as he walks, but his jet-black hair and wide shoulders are unmistakable. It's Ben! The boy who thought I was his sister. The boy Mak said she didn't really know. Why is *he* at Grandma's funeral?

I press my nose to the window but I let the cab speed

on. Right now I can't face Mak or the boy: I'd only end up causing a scene at Grandma's funeral. I feel so drained; my head is banging. I just want to get home.

I arrive back at the house and head to the utility room to see Arthur. I ache to cuddle with him. Just one little sign that he knows me and I'll be able to get through the rest of this horrendous day.

He's got his nose in his food bowl. I wave his leash at him, saying brightly, "Let's go for a walk, Arthur. Come on, let's chase the squirrels."

He looks up from his food and whimpers as if I'm about to beat him.

"Stupid dog!" I slam the door. I can't stand his rejection any more.

By the time I've gotten changed and remembered to take my meds for the tremors, it's five o'clock. The funeral will have finished. Grandma will be buried and people will be eating canapés and making small talk at the reception. I can't imagine how Mom must be feeling. It must be hell for her, knowing that she ignored all those calls from Grandma; that she threw her out of our house. Grandma might still be alive if it weren't for us.

I head to Mom's writing bureau in the library. I need some good writing paper, not the cheap lined stuff I've got upstairs. I'm going to write a letter to Grandma. I'm going to tell her how sorry I am. I'll take it to her grave tomorrow and bury it under the mound of earth that will be piled over her coffin.

The little key is stuck to the underside of the bureau. I've seen Mom get it from there a hundred times. I unlock it and pull down the ornate desktop that rests on two extending brass arms. Inside the bureau are piles of neatly stacked paperwork and drawers full of paper clips and staplers. In one of the drawers, I find a pad of thick light-blue writing paper. I pick up a pen and open the pad, revealing a crisp, fresh page. The pen glides over the paper like skates on ice.

Dear Grandma,

I want you to understand just how sorry I am that I wasn't brave enough to tell you the truth myself. I know that you would have been shocked, and you wouldn't have approved of what Mom and Dad did, but your love for us all would have overcome that. You would have loved me no matter what they did to keep me alive. I'm ashamed that we let you believe that I had died. All the lying and deceit robbed us of spending happy times together; instead, the stress I caused you as Renee has led to this. I beg for your forgiveness. If I could turn back time I would show my faith in you and tell you the truth.

I want you to know that my memories of you will always be of the most wonderful, strong woman who loved me just the way I was. Sleep well and in peace, Grandma.

I am, and always will be, your loving granddaughter, Lucy

I reread my letter. I need to try again. It's not right, too stiff and formal. I need to write from the heart.

As I lift the writing pad to tear out the page, a piece of dense white blotting paper flutters on to the desk. It's full of inky reverse writing from where it's been pressed down on a letter. Something about the shape of the impression makes me pay attention. It's hard to decipher and some of the words are smudged, but the last line jumps out at me.

Mike and Hazel

My heart begins to pound. I race up the stairs and hold the blotting paper in front of my dressing-table mirror – the words reveal themselves. My belly twists. I know instantly what it says.

CHAPTER 34

IT'S US

I tremble with rage as I unlock the dressing-table drawer. The fake letter from Amy's parents sits next to my old hairbrush. This drawer is meant to be for treasures, but I've been fed lies.

"How dare Mom do this to me. She let me think I knew you!" I hiss at **her** reflection in the mirror.

This letter made me believe in a girl named Amy who doesn't exist: a girl created by Mom to keep me quiet, to make me accept this body, to manipulate me... I freeze as the thought hits me. What about the morning after my party, when I told Mom about Ben; about him thinking I was his sister, Hayley? Mom didn't miss a beat before telling me it can't be anything to do with the donor because we have the *letter*; we have "Amy" and Amy doesn't have a brother...

My mind claws back every last detail of that conversation. Mom was so quick to lie to me. She tried to put me off asking

Mak about him. She was adamant that Ben was drunk and confused and that I should just forget about him. But she *knew* the letter was fake, so she must have known there was a possibility Ben was connected to the real donor. So what is it that she doesn't want me to find out?

I fumble for my cell and call Mak's number. I've got to speak to her. I need to meet Ben. He needs to explain to me why he's here.

"Hello," Mak answers.

"Makayla, it's Renee – please don't hang up," I say hurriedly. "I saw Ben with you at the funeral. Are you still together? Can we meet up?" I try to get it all out before she has a chance to cut me off.

There's the sound of muffled voices. She must have her hand over the receiver while she talks to someone else. Seconds pass and then she says, "Yes. Ben is with me. I agree, we need to talk. We're in Rocky Road Café in Montrose. Do you know it?"

"Sure." I feel sick with nerves. "I'll be about twenty minutes. You'll wait for me, won't you?"

"We'll be here," she says ominously.

My cab pulls up alongside the café. I spot them right away. They're sitting at one of the sidewalk tables under a red-and-white canopy, sipping Cokes and talking intently.

I approach them with my heart in my throat. Ben stands up as soon as he sees me. His brown eyes widen. He reaches out to me but then stops himself, letting his arms fall by his sides.

"Sit down," Mak orders. Both of them can't take their eyes off me. I shift in the chair, my mouth dry.

"Why did you put those playing cards in Mrs Kendal's coffin?" Mak's voice is full of curiosity rather than anger. I don't know how to answer. Mak is the only other person who knows the significance of those cards. If I tell her the truth she'll just think I'm a liar and walk away. "Did Mrs Burgess tell you about the bridge hand?" she asks sharply.

I shrug awkwardly, looking down at the table to avoid her burning stare. I've got to take control of this. I don't want to be interrogated by her; I came here to get answers.

"Ben, why did you think that I was your sister?" I ask in trepidation.

Ben's eyes fill with tears. "Because my sister is missing and you look the image of her, apart from your eyes and your hair color."

I feel the blood leaching from my skin at his words. I force myself to speak.

"When did she go missing?" I ask, my words shaky.

"Over a year ago, from Leeds; that's where I live in England. There was no reason for her to run away. She was happy . . . doing fine. The police haven't been that interested. They reckon that seventeen-year old girls who go missing from our estate have just run off with some bloke or other." He looks upset . . . angered.

"So how come you came all the way here to see me?" I ask, hanging on his every word.

"Someone sent me a YouTube clip called 'Buckaroo Babe' –

it was of you, right?" Ben stares at me unblinkingly.

I clasp my hands together, trying to appear calm. He's seen the video Tanya took of me being thrown off Moonshine.

"I showed it to the police and forced them to get in touch with the Houston authorities to have you checked out. Apparently, they sent a cop around to see you at your house. They told me that you weren't Hayley ... that you had ID and that you didn't even have brown eyes like my sister." He shakes his head despondently.

I feel woozy. I grip the table, trying to stop myself from falling forward. It wasn't Mak or Grandma who sent Officer Parnell to our house; it was Ben. They were checking that I wasn't Hayley ... a missing girl. Did Mom know this? Did Officer Parnell tell her? "What's wrong? You look sick." Mak's voice makes me straighten myself up. I've got to stay focused. I need to find out more.

"It's just a shock to know that the police were looking for a missing girl," I rasp, turning my gaze on Ben. "Why didn't you believe the police when they told you that I wasn't Hayley?"

He sighs deeply, putting his head in his hands. "I just couldn't let it go. I kept obsessing that this girl ... you, may have been wearing colored contacts and that the cops hadn't checked properly." His face twitches with stress. "I had to see for myself, but I wasn't thinking straight. I haven't slept properly since the day Hayley disappeared. I've spent too long feeling useless, helpless; telling my mum that I'd find her when there was nothing to go on. At your party I looked into your eyes hoping to see Hayley, but you didn't know who I was, you don't wear contacts . . . you don't even sound like my sister," he says, on the verge of crying.

"If you don't believe that I'm Hayley then why are you still here?" I ask gently.

"Because I've told him what you said to me in the graveyard," Mak says solemnly. "About being Lucy . . . about being given a body transplant. You told me that they took your brain and eyes and put them in another girl's body and then you told me it was all lies." She sounds like she still doesn't believe it, but then part of her must, otherwise why tell Ben?

Ben shoulders shake as tears roll down his face. "Listen to me – knowing that my sister is out there somewhere . . . in danger . . . suffering, is driving me insane, *so* insane that I'll follow *anything* that could lead me to her, no matter how crazy it sounds. So, I want you to *see* my sister, Hayley Turner, and then I need you to tell me whether what you said to Makayla in the graveyard is true." He holds his phone in front of my face.

I soak in the face that fills the screen. The pretty girl's image stares back at me, smiling and carefree. I know every inch of this face. I know the scar across the eyebrow, the slightly uneven white teeth, even the dimples in the cheeks. There's no doubt in my mind – it's **her** . . . it's me . . . it's us.

My breathing is like machine-gun fire as I'm transfixed by Hayley's photo. Terrifying questions shoot around my mind.

I stand up unsteadily, knocking the table and causing the Cokes to spill everywhere. "I've got to go," I mutter.

Mak and Ben bolt out of their chairs.

"No!" Ben exclaims, standing in my way. "You can't go. What is it? You've got to tell me!"

I can't tell him . . . not yet. There are too many questions I still need answering to understand what's happened . . . *how* it happened. I've got to talk to Mom and Dad. They need to tell me the truth. I've got to know how a missing girl's body ended up being used by Dr Leo . . . by me?

I skirt around Ben and start sprinting down the sidewalk, shouting back to him. "I *promise* that I'll talk to you, but not now . . . not yet."

CHAPTER 35

DRIVE

I turn the key in the front door and brace myself to confront Mom and Dad. The hallway is empty. The house is full of silence.

"Mom . . . Dad, are you home!" I call out, but only Arthur's barking from the utility room answers me.

My whole body is knotted with stress as I climb the stairs. I'm desperate to question Mom and Dad but I dread their answers.

I enter their bedroom and search in Mom's closet for my laptop. I know that she keeps it hidden in here. I feel the laptop's shape under Mom's pile of cashmere sweaters. I take it into my room, close the door and sit on the bed.

I close my eyes, just for a moment, brace myself and then type the words into the search engine: *Hayley Turner, missing, brother Ben Turner, Leeds, England*. I gnaw at my lip as a page of results appears. The top link is from the *Leeds*

Chronicle dated three months ago. The headline reads *No trace of local girl, Hayley. Desperate family appeal for any new information.* I click on it and her photo appears, taking my breath away. I notice how similar her brown eyes are to Ben's. How prettily her long jet-black hair frames her heart-shaped face. I touch my blonde wig, thinking of the mop of thick black hair beneath it. I fix my eyes on the article.

The family of seventeen-year-old Hayley Turner made another desperate plea today for any information on her whereabouts. Local girl Hayley went missing nine months ago after failing to return from a night out with friends in the city centre. No trace has been found of her since. Police have been unable to find any evidence of an abduction, but say that they cannot rule it out. Hayley's mother, Natalie Turner (38), and her brother, Ben Turner (18), made a tearful appeal for any fresh information. Natalie says, "We've never believed that Hayley would have disappeared without contacting us. She was happy girl who loved her home, family and friends. We are desperate for any leads that may help us find our lovely Hayley."

My hand is clasped over my mouth, my head shaking from side to side.

I breathe deeply, trying to stay in control, as I move on to a link for "Finding Hayley", a Facebook page run by Ben.

I read Ben's last post: *The US police have visited the girl in the "Buckaroo Babe" video and have concluded that it isn't Hayley. I can't believe it. I was sure it was her but please keep looking. Send me anything you see that might give me a lead. Please don't give up on Hayley. Thanks as always.*

My gaze is drawn to the title of YouTube clip posted on his page: "Hayley at the Regional Finals". I press play and suddenly Hayley is no longer just a photograph; she's in front of me, walking and talking, bursting with life and personality. She bounces to the end of the run-up. Look at her feet! I walk just like her; she moves like a ballerina. She sprints along and vaults over the horse with such power and fearlessness, landing with precision and elegance, her arms and body stretched and arched. A burst of applause rings out around the stadium; the judges' table hold up all 9.975s; she looks over at the camera and gives a cheeky wink, her brown eyes twinkling. The camera cuts to her mounting the beam and performing a faultless, gravity-defying routine of fluid beauty. She performs a double somersault to dismount and again the crowd responds, going wild as the judges hold up four 10s. Hayley punches the air and runs towards the lens, flinging her arms around the cameraman.

"How about that, Benny Boy?" Her voice is husky like mine, but her accent sounds like Ben's.

"God, you're going to be even more unbearable to live with," I hear Ben laugh.

The camera cuts to the medal ceremony. The filming becomes unsteady as Ben whoops and cheers as his sister takes first place on the podium, her smile a mile wide.

I can't stop my body writhing with sobs; tears splash on to the keyboard.

I grip the laptop, lecturing myself. I've got to keep reading. I need to find out as much as I can before Mom and Dad get back. I scroll down the page, my blurred eyes widening as I read a post from months ago.

> I'm still looking for any information about a clinic
> in the Yorkshire area that my sister was attending.
> Apparently, it was carrying out research into teenage
> health. If you were paid to undertake health tests, or
> were involved in any way, please get in touch.

A clinic in the Yorkshire area? Why does that sound familiar? I massage my forehead, trying to remember . . . I know where I've seen those words before. In the school computer room, reading through the results for Dr Radnor.

My fingers struggle to type in the new search, hitting the wrong keys in my panic: *Leonard Radnor MD, grant, UK, Yorkshire, clinic teenage health and neurological development.*

Two links appear. The first I've already seen on the school computer, the second is the home page for the clinic. It says that the "West Yorkshire Research Clinic for Adolescent Health is now closed". I click hastily on the other tabs on the home page. Under the list of staff it reads "Clinical Director Dr L. Radnor, professor of neurological surgery".

I stare at the screen in horror. My mouth opens but I can't make a sound.

"Renee, are you up there?" We're home!" Dad's voice shakes me up, cutting through the blankness of my shock.

Fury wells up in me. I grab the laptop. I pick up the letter and blotting paper from my dressing table, put them in my pocket and charge down the stairs to face them.

"Oh, honey," Mom says, looking alarmed. "Are you okay? I'm so sorry that you couldn't come to the funeral."

"Have you heard any more from Amy's parents?" I ask abruptly, my voice icy.

Mom looks taken aback for a second, but then she answers confidently. "Hazel and Mike, you mean? No, we won't hear anything else. We were lucky that Dr Radnor let us have that one letter."

"This letter?" I hold it up.

"Yes, that letter." She's looking at me nervously.

"So what's this?" I hold up the blotting paper. "I found it in your bureau, Mom."

"It looks like nonsense," Dad says wearily, taking his jacket off and loosening his black tie.

I can tell Mom recognizes it right away but she still tries to hold my gaze as she twists her wedding ring around her finger.

I turn on Dad. "Were you in on this? Did you know that *she* wrote this letter pretending it was from the donor's parents?"

Dad seems to suddenly realize what I'm talking about. His mouth twitches. "I'm so sorry, Lucy. Your mom only told me after you'd been given the letter. It was too late to do anything then."

"Lucy, you were desperate to know about the donor. I knew how much it would help you to have a name ... to feel a connection with her. I didn't see any harm. It made you feel so much better. Dr Radnor was furious with me when he found out at the clinic, but I made the right decision," she says without a flicker of guilt.

"And what other decisions have you made for my own good?" I lift the lid of the laptop and play the clip, holding it up to Mom.

Her hands fly to her mouth as she watches the video of Hayley in the gym.

"It's Hayley Turner, Mom, the girl whose body I was given. Look at her ... look how full of life she is."

Dad takes the laptop. He shakes his head sadly. "So this poor girl is your donor? How did you find out her name, Lucy?"

"Hayley's brother was at my party, checking if I was his sister."

"What?" Dad exclaims. "Why?"

I look across at Mom. She stands in silence, her eyes enormous.

"Ask Mom," I reply.

"Gemma, what's going on?" Dad asks, bemused.

I tear Mom's hands from her mouth. "Answer Dad! Did Officer Parnell tell you about Hayley? Have you known since then?" I demand.

She sinks into the armchair in the hallway, nodding her head slowly. "When I went outside with her, Officer Parnell showed me a photo and told me that she'd been asked to investigate a missing person case. I knew as soon as I saw her photo that she was your donor."

"What? The donor was a missing person? You've known about this for weeks and didn't tell us?" Dad says in disbelief.

"It was best you didn't know. It would only have caused stress and Lucy was making such great progress. I didn't even tell Dr Radnor the real reason the police stopped by," Mom replies weakly.

"Why not, Mom? Were you too scared that he'd tell you the truth of how a missing girl from England ended up as my donor?" I say accusingly.

"We can't jump to conclusions. None of this means that Dr Radnor had anything to do with Hayley going missing. It's more likely that he ended up using her body without knowing where she'd really come from." She sounds like a defense lawyer in a courtroom.

I shake my head at her. "You're wrong, Mom. Dr Radnor didn't just know where Hayley came from, he organized it."

"How can you say that? What proof have you got?" Mom says tensely.

"He set up a clinic in England that was supposed to be researching into teenagers' health. Hayley Turner was being paid to undergo tests there and then she disappeared. What do you think those tests were for, Mom?" I strain to keep my anger under control.

Her face is paper white; she doesn't reply.

"Dr Leo was testing teenagers in the UK to find the best

284

body to use for me. Poor Hayley must have been the one he chose. I can show you the clinic's web page. You'll see he's listed as the clinical director." I put the laptop in front of Mom but she won't look.

"No. There must be some other explanation. We can't be sure that you're right," she says desperately.

Dad looms in front of her, looking sickened. "But what were the chances of Radnor getting such a perfect donor at just the right time? Look me in the eye, Gemma, and tell me that hadn't crossed your mind."

"Shut up, Lewis! Shut up!" Mom snaps, pushing him out of her way.

"We never questioned Radnor properly about donors because the truth is, we didn't want to know; you were just so obsessed with getting a body; with keeping Lucy alive at any cost," Dad says to her, his voice full of self-loathing.

Mom rises up to face him. "At least I loved her enough to *want* to keep her alive. I practically had to force you to agree to the operation," she replies venomously.

Dad turns to me, blocking Mom out. "Lucy, just because I didn't want to put you through the transplant, it doesn't mean I don't love you just as much as your mom does. Maybe it shows I love you even more," he says passionately.

"How dare you, Lewis!" Mom bawls, her face twisted in rage.

I can't believe that they're arguing like this after what I've just told them. Can't they see what's important? Haven't they realized what we have to do now?

"Enough!" I shout, taking out my phone. "We just can't stand around talking about this. A girl has been killed. I'm calling the police. Let them arrest Radnor and investigate. Then you'll see that I'm right."

"No!" Mom lunges at me, knocking the phone out of my hand. It smashes against the marble floor.

"What are you doing?" I shout at her, flabbergasted.

"We can't have the police involved," Mom says, getting on her hands and knees to pick up the pieces of the broken cell.

"Mom, I know that it's been Grandma's funeral and that you're under a lot of stress, but we need to call the police about Radnor." I speak to her like I'm talking to a child.

"I'm sorry, Lucy. No!" She shakes her head. "Now please go up to your room and leave this to me."

I look at Dad for support but he seems stunned by it all. He sits down on the stairs, staring into the distance.

I don't know what's going on in Mom's head, but if they won't do the right thing then I will. I need to get out of here and call the police, but if I try and run Dad will catch me before I make it to the end of the drive... I glance at the keys to my new car, hanging from a hook by the front door. My heart is beating out of my chest as the idea grips me. I know it's dangerous but it's my best chance: I sprint over and lift the keys off the hook, pressing the button on the video intercom to open the driveway gates. I run outside to the carport and zap the BMW open. I fling myself into the driver's seat, locking all the doors with fumbling hands. Dad

286

rushes over, still looking dazed, trying to peer through the car window.

"Lucy, don't lock yourself in. Come back inside. We need to talk this through. We can make a decision together about what to do," he pleads.

I turn the key in the ignition and the engine fires up.

"For God's sake, get out of there. You're in shock."

I try to remember what I did when Dad let me drive around the parking lot. I take in the controls on the dash, the pedals, shifter, brake. My foot presses down on the gas, revving the engine. I can do this. It's just like driving a powerful go-kart.

"Lucy, open the door." Dad bangs on the window. "You'll get yourself killed!"

I keep revving as I put the car into reverse, lower the parking brake and rocket backwards. Dad throws himself out of the way. I swerve on to the lawn, churning up the grass as the wheels spin. I put it into drive and get on to the tarmac, but the steering wheel is so sensitive that every time I turn it the car swings from side to side.

I'm approaching the last bend too fast. I hit the brake and swerve, plowing through flower beds. I slow down and regain control, straighten up and get back on track.

I can see the towering iron gates, but instead of opening they're beginning to close. Dad must have pressed the gate button again. They swing in slowly. If I speed up, I can make it through.

My knuckles are white around the steering wheel as I

press the gas pedal to the floor and the car storms towards the narrowing gap. There's a vicious jolt as metal hits metal. The airbag explodes into my chest and face. The sides of the car squeal as they scrape along the jaws of the gate.

I'm dazed, but I keep pumping the gas pedal, willing us to break through. The car tries to inch forward; the hood buckles, steam rises from the engine, choking fumes flooding the inside. I pull at the door handles but they're clamped shut. The electrics won't work; I can't get the windows down. I've got to get air.

The windshield starts to crackle from the pressure of the gates. I shuffle into the center, lean back, and raise my legs so that the soles of my shoes are on the glass. I spread them out as wide as I can and kick and kick and kick! The windshield peels out from the frame, taking the fumes with it. I gasp in the fresh air, collapsing over the hot, hissing hood.

CHAPTER 36

DOING WHAT'S BEST

My eyes flicker open. I'm warm, wrapped up in bed. Shafts of daylight find their way into my bedroom through gaps in the drapes. I'm wearing fresh pajamas and I can smell the sweet scent of freesias that have been put in a vase on the bedside table.

As I lift my head off the pillow, the whole room spins. Slowly the trauma of yesterday filters through. My head pounds as I think about Hayley.

I need painkillers. I crawl out of bed to the bathroom. The cabinet mirror reflects back purple bruises on my forehead from the impact of the car airbag. I open the cabinet door. It's been cleared out: no painkillers, no drugs, no scissors, not even a razor. Is Mom worried that I'll try and overdose ... slit my wrists or something? Is that how she thinks I'll handle this? Doesn't she understand, I've got no intention of harming myself. Hayley's brother is looking for her, living in hope that she'll turn up alive. If I kill myself, Ben and his mom will never know what happened to her. I have to tell them, no matter how horrific it is for them, they need to know the truth and Radnor needs to be locked away forever.

I lean heavily on the furniture as I struggle to the door and turn the handle. The door doesn't budge.

"Hey! Hey! Open the door." I bang with my fists.

Footsteps run up the stairs. A key turns in the lock. The door opens and Mom and Dad stand grey-faced in the doorway.

"Get back into bed, Lucy," Mom orders.

"How dare you lock me in?" I growl.

"We've done it for your own good. You've been lucky; you could have been killed," Dad says.

"That was madness, Lucy. I don't know what you were thinking. Where were you going?" Mom asks earnestly.

"To tell the police about Radnor ... about Hayley."

"We can't let you do that." Mom tries to hold my hand, but I pull away in disgust. She can't be serious.

"Mom ... Dad, we should tell the police together." I speak slowly, trying to get through to them. "You've got to let Hayley's family know. Imagine if it was you, looking for me, not knowing if I'm alive or dead; it's unbearable. You owe it to that family to tell them the truth. And Radnor ... he's got to be arrested, now!"

Mom shakes her head, sadly. "Listen, Lucy, our hearts

go out to that poor girl's family, but telling the authorities won't bring her back; it'll just mean that they'll find about the transplant . . . about you."

I throw my arms up at her. "Don't you understand what Dr Radnor has done? He ran tests on Hayley like she was a lab rat. He abducted her from England and brought her to his clinic in El Paso for *me*. You do realize that Hayley would have been hidden in that clinic when I was there, dying. He probably kept her sedated while he continued to prepare her body for the transplant." I stare at Mom as I talk, desperate for her to see the evil Radnor has done. "He told us that the *donor* was brain-dead, but Hayley wasn't; she could have been alive right up to the moment he cut her skull open in that operating theater." I crumple on the bed as my mind plays out all the horror Hayley was put through.

Mom's face is tinged with green, her eyes watering. She rushes to the balcony doors and opens them, taking deep gulps of air. Dad walks to her side and puts his arm around her, whispering intensely. She nods as tears roll down her face.

"Your mom and I need a little time to think things through," Dad says, shakily.

"But there's nothing *to* think through. Call the police now!" I demand.

Silently he guides her out of the room and locks the door behind him. I'm appalled by them. If they need to think about this for even a second, I know that they'll just be convincing themselves that they can't go to the police.

I struggle on to the balcony and keep watch, hoping that someone will come by the house. After fifteen ... twenty minutes my throbbing head is struggling to concentrate, but then I spot Jim walking up from the stables. My heart leaps. He'll help me.

"Jim!" I shout as loud as I dare.

Jim sees me and walks up to below the balcony. His face is riddled with anxiety.

"Hi, Miss Renee. How are you feeling?"

"Jim, I need your help. They've locked me in the bedroom. Can you get me out? Can you call the police and tell them to come to the house?" I know I must sound crazy to him but I have to try.

Jim tips his hat back. "I don't think I can do that for you. You see, you need to rest; get better. Mr and Mrs Burgess are looking after you; doing what's best for you. That was a nasty business with the car. We don't want to see you getting hurt again."

"Please, Jim! I don't know what they've told you, but it's not true. I need to talk to the police." I want to look in control but my voice is shrill and my eyes must look wild with anxiety.

Jim swallows hard. "When you're feeling a little better maybe you'd like to come back to the stables? You don't need to touch the horses. You could just help me muck out. Would you like that?"

"They're holding me prisoner. Just get the police," I screech at him, losing it.

His tanned face flushes with embarrassment. He lowers the brim of his hat and disappears into the house. I wait anxiously, watching the door. A few minutes later he reappears outside the house. I call out to him manically, but he doesn't look up; he just keeps walking.

I rush to the bedroom door and bang on it again and again until my fists ache and my head is going to explode.

I hear the key turn and the door swings open. Dad enters carrying a tray of snacks and pills.

"Jim's worried about you," Dad says, putting the tray down. "We'd already told him how fragile you are. He doesn't want you trying to hurt yourself again."

"You can't do this!" I lash out at him but he grips me in a bear hug. I grunt as I fight against him, but he holds me until I'm too exhausted to struggle any more.

"That's enough!" Dad says firmly. "I've brought you some painkillers; you look like you need them. But you're going to have to promise to stay calm. Will you stay calm?"

I'm desperate to get rid of this headache ... to be able to think clearly. I nod and he releases me, my body sagging. Dad lifts me up into his arms like I'm a little girl. He gently places me back into bed and tucks the soft covers around me. He looks wiped out. There are deep lines on his forehead that I've never noticed before and dark shadows under his blue eyes. He passes me pills and a glass of water. "I've got your medication for the tremors as well. Come on, get them down your gullet."

I obey, relieved. Sighing deeply, he sinks on to the bed

next to me and takes my hand. Despite my fury it feels good to have his hand around mine.

"Lucy, I know that all this is shocking ... horrific, but we've got to get through it." His voice is becoming stronger as he speaks.

"Please tell me that you're going to the police," I say, already knowing the answer.

Dad strokes my hand, looking down at the bedclothes. "Your mom and I have thought through every scenario. You can't see it now, but there will come a day when everything will be better – but that won't happen if we tell the police about Hayley."

I flush with anger. "No! This is bullshit! How can you *not* tell them when you know what Radnor has done?"

"We've made our decision for your sake. The consequences of telling the police won't just mean that Radnor ends up in prison; your mom and I will end up there too, and that will leave you all alone, with no one to protect you. Doctors would want to study you. The media would hound you. We can't let that happen."

"I don't want you to go to prison and I don't want to be left alone, but don't you dare say that you're doing this for my sake," I spit.

Dad's eyes fill with tears. "It's not just you that we have to think about, Lucy. It's your mom. I know how angry you are with her, but everything that she's done has been out of love for you. If we tell the police about Radnor ... about Hayley, your mom will not be able to survive in prison. The thought of being separated from you, of leaving you unprotected – it will kill her."

I snatch my hand out of his. How dare he emotionally blackmail me, try to make me feel like Mom's life is in my hands.

"Lucy, please don't be angry with me. I'm just telling you the facts. If you don't care about what will happen to you or me, then please think about the consequences for Mom. You can either destroy her by telling the police or give this family a chance by keeping quiet and looking to the future. You decide."

I recoil as he kisses me on the cheek. "For now, the door stays locked, for your own safety. You just get some rest; everything is going to be fine."

CHAPTER 37

THE CALL

I turn the TV off and roll over on my bed, burying my face in the pillow. The sun is going down and I've been rushing to the balcony at every noise I hear outside, but no one has come to the house since I saw Jim this afternoon. Mom and Dad must be keeping people away. I wonder if Mak has tried to visit. She and Ben must be desperate to know what's going on after the way I took off at the café.

Mom and Dad have been taking turns to check up on me. They come in here, all soft voices and apologetic faces. They sit on the side of the bed and tell me that they know how difficult this is, but they have no choice. "Telling the police won't bring Hayley back, but it *will* destroy this family. I can't lose you after all we've been through." Mom keeps saying it like a mantra. Maybe she thinks that if she repeats it enough I'll be brainwashed into believing it.

I hear the sound of Mom's high heels coming up the

stairs. She's just on the other side of the door when her cell rings. She answers it, saying unsurely, "Makayla! It's good to hear from you."

My pulse starts racing. I scramble off the bed and put my ear to the door. I'm tempted to start shouting out, hoping that Mak hears me, but I bite my tongue, knowing that Mom would just end the call right away and then phone Mak back, making up some excuse. I need to keep quiet and try to listen.

"Well, no wonder you can't get through to her, Makayla. Renee's cell is broken. We're in the process of getting her a new one." Mom lies so effortlessly, but the knowledge that Mak has been trying to contact me fills me with hope.

"Really . . . well, I must say I'm a bit surprised that you've been trying to call, Renee. I didn't think you'd ever want to talk to her again after what she did to you," Mom says manipulatively.

There's a pause as Mak replies and then I hear Mom say, "Well, that's very forgiving of you. I'm sure she'll be pleased that you've decided to try and be friends."

I press my ear harder against the door, trying to steady my breathing. Mak obviously isn't telling Mom what she knows. Does this mean that Mak doesn't trust her?

"I'm afraid that you can't speak to her. Renee is asleep right now. She's got some *horrible* stomach bug." Mom sounds full of sympathy, but Mak isn't giving up.

"No, there's no point calling back tomorrow. I reckon she's going to be laid up for a few days with this thing. Why don't I get her to call you when she's feeling better?" Mom is speaking too quickly. She's trying to rush Mak off the phone, but Mak keeps talking.

"Thank you, Makayla." Mom's voice cracks. "It *was* a lovely service. I think Mama would have approved... Yes, I remember you and Lucy playing bridge with Mama. She used to love teaching you both." Mom's impatience is seeping through her tone.

Mom gives a fake laugh. "You weren't bad at all. It's a complicated game."

Mom can't restrain a frustrated sigh. "No, honey, I don't know what Mama's 'dream hand' was. I'm not a fan of bridge so Mama never bothered discussing it with me... Makayla? Makayla, are you still there?"

My hand tightens on the door handle; my belly flutters. Mak must have asked her about the bridge hand – the one I put in Grandma's coffin. She's checking if I got the information from Mom. I've got to shout out to Mak. I've got to let her know what they're doing to me.

I bang my fist on the bedroom door, hollering, "Mak, it's Lucy, you've got to help me!"

Immediately the key clicks in the lock and the bedroom door is shoved open, knocking me backwards on to the floor. Mom stands over me, looking infuriated. "Stop it, Lucy. Makayla didn't hear you. She'd already put the phone down on me. Now, why would she hang up on me like that?"

"How should I know?" I snarl at her, praying that Mak believes me now.

CHAPTER 38

THE OFFICE

The hands on the clock click to three a.m. The house is silent. I've slept fitfully but at least my head feels clear now. They've left my next dose of meds for the tremors on my bedside table with a glass of water. I swallow the pills and get out of bed, stretching my stiff limbs. I've been praying that Mak would have sent the police, but it's been hours since her call with Mom and no one has arrived. I can't just sit here and wait in the hope that Mak has contacted them. I have to do something. I get dressed in the dark, tightly tie the laces of my sneakers and lift a pair of leather gloves out of a drawer. They slip on to my hands like a second skin. I stroke the photo of me and Grandma on my dressing table. Opening the doors, I step out on to the balcony. The night is so clear, the inky sky is studded with bright stars.

I brace myself and climb over the balcony. Keeping ahold of the platform, I plant both feet on the sloping roof of the veranda. Stretching an arm across, I try to reach the drainpipe fastened to the wall. The fingertips of my gloves are tantalizingly close but I can't get a grip on it; letting go of the platform I make a lunge for the pipe. I miss, losing my balance, my feet slipping down the sharp slope. I hold in a shriek as I slide off the edge of the veranda roof, frantically snatching at the air. My hands find the gutter and I cling on to it, breathing heavily, regaining some control before I let myself drop to the ground, bending my knees and rolling on to my side to soften the impact. I anxiously watch the house for movement but it stares back at me, silently. Even Arthur hasn't woken up.

I creep around the side of the house and stand outside the window to Dad's office. Pressing my hands on the frame of the sash window I push up, breathing a deep sigh of relief as the window slides open. I climb into the office and sit at his desk, turning on the lamp and picking up the landline phone, my fingers hovering over the numbers. Once I hit those three digits, there'll be no going back. But that's what I want, isn't it? Dr Radnor needs to be locked away. Hayley's family need to know the truth.

I press nine ... one ... my fingers hesitate. My eyes are caught by the framed photo on the desk. It's me, Dad and Mom in Florida. We're in the ocean with our arms around each other. I'm deathly pale and bald but there's laughter all over our faces. In the middle of us, like another member of the family, is a dolphin, posing for the camera; his head out of the water, his mouth open in a massive smile. I love this photo. I never knew Dad kept it on his desk.

I don't know what to do. Making this call could send Mom and Dad to jail and leave me on my own. I suddenly feel jittery ... unsure. Can I really do this to my parents, to myself? It won't bring Hayley back, but it'll destroy my family – what Mom keeps saying is true, but what about Ben and *his* mom? How can I let their torture continue forever?

I'm getting flustered by my own indecision. I stand up too quickly and the swivel chair topples to the floor with a thud. I hear Arthur start to bark furiously outside the door. The padding of his paws on the wooden floors is loud as he speeds towards the office. He's right outside, growling. I try the handle even though I know that Dad always locks his office.

"Arthur, shush. It's Lucy. Be quiet, boy; it's only me," I whisper through the door.

My plea doesn't stop him. He starts scratching at the door, each bark like a foghorn. He'll wake Mom and Dad. They'll be down any second. I have to get out of here! I turn off the desk lamp and pick up the chair.

"What's wrong, Arthur?" Dad calls out from upstairs.

Adrenaline pumps through me as I climb out of the office window, shutting it quickly behind me, and race to the front of the house. My body aches as I begin to scale the drainpipe leading up to the veranda roof but as I climb I feel hands grab my legs and pull me down to the ground. Dad looms over me, his face heavy with sleep and lined with stress. "What the hell do you think you're doing?"

CHAPTER 39

TREMORS

They've kept me in my bedroom all day. I've been pacing the floor like a caged animal, trying to figure out how to get out of here now that they've locked the balcony doors. I keep daydreaming about the cops arriving at the house. Surely Mak would have called them? She must have enough doubts to ask them to come by and check things out. After all, she told Ben about me saying I was in another girl's body. She phoned and asked Mom about the bridge hand – somewhere, deep down, Mak must know what I told her in the graveyard is true. I have to believe that.

Mom came in this morning with pancakes, juice and a wholesome smile, like all this is perfectly normal.

"I wish you hadn't pulled that stunt last night, Lucy," she says, her lips pursed in disapproval.

"It wasn't a stunt," I reply with disdain. "I was trying to do the right thing because you won't."

"I am doing *the right thing*. Keeping our mouths shut is the right thing to do for you . . . my daughter. You're all I care about," she says, looking at me with no trace of guilt. "I won't have you taken from us. Without our protection, you'll be treated like some kind of . . . of. . ."

"Say it, Mom, say it!" I seethe. "Some kind of freak! That's what you mean, don't you?"

"Of course not! You're not a freak. You're still Lucy. We've always got to remember that this body you were given is just a shell."

"Come on, Mom," I bristle. "You of all people don't believe that. A body isn't just a shell. It's part of who you are, how you feel about yourself; how others see you, even how they treat you, and this will always be Hayley's body, not mine."

"But you still have *Lucy's* personality, *Lucy's* thoughts. They haven't changed," she insists.

"Who are you trying to kid? I don't know what my personality is any more. I'm not Lucy Burgess, I'm not Renee Wodehouse, I'm not Amy, I'm not Hayley Turner! What you've done to me has screwed up the only part of *Lucy* that was left." I feel my chest tightening.

Mom leans in, trying to wrap her arms around me. "Please don't say that, Lucy. I did this for you."

I shove her away. "No, Mom! You did it for yourself, because you weren't brave enough to let me die, and now look at the consequences. A girl has been murdered for me."

I watch her face twitch, as if she's going to break down,

but then she recovers, composing her features again, blocking out what I've said. She turns on her heel, saying shrilly, "Eat your pancakes before they go cold." She hurries out of the room, turning the key in the lock.

I've been watching out of the balcony window all day, but the only sign of life has been a van that drove up to the house a few hours ago. I banged on the window but it kept going. I bet Mom told them to park around the back where they can't see me.

When I put my ear to the bedroom door I can hear the sound of banging and drilling coming from downstairs. I can't figure out what they're doing. It's driving me insane not knowing what they're up to.

At lunchtime, Dad unlocked the door and brought me a bowl of spaghetti and my meds. At least he has the decency to look like crap; like this might actually be affecting him.

"Dad, what's happening downstairs?" I try to sound casual. I need to break through the barrier he's thrown up.

He doesn't answer.

"When are you going to let me out of here?" I ask, trying to make eye contact with him.

"Soon," he says quietly. He stands and watches me take my meds like he's a nurse on a psych ward. He leaves without saying another word, leaving me to imagine what the hell is going on downstairs.

I see the van leave just after five o'clock and minutes later Mom and Dad unlock the bedroom door.

"Come on, Lucy." Mom holds out a hand, which I ignore.

"Where are we going?" I ask nervously as I walk with them down the stairs, relieved to be out of my bedroom.

"Somewhere that you'll be more comfortable." She smiles, but I can see it doesn't reach her eyes.

A wave of panic washes over me. "Dad, what's going on?"

He isn't looking at me. A trickle of sweat runs down his face. We reach the bottom of the staircase and Mom gently puts her arm around my shoulders, shepherding me down the corridor. A couple of steps further and I see the basement door, but it looks different. Two heavy bolts have been added to it: one on the bottom and one at the top.

"No!" I turn to run but I feel Dad's arms grip me and lift me off my feet.

"Lucy. Everything's going to be okay," he says, carrying me down the basement steps as I kick and scream.

I thump him on the shoulder and he drops me on to the sofa like he's releasing a wild cat.

I look around frantically and notice them right away: two caged surveillance cameras, high up on opposite walls.

"Oh my God! You're going to keep me down here and watch me?" I gasp in disbelief.

"The cameras are only so we can see that you're safe. You'll only need to be in here until you come to your senses," Mom says, her voice unnaturally sweet.

"You really haven't thought this through, have you?" I hiss. "It's not going to look good for you when someone finds out that you've locked me in the basement."

"There's no one *to* find out. No one is looking for you,

Lucy." Her soft tone can't disguise her threat. I can't believe Mom is talking like this – she's scaring me.

"You're wrong," I fight back, jumping up from the sofa. "Mak knows that I told her the truth about the body transplant. She'll make the police come here and they'll find out everything. So, *you'd* better tell them before Mak does, or it will look even worse for you and Dad."

Mom stands back from me, clasping her hands together like she's about to deliver bad news. "I'm sorry, Lucy, but the police won't be coming. Monica phoned me. She told me that she's very concerned about Makayla," Mom says gravely.

"Why? Is she sick?" I garble, imagining my friend in pain . . . suffering.

"No . . . not physically, but Monica is worried that Makayla is having some kind of mental breakdown. You see, Monica had a call from the local police. The officer involved was concerned about a bizarre request that Makayla made, asking them to investigate a girl who, she claimed, may have had a body transplant."

I cover my face with my hands. Poor Mak. I *did* get through to her, but no one believes what she's saying.

"Monica is distraught," Mom says, solemnly. "She's going to get Makayla counselling to help her through the trauma of losing Lucy and the lies Renee told. She feels guilty that she didn't get Makayla the support she needed earlier."

I feel blood rushing to my head, making it pound. No one is coming to help me! What do I do?

I look pleadingly at Dad but he sits down heavily in the

armchair, running his hands down his grey face. "I'm sorry, Lucy."

Suddenly Mom's whole demeanor changes. Her face brightens as she starts to point out features around the room like she's selling me real estate. "You love this den," she enthuses. "You'll be very comfortable here. You've already got a nice bathroom. This sofa pulls out into a great bed. I've put my running machine in here for you. I had to take out the pool table, but you've got the home theater system of course, the game console, there's Dad's vinyl collection, and a whole lot of books."

"Why are you talking like this is some kind of treat for me?" I ask incredulously, but she just continues regardless.

"I'll bring your clothes down and your make-up. And how about I get us a foot spa? We could have pampering sessions together," she trills.

I throw my hands up in disbelief. "What planet are you on? I'm not going to have pampering sessions with you! You're keeping me a prisoner in a basement. Dad, you know that this is madness. Tell her . . . tell her!"

"It's only temporary, until you realize that it's best for you, and for us, to keep our mouths shut and get on with our lives." Dad's voice is weak and unsure. "You may think that you're doing the right thing, Lucy, but how can it be, when the consequences will be so devastating for this family?"

"You had better let me out of here now or you can forget about us being a *family*, because I'll never forgive you. I won't want to know you." I spit the words at him.

"You will," Mom says confidently, plumping a pillow on the sofa. "Because you'll realize that everything we do is out of love for you. We'll get through this and move on, you'll see. Now, why don't you put a movie on? We'll be back in an hour with your meds and some dinner."

They're frightening me; they really mean to go through with this. I charge at them, barging my way up the stairs, but Dad is right behind me. He pries my fingers off the handle and holds me back as they slip through the door and slam it shut. I hear the bolts being shot across. I bang my fists against the wood.

"Let me out of here!"

"We love you, baby. This is for your own good. Everything will be okay when you start thinking straight," Mom says calmly.

I look around for an escape route, but I know this basement so well. There's no way out except through that door. The frosted windows in the outside wall are far too high to reach and too narrow to get through. My whole body bubbles with fury. I wait a few minutes to give them time to get to their little spying room, wherever that is, then I pick up the Xbox and hold it to one on the cameras.

"Hey, are you looking? Watch this." I lift the Xbox above my head and fling it to the ground, smashing it to pieces. I listen for their footsteps running back to the basement to stop me, but there's none. I unplug the projector from the shelf and dance manically around the room with it before lobbing it at the camera. It smashes against the metal cage, leaving the camera untouched. I smile inwardly as I hear footsteps approaching.

I shout at the door. "I'll smash up everything in this room if you don't let me out of here, now!"

"Go ahead," Mom's voice calls from the other side. "But I'd advise you against it; you're going to get mighty bored down there with nothing to do. You need to calm down, Lucy, and start thinking about putting yourself first. It's too late to help Hayley, but you can still help yourself."

There's no clock in the basement but I have to take my meds every six hours and they've brought my pills six times, so I reckon it's been around thirty-six hours. I never knew time could drag like this. The air-conditioning has gone off. It's full of hot, stale air down here. I've had to change into shorts and a T-shirt. I've even taken my wig off to try to stay cool. I run my hands through the mop of soft jet-black hair that has been growing all this time. It's good to feel the scar etched into the back of my scalp like a halo; it reminds me of what Radnor has done to Hayley. It makes me more determined not to give in to Mom and Dad.

Mom brought down my clothes and even the photo of me and Grandma. I asked her if she'd turned the air-conditioning off. She answered that it was broken and that they were trying to get it fixed, but I think she's lying. She'd justify any tactics to make me give in and agree to keep quiet about Radnor. I can see it in her eyes; she truly believes that she's doing this for me, and nothing I can say will stop her.

But I just have to stay strong. I know I can't get help from outside. No one believes Mak, and Ben could be back in the UK by now, having decided that the transplant story was a sick fantasy. So, I'll just have to keep working on Dad and get through to him that this is madness and that he's got to do the right thing.

I'm sprawled on the sofa bed listening to *The River* full blast on the stereo when Dad comes down the stairs laden with food.

"Hey, it's good to hear the Boss." He smiles tightly. "I've been looking up dates for Springsteen's tour. It's not until next year but I'm going to get in early, get us a couple of great seats."

I bury my face in the sweaty mattress. How can he be so deluded?

"It's pepperoni pizza for dinner." He hands me my pills and a bottle of water. I swallow them down and snatch the pizza from him. He sits on the arm of the sofa and watches me eat, his face grim.

"I called Radnor," he says solemnly. "I had to know for sure. I've been clinging on to the hope that Radnor was somehow tricked into thinking Hayley was a legitimate donor."

I stiffen. "And what did he say?"

Dad swallows hard. "When I confronted him with what we know, he didn't deny it. His only response was that he has film of me and Mom in his office, looking at a photo of Hayley and going through her medical file. The date of the footage is *before* Hayley Turner went missing."

"So what does that mean?" I ask, confused.

"It means that Radnor staged the meeting so it looks like he's showing us Hayley for our approval. It looks like we're giving him the go-ahead to abduct her and use her as the transplant body. He'd planned it as insurance to make sure that he could keep us quiet if we ever found out the truth."

My insides shake – to think that I'd been in awe of Radnor; I thought he was my savior, but really, he's nothing but a monster. He'd planned this meticulously. Has he done it before? I picture the files in Radnor's drawer; all those photos of healthy-looking teenagers, all those pages of test results. I grab Dad's arms as I realize what they mean.

"There are others!"

"What others?"

"I found files on teenagers in Radnor's office. He told me that they were patients waiting for the transplant operation, but what if they're *victims*, not patients? What if he's got one of them in his clinic right now, preparing them to be the donor for that old woman, Elizabeth?" My belly lurches at the thought of it.

Dad presses his hands on his head, like he's in pain. "You don't know that. Those teenagers *could* be his patients," he says weakly. "He's already shut down his clinic in England, hasn't he? I'm sure he'll never do this again."

"Stop fooling yourself, Dad. You've got to tell the police." I'm pleading now.

"We can't," he mutters.

"But you've got to!" I beg, trying to make Dad meet my eyes as he bows his head.

"If Radnor shows them the footage, we won't be able to prove that we didn't know how he got Hayley. The police will see that we'd already paid him to perform an illegal operation; that we were willing to go to extremes to keep you alive. They'll be convinced by the footage. They'll think we're guilty."

"Well, maybe you *are* guilty," I seethe. "I heard what you said to Mom; it was all too convenient that Radnor could get you a perfect donor just at the right time. Is that what's been eating away at you, Dad, guilt? Is that the real reason that you found it so hard to look at me, because deep down you knew that you were looking at a murdered girl?"

"Please don't say that, Lucy," he winces. "We've got to focus on what's best for you now. If I go to the police about Radnor, it will mean that Mom and I won't just be sentenced for procuring an illegal operation, we'll up in prison as accessories to murder. We'd never see you again."

As he finishes speaking, "Hungry Heart" rings out joyfully from the stereo as if it's mocking me. I scramble to the turntable and scrape the needle across the record. Lifting it off, I smash the record against the table. I grab another of Dad's Springsteen records and pull it out of the sleeve, bending it over my knee until it snaps. I pick up another and another. His precious signed copies, his limited editions. I hurl them at him, making him duck and shield himself. I stamp on them and fling them against the wall, screaming at him. "I hate you! I hate you!"

Tears fill his eyes as he hurries out of the basement.

*

312

They'll be watching me, of course, but they haven't been down for hours. They're literally leaving me to sweat. They're giving me time to worry about what would happen to us all if I told the police. They want me to dwell on the fact that no one knows I'm down here. No one's even looking for me. I have no friends and no family but them. If I want to get out, my only option is to do as they say: forget about Hayley and telling her family, forget about those other teenagers in his files, forget about stopping Radnor. Just learn to lock away these vile things in the depths of my mind and concentrate on how I can live a fake, happy life.

I know my mom. I know how terrifyingly determined she is. I absolutely believe that she plans to keep me locked in here for as long as it takes. She's used to getting what she wants; after all, Mom is the woman who wouldn't even let death win. She wants me to think that I'm powerless, but she's wrong: I hold the ultimate power; I just have to be strong enough to use it.

The hours pass like I'm wading through molasses. I hear the scrape of the bolts being released and Mom appears at the top of the stairs. It's finally time for my meds.

She ignores the floor littered with smashed records, empty water bottles and clothes.

"Look, honey, I've brought you a bottle of Coke and some chocolate bars." She holds out her palmful of pills. "Here you go."

I lurch at her, lashing out at her hand, sending the pills flying into the air. I grind each one into the floor with my bare feet; it hurts but it feels good to finally be taking control.

"That was silly, wasn't it? I'll just go get some more." Her tone makes me grit my teeth. It's the same one she'd use when I was lying in the clinic bed waiting to die, helpless and completely dependent on her.

I pace the floor waiting for her and a few minutes later she returns with another five pills.

"Now, in case you were planning to destroy this dose as well, I should warn you that the supply Dr Radnor gave us will run out in about a week. We're reliant on him to send us more, so in the meantime, I'd advise you not to waste any."

I take them from her.

"Good girl," she coos.

I stride into the bathroom and drop the pills down the toilet, then flush.

Her face clouds with anger. I can see her straining to keep control.

"I won't be taking any medication until you let me out of here and we tell the police about Hayley and Radnor." I say it with authority. She needs to know that I mean it.

She stares at me, irritated. "Okay, Lucy, if that's how you want to play this, it's fine by me. We'll see if you still feel the same when the tremors start and won't stop." She whips around and marches out.

I take a cold shower to try to cool down. I'm tired and edgy, paranoid that every twitch is the tremors coming. They're all I can think about – when will they start, how bad will they get? Radnor said that without the meds my condition will deteriorate, but what will actually happen to me? I know that Mom will be watching, waiting for the tremors to start; waiting for me to call out for the pills. I can't give in.

I need to keep my mind occupied to stop obsessing about the tremors. I skim the shelves full of books in a corner of the basement. There are thrillers, romance, fantasy, but I find myself drawn to the shelf of picture books. They're curled at the corners from being read so many times. Mom has written my name inside a few of them and, in others, I've written my name myself in big, baby letters. I take the whole pile and flop on to the sofa bed, leafing through one story after the other with their smile-inducing pictures and comforting, familiar words. *The Very Hungry Caterpillar, The Tiger Who Came to Tea, The Cat in the Hat, Where the Wild Things Are.* They feel like a loving hug. I lie back and drift away with Max as we sail to the Wild Things' island; nothing can touch me there...

I wake with a gasp. My body is on fire, pins and needles burning up and down my arms and across my chest. The sofa bed is trembling, the springs clanging. My arms are bang, bang, banging on the mattress. I can't stop them. They don't obey me. My T-shirt and shorts cling to me. The sheet is cold and damp, tangled around my legs. A sharp smell shoots up my nose. Oh, God – it's pee. I'm lying on a pee-soaked mattress! I roll off the bed in disgust, collapsing on the floor. My arms whack against the hard ground, making my shoulders judder and jaw clench with pain. I try to trap my arms beneath me but I have no control over them. When is it going to stop? The hand tremors never lasted this long. It's terrifying, but I don't want to shout out for Mom and Dad. I have to get through this. It can't go on much longer, can it? Tears roll down my face as I grit my teeth, praying for it to end.

The door opens. Mom and Dad rocket down the stairs. Dad sweeps me up, holding me tightly. My body batters against him as he squeezes hard, cradling my head into his shoulder.

Mom lifts the pills to my mouth urgently. "Take them, Lucy. It's the only way to stop this."

"Phone . . . police," I stutter through chattering teeth.

She hesitates for a second, fighting her instincts, and then she replies. "You know that I can't."

"But Gemma." Dad sounds distressed. "Look at her."

"I won't have her taken away from us, Lewis. How can we protect her if we're in prison?" Her voice quivers.

"Please, Lucy, take the pills," Dad pleads, grabbing them from Mom and holding them to my lips.

"No!" I splutter.

Mom steps back, her eyes fixed on the ground.

I don't know how long me and Dad have been locked together, but I sense a change coming over my body. The shaking calms down to jerks and then stops. I slump into Dad's chest, exhausted. He holds me up and carries me to the armchair.

"You're okay." He strokes my arm. "It's over."

"It's over for *now*," Mom says bitingly. "This is only the start, Lucy. The condition will get a lot worse if you don't take the pills."

My head lolls. I can barely keep my eyes open.

Mom feels the bed and starts to strip the sheets. "You lost control of your bladder. What else is going to happen to your body without the medication?" she says tensely. "Lewis, carry Lucy into the bathroom and I'll come help her shower."

"Don't touch me. Get out," I rasp.

"At least let me change the bedding," Mom pleads.

"Leave it," I mumble.

Mom's face twitches with anxiety as she stares me down. "Last chance, Lucy. Take your meds."

I give her the finger.

"Let's go, Lewis," she snaps.

"What? You're going to leave her like this?" Dad strokes my cheek tenderly.

"It's Lucy's choice. We've got to be strong, Lewis. We're doing this for the good of her and her future. We'll be here to look after her the moment she lets us. One day she'll thank us for this."

My body creaks as I wake up in the armchair. The inside of my mouth feels like the bottom of a dumpster. I wipe dribble from my chin and roll my head, trying to loosen my stiff neck. My clothes are rigid with stale pee. I stink. I peel myself off the chair and inspect my arms; they're covered in bruises from thrashing on the ground. How long have I been asleep?

I have no idea what time of day it is, but my belly grumbles with hunger. I grab the bottle off the floor and gulp the warm water down my dry throat. There are chocolates and cookies on the table. I shovel them into my mouth.

I shuffle to the center of the room and address the cameras. "Are you watching, Mom? Whatever happens to me next you'd better believe that I'm not giving in, so do yourself a favor and call the police right now."

There's a rumbling noise and beautiful cool air from the air-conditioning begins to blast around the tropical room. Has it just been fixed, or is Mom weakening? This small triumph brings a smile to my face.

I get showered and changed. I'm determined to appear in control for the cameras. I won't let them see my growing terror at the thought of the next attack.

My face twists in contempt as Mom walks down the basement stairs carrying a tray of food. I wonder how long can she keep this up when she looks so frail and exhausted.

"You've slept a long time. How are you feeling, Lucy?" she says sweetly.

"I've never felt better. It's just like one long vacation down here." I give her a vicious smile.

"It was terrible to see you like that yesterday." Her voice is thick with guilt.

"Yeah, but not terrible enough for you to call the cops about Radnor. Are you going to wait until I actually die? Is that your plan, to watch me die rather than do the right thing?"

She sighs, choosing to ignore my question. "Do you want to play cards? There's a pack in the cupboard over there."

I'm about to tell her to get lost, but I hold my tongue. "Okay; will you go get them?"

"Sure," she says, looking delighted.

I wait for her to walk to the other end of the room before I fly up the stairs, shutting the door behind me and shooting the bolts across. I hear her racing towards the door. She bangs on it, roaring out, "Lewis! Lewis! Stop Lucy. She got out of the room."

My eyes dart around the hallway and up the stairs, on the lookout for Dad. I reach the front door. It's locked. I run through the kitchen. They've locked the back door too and there's no key hanging up in its usual place. I can still hear Mom shouting as I sprint into the living room and grab the handle of a window. It won't turn. I try another, then another, banging my fist on the glass. It's like the whole house is in lockdown.

Dad barrels into the room. "Lucy, give me your hand. Let's go back to your den."

"It's not a den, it's a prison," I shout.

"It won't be for long. When you accept that we can't tell anyone about Radnor, we can put all this terrible business behind us."

"What happened to you, Dad? When did you become such a coward?" I'm overwhelmed by sadness. "Why are you letting Mom do this to me?"

"We're just protecting you. You're not thinking straight.

You've got to understand the consequences for you of telling the police." He corners me as I try to run left and then right. I cry out as he grabs my bruised arm. "I'm sorry . . . I'm sorry," he whimpers as he pulls me along.

He opens the basement door and shepherds me down the steps. Mom's face is like thunder. She walks past me and leaves without saying a word.

"I got you a new mattress," Dad says, desperate to make amends.

"Another mattress to pee on, you really are the *best*, Dad," I mock, bitterly.

He blushes. "We don't want you to suffer, Lucy. You can stop this right now if you choose to."

"Ditto," I scowl.

It could have been an hour, maybe two, since Dad brought down the new mattress. It's got a plastic protector on it, the kind they had on the bed in the clinic in case of "accidents". The boredom is driving me crazy. I can't relax. Every minute I'm waiting for the next attack, but in a perverse way I want it to come. Mom won't be able to stand watching me go through another trauma like that. When it comes, she'll give in. I repeat it over and over again to keep myself strong – when it comes, she'll give in.

I empty the deck of cards on to the table, letting my thoughts wander to Grandma. Grandma always tried to do the right thing. If she were here she'd tell Mom that she's ashamed of what she's doing; that Mom has lost her sense of what's right and wrong. Mom has backed herself into a corner and taken Dad with her. *Come on, Lucy. Keep busy. Keep focused.* I attempt to make a five-story tower. It keeps collapsing, but I don't mind. I've got all the time in the world, I think bitterly.

I've completed the fourth story of the tower. I try not to make any sudden movements as I place the final card on top but my hand starts to quiver, bringing the tower tumbling down. Oh, God, it's happening again. I breathe deeply, trying to keep calm, but I can feel the tremors rapidly building into full-blown shaking. My head is thrown back as my whole body goes rigid. There's a terrifying pressure behind my eyeballs like they're going to be pushed out. I squeeze them shut, begging for it to stop . . . my body goes limp and I cling to the chair, panting. It feels like snot is running out of my nose but I taste the blood on my lips. It flows off my chin and on to the duvet that's wrapped around me. The pressure behind my eyes eases. In the deathly silence, I to listen to my body, trying to pick up any sign of a tremor. Eventually my shoulders relax. I slump forward and hold the bridge of my nose to stop the blood flow.

I hear the clatter of Mom and Dad hurrying into the basement.

"Thank God it's finished," Dad is saying to Mom.

But I sense it rising again, like a storm rolling in. I stare at them helplessly as I'm thrown forward on to the ground. My body writhes, my head banging against the ground. Dad tries to pick me up but my flailing limbs hit out at him. He puts a pillow on the ground and eases my head on to it.

It feels like an eternity before my manic body wears itself out and comes to rest. I'm aware of Mom and Dad hovering over me as I lie on my back, exhausted, dazzled by the lights overhead.

I feel the wetness of Mom's tears falling on my face as she strokes my hair. "Please stop this, Lucy. No more."

She takes the meds out of her pocket and cradles me in her arms.

"Do you understand how dangerous it is for you? Take them, baby."

I stare at them longingly – five pastel-colored magic pills that will make all this stop. The feeling of that pressure behind my eyes was terrifying. A choking fear grips me – I don't know whether I can take another attack.

"Go on, Lucy, please take your pills," Dad begs.

I summon all my energy. "Call the police first," I whisper.

Mom lets out an anguished cry. "Enough! Lewis, hold her down."

"No, Gemma." He sounds shocked.

"She's got to have them. Pass me the water. Hold her head steady," she orders, her nostrils flared.

"But what about next time and the time after that? We can't force-feed her pills every six hours." Dad takes Mom's arms, trying to reason with her.

"If that's what it takes then we'll do it." She pulls out of his grip and opens the palm of her hand containing the pills.

"We can't!" He says it less forcefully as he stares at me. I must be a shocking sight, lying on the ground, battered and helpless.

"Now is not the time to have doubts, Lewis. Do you literally want to sit and watch your daughter kill herself?"

Dad's eyes swim with tears as his hands press hard on either side of my head.

"Okay, open your mouth, Lucy." Mom's face looms down at me.

I clamp my mouth shut. My face twitches with rage. She grips my bottom lip and yanks it down. I grit my teeth together, trying to pull away, but Dad's hands press harder.

I elbow her in the stomach, sending her toppling backwards.

"Pin her arms down," she rasps.

One of Dad's arms locks across my arms and chest; the other holds my head into his shoulder.

She comes at me again, but I kick out at her. She sits on me, her hands all over my mouth. I snap at her, latching on to her little finger. I bite down, drawing blood. She shrieks. Her hand whips through the air and slaps my face. My mouth opens in shock, releasing her finger. Mom's features screw up as she pulls my nose up and pushes down my bottom lip until I can't keep my teeth clenched any longer. As soon as my teeth part she stuffs in the pills, followed by a cascade of water from the bottle. There's too many; they're stuck in my throat. She's clamping my mouth so that I have to swallow, but I can't. I'm choking. I'm drowning. I gag and gag. My eyes bulge, my face feels like it's going to explode. I can't breathe. I can't breathe!

"For God's sake, she's choking, Gemma!"

Dad releases my head and pushes Mom away from me. He thumps me on the back, sending the pills spewing out of my mouth on a wave of water.

I gasp for air, looking at Mom in horror. Her hand trembles over her mouth.

"I'm sorry, Lucy," she whimpers.

I scramble along the ground, getting away from her. She's crazy . . . dangerous. "You could have killed me," I splutter.

"I just want you to take your pills. I'm trying to stop you suffering," Mom sobs.

"We can't go on like this, Gemma." Dad's voice is shaking. There's silence. A moment of calm.

"You're right. We can't go on like this," Mom echoes.

What does she mean? Is she giving in? Have I won?

CHAPTER 40

THE ONLY ONE
WHO CAN HELP

I slump in the armchair, staring at the congealing fat on the burger and fries that Mom brought down hours ago. I can't eat it. I doubt I could even swallow it. My throat feels tight and my belly is mangled with tension. Why am I still down here? Why haven't they called the cops?

It feels like I've been trapped forever. I've got to stay strong, but I'm exhausted. I've had two more attacks and each time they're getting worse. Only Mom has come to see me, begging me to take the pills, but no Dad, no holding down, no force-feeding. Just Mom, her arms wrapped around herself as she watches me thrashing and shaking, my head ready to explode, blood streaming from my nose. How can they not give in when they see me like this?

I hear noises – muffled voices come through the door

at the top of the steps. I sit up, listening hard. It's not just Mom and Dad. There's another voice. Someone's with them. A cop? I shoot out of the chair, overwhelmed with relief. At last they've called the police!

But instead of a cop, I see *him*. Radnor marches down the steps in his expensive suit, coming towards me like he's in charge. The sight of him ignites fury in me. I run at him, throwing punches at his chest. I want to hurt him; I want to cause him pain after all he's done to me ... to Hayley.

He grapples with me and locks his arms around me, whispering in my ear, "It's okay, let it all out."

I bend my head back and I spit in his face. He releases me in disgust and wipes his cheek, holding my stare.

"How could you bring *him* here?" I bawl at Mom and Dad.

"What choice did we have, Lucy? Dr Radnor is the only one who can help us," Mom says, holding up her arms helplessly.

"He's a murderer!" I declare. "Don't let him touch me."

"We don't want him here either, but we're trying to save you," Dad replies, looking at Radnor with pure contempt.

"Sit down, please, Renee. Listen to me," Radnor says calmly.

"My name is Lucy ... it's always been Lucy!" I say, standing in front of him defiantly.

"Sorry ... Lucy. Look, I know that you can't understand what I did and that you want to go to the police, but you know how much I care about you and I'm here to help. It's upsetting to see you in this state." His face is a picture of concern, but I know it's fake. He only cares about me because I'm priceless to him: a living, breathing ad for his transplant operation.

"You murdered Hayley Turner. You used her body for me." I fight back tears. I won't cry in front of this monster.

"Believe me, I understand why you're appalled, but there was no other way of getting you the perfect donor. Time was running out for you and your parents were desperate."

"Don't use us as an excuse for what you did," Mom protests, her face flushing.

Radnor gives her a look of disdain. "You got what you wanted, didn't you?"

"And have you got another victim ready to use for that old woman I met at the clinic?" I ask, squaring up to him. "Those files of teenagers that I saw; they're not patients, you're going to use their bodies like you used Hayley." My belly twists at the thought of it.

"You've been kept down here too long. Your imagination is running wild." He shakes his head in disapproval, but he can't hide his lies from me.

"Have your rich old clients put in their orders? Age, hair color, no hereditary diseases, of course. Will you charge more for the pretty victims ... the handsome victims? I'm sure that none of your patients want to wake up ugly!" I say, scathingly.

"Lucy, this isn't some vain cosmetic industry. You better than anyone know that I can defeat death with my operation. What I've achieved is bigger than you or me or any individual. You need to think about all the lives that I can save."

"But you can't *take* a life to save a life," I cry. "I didn't want someone to be killed so that I could live."

"It won't always be like this," he says adamantly. "Humans have a primal desire to live for as long as possible – that's why, one day soon, society will be ready to embrace my incredible achievement and then the government could enforce the compulsory donation of brain-dead patients. Once that happens, Lucy, I'd have a rich supply and I wouldn't be forced to take extreme measures." He puts his hands on my shoulders but I shrug him off in disgust.

"*Extreme measures?* Is that what you call murder?" I can't believe that he's trying to justify what he's done.

"Look, I don't want to fight," he says gently. "I came here today because you need me."

"I don't need you!" I deny it violently.

"But you do, Lucy. As you've already experienced, if you stop taking the medication the impact is devastating. If you continue to refuse the pills, you'll deteriorate rapidly. You'll lose bodily functions, control of your bladder and bowels. Your coordination will be severely impaired. You'll suffer extreme headaches and dangerous pressure on your optic nerve that will eventually lead to a brain hemorrhage. What I'm saying is, if you keep refusing to take your medication you will die soon, and it will be a painful and distressing death."

His words rock me back on my heels. I feel for the armchair and sit down unsteadily. I know that he's not bluffing. I can feel the attacks getting worse each time, the pain becoming more and more unbearable.

"Now do you understand, Lucy? This isn't a game. You've got to stop," Mom begs. "Each time you have an attack you're playing with your life. The next attack or the one after that could kill you."

Radnor crouches down to me. "Your parents and I are in agreement. The only option is for you to come and stay at the clinic. There, I have all the medication you need to keep you healthy, to make sure that your life isn't under threat. You'll never have to experience these terrible effects again. Do you remember when you were first in the clinic and we spoke about the pain and the fear that you felt when you thought that you were dying? You can't put yourself through that again. You've come too far to give it all up now."

"We'll be with you, Lucy. Dr Radnor has said that I can move into the clinic. I'll be there for you every single day," Mom says with forced brightness.

"So you've already agreed that he can keep me a prisoner?" I look at Mom in disgust. How could they give me to him, knowing what he's done; what he is?

"You won't be a prisoner. You'll have lots of freedom. When you settle down, we'll go on shopping trips, to the movies, and it won't be forever. I promise," she pleads.

"Did you agree to this too, Dad?" I turn to him, my voice accusing.

He can't look at me. "I don't see what other choice we've got," he replies. "You've got to start taking your medication."

"You know why he's so desperate to stop me dying?" I say.

"Because you're my patient," Radnor replies, sounding so

329

sincere I wish I could believe him.

"No, it's because you think that I'm your creation and you want to parade me in front of all your clients who will pay you millions to help them cheat death."

"Don't ever say that, Lucy. You are not his creation. You are *my* daughter!" Mom says.

"What are you planning to do, *Dr Leo*?" I spit the name out with contempt. "See if I can get pregnant? Give birth to a healthy baby? Won't *that* be something for your clients to get excited about?" I look him straight in the eyes, but his expression is inscrutable.

"Stop this talk, Lucy. I'd never let him do anything like that to you," Dad says fiercely.

"Wake up, Dad! You're making deals with a man who has people murdered for his operations. He wouldn't think twice about using me and he wouldn't let you stop him."

Radnor stands up, looking exasperated. "You're being hysterical, Lucy. I'd never harm you. I'm here to offer you a future instead of death. So what do you say? Will you come to the clinic and let me help you?"

I try to stop the thought of dying overwhelming me. I have to think clearly . . . logically. Why do I even need Radnor? He isn't the only doctor in the country. I can get my medication from someone else. There's no need to go with him.

He looms over me, studying me like he's reading my mind. "You think that you can survive this without me. *You* think that another doctor can provide the medication to keep you alive. But you're wrong. No one else knows about the drugs that I've developed for your condition. You can't just go to a pharmacy or get a prescription." He shakes his head solemnly. "I'm sorry, Lucy, but if you don't come with me today, I swear that I'll destroy my entire supply of your medication; I'll shred and delete every note so, even if a pharmacist does figure out what you need, you'll be dead long before they can develop them."

"No." Dad's voice is desperate. "You can't destroy her medication. This isn't what we agreed to."

"Mr Burgess, I need to do everything possible to encourage Lucy to make the right decision. She must understand that she will die if she doesn't let me help her."

"Please say that you'll go to the clinic ... *please*, Lucy." Mom touches my arm, but I wrench it away, burying my head in my hands.

"I need you to think the situation through, Lucy." Radnor's voice is deep and smooth. "What would you achieve by informing the police and allowing yourself to die? Your parents will go to prison as well as losing their daughter, you will cause Hayley's family untold grief by telling them the truth, and yes, I might be locked up, but you'd have prevented me from saving the lives of countless other people in the future. How can that be the right thing to do?" His words worm their way into my mind. "I think that we should give Lucy some space to reflect on her decision now that she fully understands the consequences. I'll be back very soon, Lucy."

He leads Mom and Dad out of the basement. I shrink into the armchair, wrapping the bloodstained duvet around me. I look blankly around the den; this prison suddenly feels like a tomb.

CHAPTER 41

THE HOME VISIT

How long has it been since Radnor left me here to "reflect on my decision"? Ten minutes ... fifteen? Too long to spend with these terrible thoughts.

I look up at the surveillance cameras. Is he watching me, waiting for me to crack? I crouch in the armchair and pull the duvet over my head, hiding me from view, cocooned in the darkness. I won't give Radnor the satisfaction of watching my torment.

I want to be brave – do the right thing – but all I can think about is how I'll die. How many more attacks before the one that kills me? How long will the pain last when every second of it feels endless? My life is going to end with me thrashing around in agony, screaming in pain. Would it have been better if I'd died all those months ago? Then none of this would have happened.

I start to gently rock back and forth, trying to comfort

myself. I don't want to die!

But it's so easy to stop all this, isn't it? I just need to say yes to Radnor. But could I live with myself? Could I live with the guilt of letting Radnor get away with murder? But why *do* I feel guilty? It's not as if any of this is my fault. Mom and Dad are so sure that keeping our mouths shut is the right thing to do. If they can live with that decision, then why can't I? Maybe Radnor will keep his word. He won't touch me . . . use me. Maybe I could learn to shut out all of this horror and go on to live a happy life, never telling anyone about the transplant or Hayley.

I feel my body rocking faster. My hot, panting breath is stifling under the duvet.

And what if Radnor's telling the truth about those teenagers and they *are* just patients? Maybe no one else will be killed. Say Radnor is right – that only bad will come from telling the truth? What will happen to what he's achieved? His surgery could lead to so much good; give life back to dying kids; end so much misery and grief. Who am I to stop it? I don't want to die.

This isn't fair! It's not right! Why should I suffer? None of this is my fault! I've done nothing wrong. I don't want to die!

I throw off the duvet, gasping for air. My terrified voice booms around the den. "I don't want to die!"

Radnor appears on the stairs within seconds. "It's okay, Lucy. That's all you need to say. Let's get you to the clinic." He walks over with his arms outstretched.

I shrink back in the armchair, away from his touch. "I can't come," I whisper.

"If you don't want to die, then you *have* to come."

"I couldn't live with it." I stare through him, locked in my thoughts.

"With what?"

"Knowing that I'd betrayed Hayley and her family. Knowing that there'll be other victims. Every day I'd know that I could have stopped you, but instead I allowed this to carry on. I'd be in hell in here." I jab at my head. "I'd be trapped with the guilt forever."

He crouches down to me. "That's not true. It's a choice whether to feel guilty or not. You have to be mentally strong, Lucy. You can't change what happened and I promise that there won't be any more casualties." He's only inches away from me. Despite my repulsion for him, I can't help staring at his handsome, untroubled face, thinking about the hideousness it hides.

I pull away from him. "You lie as easily as you breathe," I say with venom.

"Lucy, we both deeply regret what had to happen to Hayley, but the best thing you can do for her is to live a happy and fulfilling life. You owe Hayley that."

I push myself out of the chair and stand to face him, my voice quaking. "I know exactly what I owe Hayley and that's why I won't be coming with you to the clinic. You were right – before the transplant, when I was terminal, I was terrified of dying, but I was trying to accept it because I thought that I didn't have a choice. Now you're giving me a choice between life and death and I'm still terrified, but I choose death rather than let you use me and Hayley. I won't let you murder anyone else for your operation. You will not stop Hayley's family knowing what happened to their daughter. I will die and when the police investigate, you'll be put in prison where you belong." I fight to stop myself shuddering at my own words. He has to know that I'm strong enough to go through with this.

He clenches his jaw; the warmth evaporates from his brown eyes. He doesn't argue with me. He doesn't beg. He just leaves without saying a word.

Time stands still as I lie on the hard floor. I feel myself slipping towards sleep when suddenly a noise cuts through my exhaustion. I sit up, woozy and disoriented, wiping a trail of saliva from my mouth. I look around the room, trying to figure out the direction of the sounds. They aren't coming from beyond the basement door; they're coming from outside the house. I strain harder, desperate for some sign of who it might be. The noises continue and I finally understand what it is. It's the sound of footsteps. People are walking outside the basement.

Adrenaline pumps through me as I scramble to my feet and scurry to the narrow frosted windows high up on the outside wall of the basement.

I start to call out as loud as I dare, terrified that Radnor might hear me.

"Is there someone there? Please! Help me! I'm locked up in the basement. Help me!"

I hold my breath as the sound of the footsteps stops. The light from the frosted glass is suddenly blocked out as a shape appears at the window. Someone is on their knees, trying to peer through.

"Hello?" she says in a hushed tone. "Is someone down there?"

I gasp with joy, relief flooding my body. It's Mak!

"Mak! Mak!" I have to stop myself from shouting. "It's me. I'm in the den. They've locked me in here."

"What the hell! Why have they locked you in?" I wince. Her voice is too loud.

"Mak, don't shout. They'll hear you," I plead. "Do they know that you're here?"

"No, I asked to see you but they wouldn't buzz me through the gates. I came around the back way, through the stables. I wanted to see you." My heart leaps at her words.

"Mak, call the police!" I hiss.

There's silence. What's she waiting for?

"Mak! Can you hear me? I know that you can't see through that glass, but I promise that they've got me locked up in here. You've got to call the police."

"How do I know that you're telling the truth?" Her voice has hardened. "You've told so many lies. My head is spinning trying to figure it out. I've already tried to get the police involved. I'm not calling them again until I know what's really happening here."

I massage my forehead, picturing how close I am to getting out of here . . . to stopping Radnor, if only Mak would believe me.

"Okay," I sigh. "Try the windows at the back of the house. One of them may be unlocked. Come into the den but *don't* let anyone see you. You can't trust Mr and Mrs Burgess, do you understand?"

She doesn't answer, but as the sound of footsteps fade, I hear her talking to someone . . . she's not alone!

I wait at the bottom of the basement steps, grinding my teeth. Minutes pass like hours. It's been too long. She must not have managed to get into the house. I try not to let my mind think about the other option, but a small voice whispers it coldly at the back of my mind . . . what if they caught her? No. Calm down, think straight, Lucy. I would have heard shouting if they'd seen her. I've got to be patient.

I smooth down my matted hair and brush embedded food from my T-shirt. I can't stay still. Finally, I hear her hushed voice from the other side of the door.

"Oh my God, there are locks on Lucy's den."

I put my hand to my mouth to stop myself crying out as I listen to the metal bolts sliding open. I suddenly run into the shadows at the far end of the basement, realizing that it'll be too much of a shock if I'm the first thing Mak sees. I must look like an abused animal. I can't chance Mak going hysterical and shouting out.

I watch the door open slowly and silently. My mouth drops as I see Ben standing behind her. She ushers him in and carefully closes the door. They stand at the top of the steps, bodies rigid with tension. I see their eyes dart around the basement, see their expressions wrinkle with confusion as they survey the floor, littered with smashed records, empty water bottles and abandoned burger cartons.

"What the hell is going on?" Mak whispers, dread spreading across her face.

They walk down the stairs in silence and peer around the dimly lit room.

CHAPTER 42

NOT HER ANY MORE

Ben heads in my direction, staring at the smashed Xbox and picture books scattered on the ground. I step out of the shadows, my finger on my lips. "Shush!" I hiss as he recoils at the sight of me.

Ben's eyes are enormous. He stares at me but then grabs ahold of my hand like he'll never let it go.

Mak rushes towards me, her face is screwed up like she's in pain. "What's happened to you?" she gasps. "Why have they locked you in here? Why are there cameras on the walls?"

I wince, realizing that Radnor could be seeing all this.

"You've got to move. Quickly. Come on. They might be watching." Ben clings on to my hand as I hustle them into the bathroom, out of sight of the cameras.

"Did anyone see you?" I ask urgently.

"No, we got in through a window down the hall. We heard voices in the living room, but no one saw us. What the hell is going on?" Mak asks. "When I buzzed at the gates, Mr Burgess said that you'd left a few days ago, but I knew he was lying. Why have they done this to you? Have they gone insane?"

I can't answer. Ben is facing me as if he's in a trance. He raises his hands just above my head and then lowers his fingertips and gently runs them along the scars on my skull and down the back of my neck. I let him do it – he needs to do it. He swallows hard, the muscles in his face twitching, but then he seems to recover as his finger traces over the scar through my eyebrow. A smile flickers on his lips. "Do you remember how you got that scar?"

I don't answer – he doesn't want me to.

"You, clinging to the back of my bike on your roller skates; letting go on that hill and crashing into the bus shelter, a ride in an ambulance and eight stitches later you had me running round after you for weeks. Mum tried to blame *me*, of course, but you wouldn't let her. You said, 'Leave our Ben alone. It wasn't his fault. I was the one who let go of his stupid bloody bike.'"

Tears are pooling in my eyes. He puts his arms around me, squeezing so tightly I can hardly breathe. I feel all his love and agony in this embrace. It's unbearable.

There's a scraping sound from the top of the stairs. Ben's arms drop from around me. I hear Mom's panicked voice.

"Lewis, did you forget to lock the door? What if she's gone!" I hear her pushing her way down the steps.

"Listen," I whisper to Ben and Mak, "you need to stay in the bathroom. Don't make a sound. Wait until they've taken me and then get out and call the police."

"I'll call them now," Ben says, taking his phone out. He looks at it in alarm. "There's no signal!"

"You can't get a signal down here," I whisper. "You have to get out of the basement to make the call.

"But listen," I continue, trying to appear calm, "promise me that *whatever* happens, you won't come out of this room. Do you understand? They can't know that you're here."

They both look terrified as I walk out of the bathroom shutting the door behind me.

"Lucy! Lucy!" Mom shouts down into the room, Dad at her side.

"What?" I reply flatly.

"Oh, thank God." She races down the stairs and right up to me, a tower of tension. "Enough of this madness, Lucy. We're your parents and we're not going to watch you kill yourself. You're coming with us to the clinic. Dr Radnor has a dose of your medication all ready to give you before the journey."

"Okay," I say.

"What do you mean, 'okay'?" She pulls up in surprise.

"Okay, I'll go to the clinic," I say solemnly.

She flings her arms around me. "Thank you, Lucy! You're doing the right thing. I'll make sure that you never regret it.

You have so much to look forward to."

Dad looks at me curiously.

I wriggle out of her embrace, turning away.

"I got you fresh clothes. Why don't I help you take a quick shower? You don't want to travel feeling lousy." Mom beams.

"I don't need help. Leave me alone to get cleaned up. I'll let you know when I'm ready," I say coldly.

Dad takes Mom's elbow. "Come on, Gemma. Leave Lucy alone."

"Of course. I'll see you in a minute. I love you, baby!" she calls out as she leaves.

I open the bathroom door in trepidation, knowing that now, Mak and Ben can be in no doubt about the truth. I gnaw at my lip as I see Mak's shaking hands covering her mouth. Ben is next to her, his head bowed, eyes closed. I feel helpless. I can't say anything to make this right for him.

"Lucy?" Mak asks shakily.

"Yes, Mak. It's me. It's Lucy." I nervously put my hands out to her.

She throws herself at me. Clinging to me. "Lucy. Oh my God, Lucy!" It feels amazing to hear her call me by my name.

"I wasn't lying, Mak. I was trying to reach you," I whisper as we bury ourselves in each other.

"I know. I'm so sorry. I let you go through all this on your own," she splutters through tears.

"It's okay." I kiss her cheek. I don't ever want to be parted from her again, but I reluctantly pull away, knowing that I have to face Ben.

"Ben," I say gently as if waking him. He raises his head, opens his eyes. "Ben, I'm so sorry. You understand that I'm not Hayley, don't you?" My voice is soft, but I know how devastating my words must be to him. He seems to be looking right through me. "I promise that once we're safely out of here, I'll tell you everything, but first we've got to get out. My parents have lost it – they're dealing with someone very dangerous. If you're found, I don't know what would happen."

Ben seems to come out of his reverie and focuses on me. "No! I'm not going anywhere until you tell me what happened to my sister." His voice is full of desperation as his eyes search my face frantically.

"Ben, you *know* what happened to Hayley," I whisper gently. "Please let's not do this now."

His face darkens; his tone is menacing. "We have to. I need to hear it from you. I want to know everything!"

I close my eyes, trying to gather my strength. I'm going to have to do this. "If I tell you, you have to stay calm no matter how shocked you are. No matter how difficult this is to hear. Can you do that?"

"Yes." I hear the dread in his voice.

I step away from him, afraid of the words that I have to say.

"I know you see Hayley when you look at me, but it's not her any more. I am Lucy Burgess. Hayley is dead."

He rocks back like he's been punched in the face. The veins on his neck pulsate.

"Ben, I was dying of cancer; my parents were desperate to

save me. They asked a surgeon to perform a body transplant on me. I didn't know they were going to do it, I swear. And my parents thought the surgeon used a genuine donor. But the doctor who did this had Hayley abducted and used her body for me . . . for Lucy Burgess." My voice breaks as the words strain to come out.

Ben looks stunned. I can't imagine how unbearable this is for him to hear, but I have to continue.

"They put my brain in Hayley's body and they kept my eyes. You've looked into them before, Ben, at my party. They're the wrong eyes, so you thought that you'd made a mistake, but you didn't."

I rush out of the bathroom and bring back the photograph of me and Grandma.

I hold it up to him. "Look, this is me. I've got the same eyes. Lucy's eyes . . . my eyes in Hayley's body."

He takes the photo from me, soaking in the image, then staring into my eyes.

"My parents locked me down here because I found out the truth and I wanted to go to the police. I couldn't stand the thought of you looking for Hayley for the rest of your life, hoping that she was alive. I'm so sorry, Ben."

There's an ominous silence as he stands, paralyzed. Then it hits him like a tsunami.

He hurls the photo frame into the wall, shattering the glass. He falls to his knees, loud sobs shuddering through his body.

I kneel down to him, feeling the heat of his pain and

anger. "Ben, you have to keep quiet. I'm sorry . . . I'm sorry."

He leans his head into my shoulder. I stroke his thick mop of hair as if he's a little boy.

"Lucy, they're expecting you." Mak's voice breaks the moment. "You've got to go upstairs. We need to get out of here and call the police."

I nod. I don't want to leave him like this but I've got to, for all our sakes.

I have to keep it together. I disentangle myself from Ben as Mak takes over, holding his hand in silence. I quickly go into the shower cubicle to change into the clean clothes.

Mak hugs me tightly as I go to leave. "I've missed you so much, Lucy."

"I've missed you too," I whisper, determined not to cry. "Look after Ben. Make sure he gets out of here." I leave him crouched with his head in his hands. Mak wraps her arms around him.

I bang on the den door, shouting, "I'm ready!"

As the door swings open I'm surprised to see Arthur. He runs past Mom on the steps and sniffs the air. He sweeps around the room and stops at the bathroom, barking madly.

"What is it, Arthur?" Mom asks.

"It's nothing. He's picking up all kinds of smells down here." I feel sick as he starts scratching at the door.

"Arthur . . . Arthur, come here!" Mom calls, going to get him.

As she reaches the bathroom she grips the door handle. "Look, there's nothing in here, silly dog," she says, pulling it down to look inside.

345

"Mom, I don't feel well!" I cry out, desperately trying to distract her. "I think I'm going to have another attack."

"Okay, honey, I'm here. Don't worry, it's going to be fine." She can't disguise the fear in her voice.

I try and hide my relief as I see Mom let go of the handle and grab Arthur by the collar, dragging him away.

She chaperones me out of the basement and shoos Arthur down the corridor. She turns and automatically slides the bolts across the door. My heart stops.

"Lucy, are you okay?" Dad is striding towards us.

I ignore him and stretch up to unlock the top bolt but Dad takes my hand and pulls it away.

"She's got another attack coming on," Mom says, urgently.

I spin around in a panic, lurching towards the door. I've got to undo the bolts. They've got to get out and call the police.

"Come on, Lucy, Dr Radnor's got your meds," Dad says, sounding concerned.

I try to struggle out of his grip, ordering him to get off me.

"She's getting hysterical, Lewis," Mom says. "We've got to stop the attack."

They take me by the arms and haul me away from the basement.

CHAPTER 43

YOUR FAULT

My mind is frozen. I can't think. I know I need to get Mak and Ben out of the basement but there's no time. I see Radnor standing in the hallway. There's a stack of suitcases piled by the front door.

"Lucy needs her medication, *now!*" Mom says, dragging me towards him.

Radnor gives me the pills and a bottle of water. I swallow them down, desperately trying to figure out what to do next. Does anyone even know that Mak and Ben came here? If I leave this house they're going to be trapped down there and no one will know what happened to them or me.

"The pills will stop the attack," Radnor says. "She's quite safe to make the journey. Let's get the cases in the car. Lucy should travel with me."

"Then I'll travel with you too," Mom says firmly. "Lucy needs me. Lewis can follow in his own car."

I need to stop this. I can't get into that car knowing that no one has told the police, knowing that no one is coming to stop Radnor and release Mak and Ben. "I'm not going," I blurt out.

My words make them stop in their tracks.

"Of course you're going," Mom replies with a manic smile. "You made the right decision. Now, let's not start playing games again."

"I'm sorry, Mom. I'm staying here."

Radnor's face darkens. "I've tried to reason with you. It would have been better for all of us if you'd come willingly but, in your own interest, I need to take the decision out of your hands." He opens the black briefcase by his side and takes out a syringe and needle. He addresses Dad. "Would you please hold Lucy still? It's just a mild sedative."

"Why are you giving her that?" Dad asks, alarmed.

"It'll keep her calm during the journey. Once we're at the clinic we can reduce the sedative and everything will return to normal," he says, screwing the needle into the fluid-filled syringe.

I shout wordlessly in fury as Mom grabs me.

"Lewis, help me keep her still." She strains as I struggle against her.

"No, Dad, don't let them do this to me!" I plead with him.

He looks at me with pure anguish. "But, Lucy...?"

"Please, Dad!" He hesitates as Radnor grips my arm, choosing a vein.

A growl makes us all turn as Arthur runs into the

hallway, baring his teeth at Radnor. Radnor lashes out at him warningly, but Arthur leaps up and locks his jaws around Radnor's arm. The syringe drops to the floor but Radnor kicks Arthur in the belly, sending him whimpering out of the hall.

I can't hesitate. I use the distraction to tear myself out of Mom's grip, pushing her against the wall, bolting out of the front door. As I run through the grounds I hear them storming after me. My name chases me through the air as Mom calls out, begging me to stop. Adrenaline surges, but I'm weak from the tremor attacks. I stumble on uneven ground, falling into a bed of nettles amid the paddock grass. I feel the pain of their sting on my face, arms, hands. I scramble up in a daze, propelling myself onwards as I hear them closing in on me.

I see the stables looming towards me and I call out for Jim again and again, but there's no answer. I stagger around the empty cobbled yard shouting his name, but the only response is the whining and snorting of the horses in their stalls, distressed at my presence.

"There's no one here, Lucy," Mom pants as the three of them surround me. "Now for God's sake stop fighting us and let us help you."

"All I want to do is look after you, Lucy. Please come with me," Dr Radnor says, beads of sweat trickling down his face. He readjusts his glasses on his nose; runs his tongue over his dry lips.

"No." I struggle for breath, turning to Mom and Dad.

"You've got to call the police. I know what will happen to you, and *me*, but he's got to be stopped. He's dangerous. He'll do this again, you know he will."

Radnor bristles. He breathes deeply, trying to appear in control, but I sense his growing rage.

"Don't be stupid, Lucy!" Mom's voice is harsh. "Don't destroy your future for something in the past that can't be changed."

Mom and Radnor step forward; closing in on me. I'm surrounded, but I tense my exhausted body. I'm ready to lash out at them, even though I know I'm too weak to fight them off.

I feel Dad grabbing my arm. I swivel around to defend myself but, instead of restraining me, he pulls me behind him protectively. "Enough!" Dad shouts, holding his hands up to halt Mom and Radnor.

All around, the horses in the stalls react to Dad's booming voice with clattering hooves and snorts.

"What the hell are you doing, Lewis?" Mom gasps.

"This has got to be Lucy's decision, not ours," Dad says sadly. "We can't go on like this. What's your plan, Gemma? Are we going to keep her locked up forever?"

I cling on to Dad but keep Radnor in my sights, watching his jaw clench and eyes narrow in anger.

Mom steps forward, leaning into Dad's face. "What are you suggesting, Lewis? That we let our daughter die?" she hisses.

"We never gave her a choice about the transplant, but

350

now she gets to choose what she does with her life and she's made up her mind." Dad's voice cracks.

"How dare you put this burden on her." Mom is talking about me like I'm not even there. "Lucy isn't capable of making the right choice. She's not thinking straight." Mom is furious, her words icy.

"Of course she's thinking straight; she's just much braver than us, Gemma." Guilt riddles Dad's voice.

I tug at his sleeve urgently. "Phone the police, Dad. Do it now." I feel a surge of love for him as he gets his cell out of his pocket.

Radnor responds by producing his phone. "Before you've even finished talking to the police I can make a call to my clinic and have all her medication, all the notes, destroyed, just like I promised. What kind of father would you be, signing your own daughter's death warrant?"

"Lewis! If you love her, you'll put the phone away," Mom pleads.

Dad looks at me – I can see him wavering.

I rub his arm. "I know you love me, Dad. You're doing the right thing. Don't be scared for me. Make the call."

Dad's face crumples; his eyes cloud with tears as he presses the first digit. I fix my stare on Radnor, ready to launch myself at him if he attempts to use his cell, but instead of trying to call his clinic I see Radnor reach into his inside pocket. As he pulls something out, I catch a glint of metal in the sunshine; I follow the path of his hand, trying to make out what he's holding, and then I see it.

"No!" I cry.

Radnor points the gun at Dad's chest. "Put the phone down, Mr Burgess, or I'll shoot." There's a quiver in his voice.

"For God's sake, put it down, Lewis," Mom shrieks.

Dad shakes his head. "I'm not letting this murderer take my daughter," he replies, his voice cracking.

Radnor pulls back the safety on the gun. I can't let this happen. I know what Radnor is capable of. My only thought is to save Dad. "Don't do it, Dad!" I plead. I look imploringly at Radnor. "Listen . . . Dr Leo," I splutter, my arms stretched out to this monster. "I'll do as you say. I'll go with you to the clinic. Just put the gun down. Leave my dad alone."

Radnor's eyes flicker towards me. He looks unsure, but his gun is still poised to shoot.

"No, Lucy, I can't let you do that," Dad says as he looks down at his cell and presses another digit.

There's a deafening bang; a high-pitched ringing fills my ears. The horses go wild.

Dad drops to the ground, his face frozen. Blood starts to seep through his white shirt.

I look across at Radnor. His skin is grey. The gun trembles in his hand.

I can't move. I can't think.

"Lewis!" Mom's voice sounds distant.

She's on her knees, lifting his head between her hands. "Lewis! Lewis!" Dad's eyes are open, but they're empty.

"Call an ambulance, for God's sake, call an ambulance!" Mom bawls at Radnor.

352

I see him level the gun at her and fire. Mom lets out a horrific cry. He fires again and she collapses on to the cobbles.

The piercing ringing in my ears is like a scream I can't release. I bend down to Mom, to Dad, my insides shaking, but Radnor hauls me up and on to my feet. His sweat-drenched body clings to mine. He whispers angrily in my ear. "This is your fault. You could have just come with me and this wouldn't have happened. How could you be so selfish, so stupid?"

I push him off me, my eyes darting around for some way out. Moonshine's head is poking over her stable door. She's shaking it like there's a swarm of hornets around her. A pitchfork leans against her stall. I lurch for it, clinging on to the door to keep me upright. Moonshine backs away, snorting and shaking her mane. I aim the pitchfork at Radnor but shock has drained any last drop of strength from me.

"I'll put this through you," I say, trembling.

He shakes his head wearily. "There's no need for this, Lucy. I'd never hurt you. We need each other."

I jab the pitchfork at him and he looks at me pityingly.

"You can hardly stand. Let's get to the clinic. It's the only place that I can keep you safe."

"Stay back!" A cold sweat blooms over my skin as I try to hold up the pitchfork and use my other hand to work the bolt across Moonshine's stall door. It swings open and I stagger inside the stall, backing the frenzied horse into a corner as she tries to get away from me.

"Come out of there," he says in a low rumble.

I jab the pitchfork at his face, but he seizes it and flings it across the yard.

I move slowly, deeper into the stall, squeezing my way past Moonshine. Putting her body between me and Radnor. Moonshine rears up, her nostrils flared in distress. The smell of hay and sweet grass sails up my nose as her muscular flank swings inches from me. Her coarse tail whips me in the face as she starts stamping her hooves frantically. A dust cloud rises, catching in my throat. I squeeze into the corner of the stall, praying that she won't turn on me.

White sweat marks start to form on her shivering coat. She swings around and jerks her head down at me, hot breath on my cheeks, whites of her eyes massive with fear as she snorts and squeals. I hold my position, not moving a muscle.

"What the hell are you doing, Lucy? Come out of there; that horse is going crazy. It's dangerous," Radnor hisses into the stall.

"I'm not coming out," I whisper, but I know he's not going to leave without me, his priceless creation.

He hesitates before speaking. "Lucy, I'm coming in to get you. You must not struggle, do you understand?"

I don't answer. I watch Moonshine's ears flickering as she hears him step into the stall. She quiets, listening, smelling his fear, her flanks quivering. He slowly skirts around her. Her unblinking eye is trained on him.

"Give me your hand," he whispers tensely, stretching his arm out to me.

As his fingers inch towards me I slowly lean back, out of his reach, trying to keep Moonshine calm. Radnor responds by lunging at me, trying to get a hold on me. Moonshine squeals. I cower in the corner, my hands over my head as the horse rears up at Radnor. He raises his arms, letting out a scream. There's a sickening crunching sound as her hooves stamp on him. I screw up my eyes as she rears up again, crashing down on his body. I have to get out of here. My legs feel like Jell-O as I inch my way behind the raging horse slamming the bolt across the door behind me.

An eerie silence falls over the stall. Moonshine calms, like a madness has passed. She stands placidly, ignoring Radnor's crushed body at her feet. I stop myself from retching and stagger over to Mom and Dad, falling to my knees, showering Dad's face in kisses, washing his still-warm skin with my tears. I lean across to take Mom's wrist, searching desperately for a pulse, gasping as I hear the faintest moan rise out of her. I grab her cell from her pocket and call 911, all the while tapping Mom's face, pleading with her to open her eyes.

"Stay awake, Mom!" I repeat over and over again. "I won't let you die! I won't let you die!"

EPILOGUE

I feel a hand land gently on my shoulder. "Hey, Lucy."

The familiar sound injects warmth into me. I don't think that I'll ever get over the relief of hearing Mak say my name.

"Hey, Mak," I reply, my voice thick with exhaustion. I stretch my body and hear the crackle of weary muscles. I've been hunched over Mom's hospital bed all day, watching for the slightest movement.

Mak pulls up a chair next to me, plants a kiss on my cheek and hands me a can of Coke. "How's she doing?" she whispers.

I stroke Mom's greasy hair away from her milk-white face. Her lips are shrunken and dry. I get out the cherry balm from the bedside table and smooth it over them. She hasn't woken up in the three weeks since the shooting. At first the doctors warned me that she may not pull through, but they don't know Mom the way I do. She may look helpless, lying here with tubes up her nose and down her throat, but I know that she'll be fighting every step of the way. She doesn't want to leave me.

"I think she seems stronger today," I reply, hopefully.

"Well, there's definitely more color in her cheeks," Mak says, encouragingly.

Nurse Becky bustles into the room and smiles at us as she checks the monitors and takes Mom's temperature. Becky has been here since Mom first got admitted. She was the one who arranged for me to have a bed in Mom's room, when she realized that I wasn't going to leave Mom's side. Each night I try to get to some sleep, but I usually just drift off in the chair next to Mom's bed and wake up with a stiff neck.

"Everything's looking okay," Nurse Becky says reassuringly. She talks to Mom as she rearranges her pillows, shifting her position in the bed. "Is that more comfortable, Mrs Burgess?"

Mom's head lolls to the side like a rag doll, and her eyes remain closed. Nurse Becky gently moves Mom's head upright. She turns to me as she goes to leave, raising her eyebrows. "Lucy, have you taken your medication?"

"Don't worry, I'll take it now," I reply, absently searching through my rucksack for the pills. Mak hands me a glass of water as I swallow them down.

"You're not looking after yourself. You've got to come home with me," Mak says forcefully.

I make a non-committal noise. I touch Mom's warm arm and my thoughts harden as I imagine Dad's cold body, all alone, in the morgue. Part of me is relieved that the police won't release him to be buried yet – I want Mom to be at

Dad's funeral. She needs to say goodbye to him and she needs to face what she did to him. To me. To our family. I'm only still here, at her bedside, because I understand that every twisted decision Mom made was out of her desperate, terrifying love for me.

I try my best to keep Radnor out of my head. Every time I picture him, I get choked up by hate and anger. Maybe I should be regretting that he didn't stand trial and spend the rest of his life in prison, but I'm glad he's dead. At least this way I can be sure that he can't harm anyone else.

Detective Cook, the officer in charge of the investigation, keeps coming to the hospital to talk to me. I trust her; she's treating me like an adult, keeping me updated. She says that the investigation is "fast moving" with more information being uncovered every day. They've traced the teenagers that Radnor had on file and found that he'd been running tests on them in clinics in South America and England. They discovered encrypted emails on Radnor's computer that proved that he was just days away from having one of the girls abducted from Honduras and brought to the El Paso clinic for a new transplant. If Dad and I hadn't stopped him, Radnor would have killed again.

The beeping of Mak's cell cuts through my thoughts. She looks down at the text, the trace of a sad smile on her face.

"Who is it?" I ask quietly, my eyes flitting to check on Mom.

Mak puts the cell away. She looks apprehensive, shifts in her chair. "It's Ben."

My belly twists with involuntary guilt and Mak senses it.

"Lucy, he doesn't blame you for what happened to Hayley. He just finds it too hard to talk to you."

"Sure, I understand," I reply, too abruptly. "I'm glad that you two are staying in touch. He needs support. How's he doing?" I dread the answer.

Mak suppresses a sigh. "He's having a really hard time. His mom is in pieces."

I run my hands down my face. Radnor's' words worm into my head: *You'll cause Hayley's family untold grief by telling the truth.*

"Maybe it would have been better if Ben and his mom had never found out what happened to Hayley. At least then they could have lived in hope," I mutter.

Mak rears up at me, halfway out of her chair. "I don't ever want to hear you say such crap again," she says. "You did the right thing, Lucy. Of course Ben and his mom are hurting ... they'll probably always hurt, but at least now they have a chance to get on with their lives and they're not stuck in hell ... waiting and hoping for Hayley to return."

Tears fill my gritty eyes. I know I've got to stop all this doubt crashing around my head. But it's so hard. I'm so tired.

A silence hangs in the air as Mak and I watch Mom, deep in our own thoughts.

I glance over at my best friend and see a coldness in her eyes. Mak has been in every day to see me, but I've noticed that she doesn't touch Mom — no strokes on the arm, no tender gestures. I know that Mak is feeling as mixed-up as me. She's angry at Mom and outraged at all she did, and yet she knows that I wouldn't be alive if Mom hadn't gotten Radnor to give me the transplant.

Mak breaks the silence, picking up my rucksack and filling it with the clothes that are scattered on my bed. "Look, you're coming home with me and I'm not taking no for an answer this time."

"I can't," I panic.

"Yes, you can," Mak says, adamantly. "My mama is coming to sit with her, and anyway, you heard the nurse; your mom is doing fine. If there's any change, we can get you back here in twenty minutes, tops."

I look at Mom, so vulnerable, so alone without me.

Mak picks up my jacket from the back of the chair. "Arthur is waiting for you at our house," she says temptingly.

I feel myself smile for the first time in three weeks. That horrific day seems to have been a turning point for me and Arthur. When he attacked Radnor in the hallway he may have just been reacting to seeing a person in danger, but I like to think that, in that moment, he saw *Lucy*. Whatever the reason, since that day, Arthur has allowed me to pet him. He doesn't seem afraid of me any more. Maybe there's hope for us.

Mak takes me by the arm. "Come on," she coaxes.

Anxiety prickles my skin. Being cocooned in this hospital room with Mom has meant that I don't have to face the outside world. I know that Detective Cook hasn't made public what really went on that day, but there must be rumors flying around the whole city about the intruder who shot Mr and Mrs Burgess.

I'm afraid to leave the confines of this place; afraid of what awaits me.

"What's going to happen to me?" I don't mean to say it out loud.

"Whatever happens, you'll always have me and you'll always have a home with my family." Mak's voice cracks with emotion.

"But how can I stay around here, Mak?" I ask desperately. "There'll be so many questions. People will try and find out the truth. And I don't even know what's going to happen to Mom if . . . *when* she wakes up."

"Don't worry about any of that. We'll just take it a day at a time," she replies calmly. "Look, we've only got one more year and then we'll be free. We can take off together before college; do a road trip to the Grand Canyon; move to New York and live in a poets' commune." She grins, knowing that her comment will make me roll my eyes. "Seriously, Lucy, we have so much living to do. Don't bail on me now. I need you."

I look at Mak's determined face. Is she right? *Can* I do this? Sitting by Mom's bedside for the past three weeks has given me so much time with my thoughts, and maybe it's *because* of all I've been through, but the one thing that I've realized is that, despite having a body that isn't my own, I know myself better *now* than I ever did before. I know what kind of person I'm capable of being.

I get up from the chair as Mak nods at me encouragingly. I hesitate, suppressing any doubts, and then I kiss Mom's forehead, saying gently, "Mak's mama is coming to sit with you. I'll be back later." As I raise my head, I think I see Mom's eyes flicker. I don't know whether my exhausted mind is playing tricks on me, but then I hear Mak.

"Did you see that, Lucy? Did you see that?" Mak gasps, pressing the button for the nurse.

I loom over Mom, too tense to breathe. I watch her lids fluttering, fighting to open, and then I see the grey-blue of her eyes, soaking me in. Her slack face comes alive with excitement. She reaches a hand up to me and I curl my fingers around it. Tears of relief pour down my face. Now I can dare to believe she's going to be okay.

Yes . . . she's going to be okay, and I'm going to find the strength to deal with whatever is to come. I need to live each day as best as I can. I need to make the most of my life.

I owe it to Hayley; I owe it to myself.

ACKNOWLEDGEMENTS

Massive thanks to my agent, the mighty Clare Conville of C+W. Despite being ridiculously busy, Clare always makes time for me, sticks with me through thick and thin, and has shown unwavering support throughout my writing of Shell.

Thanks also to the great team at Scholastic. Especially my talented editor, Sophie Cashell, for all her hard work, Sean Williams for the cover design (which I love), Roisin O'Shea and Olivia Horrox for their marketing and publicity expertize, Jessica White and Peter Matthews for their meticulous copy-editing and proofreading. Nikki Bell for making sure Shell got printed! All the sales and rights team, and, of course, Sam Smith. I'm so grateful for the commitment and passion that you've all shown for Shell.

A very special thanks must go to my daughter, Sadie. It was Sadie who first came up with an idea which then sparked off a train of thought that led me to Shell. Sadie is like a teenaged guru (only one who wears a lot of make-up and loves to party). She's my first port of call to chat through book issues and always has words of great wisdom to impart.

I'm grateful to people who read early drafts of Shell. Their feedback (even when they contradicted each other) gave me rich food for thought. So, many thanks to Julie Burke, Carrie Plitt, Sophie Wilson, Matt Marland and my son, Archie.

I consulted my lovely American friend, Renee Smith (who in turn consulted her Texan friends), to help me try and nail an authentic sound and setting. Their input was invaluable.

Hugs and kisses to Stan and Archie, who seem to have transformed from boys into burly young men whilst I was writing this book.

And last, but never least, huge love to my husband, David. His support is unfailing and in twenty-two years there's never been a dull moment. Thank you for the days!

ABOUT THE AUTHOR

Author Paula Rawsthorne first found success when she won the BBC National "Get Writing" competition with her prize-winning story read by Bill Nighy on Radio 4. She has also been a winner of SCBWI's "Undiscovered Voices" and her previous Young Adult novels have both been award-winners. She is passionate about inspiring teenagers to get reading and is a writer in residence in a secondary school for the national literacy charity First Story. *Shell* is her third novel for young adults.

Follow Paula on Twitter @PaulaRawsthorne